MARCEL PROUST

SWANN
IN
LOVE

Translated by C. K. Scott Moncrieff

and Terence Kilmartin

Preface by Volker Schlöndorff

VINTAGE BOOKS

A Division of Random House

New York

Library of Congress Cataloging in Publication Data
Proust, Marcel, 1871-1922.
Swann in love.
Translation of: Un amour de Swann.
"This translation was originally published by Random
House, Inc., and Chatto & Windus Ltd. in 1981 as part
of Swann's way, which is included in the first volume
of Remembrance of things past"—T.p. verso.
Includes bibliographical references.
I. Title.
PQ2631.R63D8713 1982   843'.912   84-7318
ISBN 0-394-72769-X (pbk.)

Volker Schlöndorff

On Adapting

SWANN IN LOVE

for the Screen

THE ADAPTATION

How does a filmmaker adapt a writer's work for the
screen? Should he follow the critical method prescribed
by Sainte-Beuve: "surrounding oneself with as much
information as possible about the writer, going over his
correspondence, questioning those who knew him—
that is, interviewing them if they are still alive, or, if
not, reading what they might have said about him"?
According to Proust, this method ignores the lessons
taught by "a somewhat deeper familiarity with another
I, different from the one we manifest in our habits, in
public, in our vices."

This *other I*, if we wish to understand it, "can be
reached only at the base of ourselves, by trying to re-
create it within us. Nothing can take the place of this
effort made by our own hearts."

A film can be as faithful as you please to the letter
of the text. But without this "effort of the heart," it

will never be more than a flat illustration.

Thus we could invoke the age-old question of "style." The way we arrange the narrative, write the dialogues, choose and direct the actors, design the sets and costumes, light and photograph them, edit the shots and the soundtrack, make the rhythm suggest the passage of time, compose the score: all of this gives the film its style. Each filmmaker has his own style, which can never be an imitation of the author's. It cannot be adopted by virtue of some arbitrary decision. If it exists, it will always be the fruit of this "effort of the heart."

In an adaptation, it is not enough to base the film on the text; one must rediscover the author's motivation, the force that made him write. I must find *in myself* equally powerful reasons. For *Young Törless*, I found them in country boarding schools, in class struggles among privileged youngsters, in my own adolescent despair, my guilt as a German and my problems at puberty. For *The Tin Drum* it was even more blatant. I didn't understand the novel until the day I walked along the little street in the Danzig suburb where Günter Grass grew up. If Grass, starting from that small, shop-lined street and that grocery store, had managed to create an entire universe, I had to remember my own childhood to join him there. I had to start from the experience underlying the book in order to tell the story in turn, through film.

THE SCREENPLAY

Proust would have had a good laugh if someone had asked him for a "synopsis" of his novel. He takes his characters at a certain point in their lives, then makes them live in time and space, without worrying too much about chronology and geography. It always feels as if you are waking from a dream when you stop reading Proust. But we know that a film needs a structure, a story told, situated in a precise time and place.

Swann in Love occupies a special place in the whole of *Remembrance of Things Past*. Although it doesn't tell a story in the strict sense of the word, we can pick up the traces of one through the characters. Swann is fascinated by Odette as an art-lover is fascinated by an object he wants to own for his collection. Odette returns his interest, but in a different way: she would like to understand Swann, to know what's going on in his head. She despairs of trying to define him; *he* is the elusive one.

Swann wants to put her in a glass case. Odette doesn't want to be a museum piece. She rebels, escapes, deceives him to save herself. Swann doesn't see that she loves him, that she is touched and elevated by the attention and consideration he shows her, which she is not used to receiving. At Swann's every kindness, she gets tears in her eyes. She asks no more than to live a great love affair with him, she says she seeks nothing better— she would even give her soul in return. But Swann would rather pay in cold cash. The dandy is, above all, a professional consumer, and Swann behaves like a good capitalist.

The confrontation of these two wills is the film's motivating force. In addition, Odette wishes to improve her social standing, which her marriage to Swann accomplishes—even as it destroys him. Let's say that they both get something out of it.

How to tell this story? Is it necessary to arrange these elements in some way?

Let's take an example: Someone introduces Charles Swann to Odette de Crécy—a woman with whom he "might possibly come to an understanding"—making

her out to be harder to get than she actually is. First
meetings. Swann finds her not devoid of beauty, but
endowed with a beauty that doesn't attract him, that
even inspires in him a certain physical repulsion. One
evening she doesn't show up as arranged. A great wave
of anxiety seizes him. He pursues her, first with his
love, then with his jealousy. Different phases of his love
follow in succession, which Bernard De Fallois named
as follows: from the first meeting to the episode of the
orchids, representing "from curiosity to attachment,"
then "from attachment to love," "from love to torture,"
and finally "from torture to appeasement."

Such a process reduces psychology to a simple mechanism, and the novel to a report. It completely bypasses
Proust's genius, which also resides in his way of telling
the story, his way of intertwining themes and states of
mind with no chronological obligation whatsoever.

Or should we, on the other hand, make a film full
of flashbacks, dissolves and other very cinematic pro-
cesses? The subject certainly lends itself to this, and it
is perhaps what many people expected, but it's not my
style. What seduced me was the very simple idea that
Peter Brook and Jean-Claude Carrière (whose "work in
progress" I took over) had: to concentrate on a single
day of Swann's love.

A day and a night that last until breakfast, and that
encapsulate an entire lifetime. To adopt a unity of time,
as Proust does with an afternoon at the home of the
Princesse de Guermantes in *Time Regained*, is to restore
to film a sense of duration.

The screenplay, which follows a single day in which
Swann, from hour to hour, sinks into night and despair,
shatters this unity of time with a cruel epilogue, which
takes place fifteen years later. Through the words of a
minor character, we learn that Odette de Crécy is now

Mme Swann. And Swann knows he's dying.

"First, the events of each hour of their lives had been told to us; up until then, the author had followed them step by step. Then, suddenly: 'Twenty years later...' Through an incidental remark spoken by a minor character, we learn that the marriage had been celebrated—we don't really know when—in this astonishing epilogue written, it seems, from above the clouds, by a person indifferent to our fleeting passions."

This text, from Proust's *Pastiches et mélanges*, conveys rather well my reaction to the epilogue of the screenplay that Peter Brook originally planned to direct.

The last sentence makes Swann's love seem no more than a fleeting passion that a dying man evokes while asking himself, like Ivan Ilych, "What have I done with my life?" And suddenly those twenty-four hours that structured the narrative are no more than the duration of a dream in which Swann's love and his desperate quest for happiness take on tragic proportions.

Sorrows are servants, obscure and detested, against whom one struggles, beneath whose dominion one more and more completely falls, dire and dreadful servants whom it is impossible to replace and who by subterranean paths lead us towards truth and death. Happy are those who have first come face to face with truth, those for whom, near though the one may be to the other, the hour of truth has struck before the hour of death! (*Time Regained*).

THE PLACE AND THE TIME

The action of *Swann in Love* takes place entirely in Paris (there is neither Combray, nor Normandy, nor any other favored Proustian spot). Swann lives on the Quai d'Orléans, Odette on Rue La Pérouse, the Guermantes in the Faubourg Saint-Germain; they go to the Opera, dine in the Bois de Boulogne, go to Tortoni's on the Boulevard des Italiens, or to the Maison Dorée, or to Prévost's. The addresses are precise. For once, Proust hasn't changed the names, and yet one doesn't think of this Paris as a real city, as one does with the Paris of Balzac or Zola. Rather, it is an imaginary place, composed of architectural fragments, of façades, of interior hues and atmospheres, of gardens and perspectives known only in dreams, in the collages of Max Ernst and in the urban landscapes of De Chirico. And although these characters ride in carriages, although they wear coats with tails, corseted dresses and hats, they belong to no specific era.

THE COSTUMES AND THE SETS

Proust compared the composition of his work at times to the architecture of a cathedral, at times to the making of a dress. He took care to study the most minute details of cut, cloth and the tailor's art. So much so that Yvonne Sassinot was able to follow his instructions to the letter when she designed Odette's dresses, which are at once beautiful and perfectly made. This avoids the outmoded and arbitrary side of costumes in period films, something that is also true of Jacques Saulnier's sets, and of Philippe Turlure's furnishings.

The portrait of "high society" in Marcel Proust's work becomes increasingly cruel. This is why we have added to *Swann in Love*—which praises its beauty and elegance—the episode of the red shoes, in which a detail of dress takes on more importance than the imminent death of a friend.

THE PHOTOGRAPHY

To follow Swann through his day, Sven Nykvist and I established a lighting plan. When the film begins and Swann awakens, it is noon; the sun is at its peak. At the Guermantes' musical matinee, the light barely penetrates into the reception rooms; outside in the courtyard, it is harsh and white. Later, during the afternoon, first in Bagatelle Park, then at Odette's, the sun slowly sets and the light becomes warmer. Later still, it slowly turns blue, darkening toward black. At the height of Swann's despair, the moon appears—a full, visible moon, which gives Paris a frozen, eternal look, making its façades as cold and hostile as the society that rebuffs his emotions. The next morning at dawn, Swann, finally free of Odette, returns home to the Quai d'Orléans, and the trees are silhouetted against an already light sky.

This plan, designed like a sundial, allowed us to give each segment of the film its own light.

THE CHARACTERS, THEIR MODELS AND THE ACTORS

"There are no keys to the characters in this book. Or rather, there are eight or ten for a single character."

Charles Swann

Charles Haas, as George D. Painter recalls, was "the only Jew ever to be accepted by Parisian society without being immensely rich. Having won entry to the exclusive Jockey Club, of which the only other members of his race were the Rothschilds, Haas appears in a painting by Tissot with other people Proust knew: the Prince de Polignac and Gaston de Saint-Maurice. Haas frequented Mme Straus's salon, and was the darling of Comtesse Greffulhe's coterie in the Rue d'Astorg. There he met Mme Greffulhe's cousin Robert de Montesquiou. Correspondingly in Proust's novel Swann is the intimate friend of the Duchesse de Guermantes, and one of the oldest friends of her cousin, the Baron de Charlus."

Swann must nonetheless be distinguished from Charles Haas, for in both his words and his feelings we often recognize the young Proust. The writer chose the external envelope of Charles Haas because of a profound affinity; but the love, jealousy and worry he fills Swann with are indeed his own. The dialogue in the great scenes at Odette's are taken word for word from *Jean Santeuil*, in which Proust identified still more fully with his hero.

To let us discover Proust's characters, whom we know so well without ever having seen them, I first thought in terms of a film with an entirely unknown cast.

We tried several times before giving up on the idea. Proust's characters have such a mythic dimension that, in most cases, only a well-known and experienced actor, one who already conveys his own mythic aura, could give them the "larger than life" quality required by the text.

Jeremy Irons possesses that distinctly "British" elegance, the spirit and finesse attributed to Charles Haas. Moreover, he allows us to glimpse the author's internal world because of his handsome, melancholy gaze, his sensitivity, the adolescent, narcissistic aspect that makes him an eternal foreigner in the world. His Swann unites Haas and Proust in the same brotherhood.

Odette de Crécy

For the character of Odette, historical documentation can provide some rather amusing details without giving us the key to her heart. As a *demi-mondaine* she is more or less imaginary. The lines Proust gives her come more often than not from the young bourgeoise in *Jean Santeuil*. As such, the character becomes the more fascinating. Painter tells us that Proust's old great-uncle, Louis Weil, was the lover of a famous cocotte, to whom he had introduced his delighted great-nephew. The young schoolboy thus passed from Gilberte to Odette.

Painter writes: "Laure Hayman was born in 1851 on a ranch in the Andes; her father, an engineer, died when she was still a child, and her mother, after trying in vain to live by giving piano lessons, brought her up as a courtesan. Like Odette, she lived in a little house in the Rue La Pérouse, with a back entrance on the Rue Dumont d'Urville.

"When Proust first met her, in the autumn of 1888, she was thirty-seven and he was seventeen. She was plump but wasp-waisted, and wore an extremely low décolletée with festoons of pearls dangling, three a side, from what little of her bosom was hidden from view. Her hair was ash-blonde, tied with a pink ribbon; her eyes were black, and when she was excited tended to open too wide, as a photograph of this period shows. In earlier photographs she is exceedingly pretty and fluffy, though quite unmysterious and not in the least like Botticelli's fresco of Jethro's daughter, Zipporah, to whom Swann compared Odette.

"The young man insisted on loading her with her favorite chrysanthemums and giving her lunch at the most expensive restaurants. Jacques-Emile Blanche hints that Proust's affair with Mme Hayman was not merely platonic: it was all a very long time ago, but Blanche, who was a friend of both at this time, was perhaps in a position to know. It would not have been the first nor the last time that Proust's relations with women were physical; and it may be significant that in *Jean Santeuil* it is the hero himself who undergoes with Mme Françoise S. the love affair which was later transferred to Swann and Odette."

It is Jean who asks Françoise the urgent questions about her lesbian affairs, which Swann takes up in turn. For both the actors and myself, these first sketches and precise indications (for example, that the woman hides her face in the man's shoulder so that he can't see her distress) were very precious. There again we have the scene in which the hero raps on the window of another house and finds himself face to face with two old men—and even, already, the "little phrase" of music.

Another model for Odette was Louisa de Mornand, for whom Proust composed this couplet:

> *Whoever can't have Louisa de Mornand*
> *Has no other choice but the sin of Onan.*

In order for us to share both Swann's suffering and Odette's will, we needed an actress who would fascinate us as much as Odette fascinates Swann.

Ornella Muti has a very strong, immediate physical and sensual presence. I understand how Swann would not find her "his type," all the while projecting his fantasies onto her. At the same time, Ornella Muti is more than simple appearance. She identifies with her role and means to defend Odette's dignity.

Ornella Muti will certainly affirm herself through the part, just as Odette, helping Swann lose himself, triumphs by making herself acceptable in society. It's like a transfer of power from a type of man to a type of woman.

The Baron de Charlus

All this happens under the amused and jaded eye of the Baron de Charlus, who is at once the accomplice of this relationship in his role as "go-between," and its victim, since he loses a friend.

Alain Delon, like any great actor, perfectly managed to capture this Baron de Charlus who is not yet the Charlus of *Remembrance*. In *Swann in Love* he is closer to the original model. It is worth our stopping a moment to consider Painter's description of him.

"Montesquiou was tall and thin—'I look like a greyhound in a greatcoat,' he would say complacently. His hair was black, crisp and artificially waved; he had beetling black eyebrows like circumflex accents, and a mustache with upturned pointed ends, like the Kaiser's but larger.

"As this strange, black and white nobleman chanted, swayed and gesticulated, he acted a whole series of puppet characters, as if manipulated on wires pulled by some other self in the ceiling.

"He made beautiful gestures with his white-gloved hands; then he would remove the gloves, displaying a simple but curious ring; his gesticulation became ever more impassioned, till suddenly he would point heavenward: his voice rose like a trumpet in an orchestra, and passed into the soprano register of fortissimo violins; he stamped his foot, threw back his head, and emitted peal upon peal of shrill, maniacal laughter. He spoke of poetry and painting, of countesses' hats, of the splendor of his race, and of himself as its crowning glory.

"All in all, Montesquiou was a hollow man. If he had used his real sensibility and intelligence to remain true to himself, he might have possessed the genius in which he so firmly believed. Instead he only dressed, collected, scribbled, quarreled, fascinated and terrorized."

The uncontested authority of the true star, the charisma of his presence allow Alain Delon immediately to become this "prodigious personality."

For all the other characters and the actors who play them, I would like to say only that their youth is not the result of a director's caprice but is faithful to the text. *Swann in Love* takes place around 1885. The narrator is still a child, Swann is no more than thirty-three years old, Odette not yet thirty (although, sold at the age of fifteen to a rich Englishman, she has lived beyond her years). The Verdurins' "little clan," like the Guermantes, are still young. Proust mentions that Doctor Cottard is thirty-two and his wife even younger.

THE MUSIC

In Proust's work, music plays a double role. On the one hand, the very style is music, more lyrical than prose. On the other, we know the importance of the "little phrase" from Vinteuil's Sonata—an imaginary sonata in which many have recognized Saint-Saëns, César Franck, Fauré and others.

Proust himself explains: "To the extent that reality served me—a very feeble extent, to tell the truth—this Sonata is (I've never told this to anyone), in the 'Evening at the Saint-Euvertes',' the charming but rather mediocre phrase from a sonata for piano and violin by Saint-Saëns, a composer I don't like. During the same evening, a little further on, I would not be surprised if in speaking of the little phrase I was thinking of the Good Friday Spell from *Parsifal*. Still during the same evening, when the piano and the violin moan like two answering birds, I thought of the sonata by Franck. The tremolos that cover the little phrase at the Verdurins' were not suggested by a prelude from *Lohengrin*, but it was itself suggested, at that moment, by something from Schubert. During the same evening at the Verdurins', it is a magnificent piano piece by Fauré . . ."

This music will exist, victorious, even after Swann and Odette are dead, putrefied, and have returned to dust. Their love will survive in the music.

Above all, we needed a piece of music that no one had heard before, with which no one had yet associated a memory: a virgin piece of music. It could only be contemporary, the work of a composer possessing the same temperament.

Hans Werner Henze has the same concern for style as Proust, first of all because he claims the same musical influences: Debussy, Wagner and Mahler. His music surprises us just as much as Vinteuil's sonata surprised the Verdurin clan, and especially the Guermantes. Henze composed his little Sonata from Proust's indications, but with a contemporary ear and musical sensitivity, without ever going in for ersatz nineteenth century.

He decided to use a full orchestra because "feelings of love are grandiose and tragic. Swann is no less than Gluck's Iphigenia or Rameau's Phaedra," he says. "I read Proust as a great work of lyricism."

Great strokes of the bow whip Swann's jealousy to a frenzy, a soprano voice accompanies Odette's sweet lies, the theme of the chrysanthemums recalls that first evening when she took leave of him by giving him a flower. A baroque organ sounds in the false splendors of a brothel, the tremolo of strings underlines his guilty conscience and trembling knees as he leaves it. In the air of madness, as Henze calls Swann's furious nocturnal monologue in the Tuileries, there are elements of *Tristan*, while the military fanfare at the end announces the onset of the first world war. And the drum beats time to Odette's victory march, which is also Swann's funeral procession.

—Paris, 19 December 1983

(Translated by Mark Polizzotti)

PUBLISHER'S NOTE:

The following is the complete text of *Swann in Love*, from the definitive English translation of *Remembrance of Things Past*. Volker Schlöndorff's film adaptation, while based for the most part on *Swann in Love*, also includes several episodes from later volumes of the work.

SWANN IN LOVE

To admit you to the "little nucleus," the "little group," the "little clan" at the Verdurins', one condition sufficed, but that one was indispensable: you must give tacit adherence to a Creed one of whose articles was that the young pianist whom Mme Verdurin had taken under her patronage that year and of whom she said "Really, it oughtn't to be allowed, to play Wagner as well as that!" licked both Planté and Rubinstein hollow, and that Dr Cottard was a more brilliant diagnostician than Potain. Each "new recruit" whom the Verdurins failed to persuade that the evenings spent by other people, in other houses than theirs, were as dull as ditch-water, saw himself banished forthwith. Women being in this respect more rebellious than men, more reluctant to lay aside all worldly curiosity and the desire to find out for themselves whether other salons might not sometimes be as entertaining, and the Verdurins feeling, moreover, that this critical-spirit and this demon of frivolity might, by their contagion, prove fatal to the orthodoxy of the little church, they had been obliged to expel, one after another, all those of the "faithful" who were of the female sex.

Apart from the doctor's young wife, they were reduced almost exclusively that season (for all that Mme Verdurin herself was a thoroughly virtuous woman who came of a respectable middle-class family, excessively rich and wholly undistinguished, with which she had gradually and of her own accord severed all connection) to a young woman almost of the demi-monde, a Mme de Crécy, whom Mme Verdurin called by her Christian name, Odette, and pronounced a "love," and to the pianist's aunt, who looked as though she had, at one period, "answered the bell": ladies quite ignorant of society, who in their naïvety had so easily been led to believe that the Princesse de Sagan and the Duchesse de Guermantes were obliged to pay large sums of money to other poor wretches in order to have anyone at their dinner-parties, that if somebody had offered to procure them an invitation to the house of either of those noblewomen, the ex-doorkeeper and the woman of "easy virtue" would have contemptuously declined.

The Verdurins never invited you to dinner, you had your "place laid" there. There was never any programme for the evening's entertainment. The young pianist would play, but only if "the spirit moved him," for no one was forced to do anything, and, as M. Verdurin used to say: "We're all friends here. Liberty Hall, you know!"

If the pianist suggested playing the Ride of the Valkyries or the Prelude to Tristan, Mme Verdurin would protest, not because the music was displeasing to her, but, on the contrary, because it made too violent an impression on her. "Then you want me to have one of my headaches? You know quite well it's the same every time he plays that. I know what I'm in for. To-morrow, when I want to get up—nothing doing!" If he was not going to play they talked, and one of the friends— usually the painter who was in favour there that year— would "spin," as M. Verdurin put it, "a damned funny yarn that made 'em all split with laughter," and especially Mme Verdurin, who had such an inveterate habit of taking literally the figurative descriptions of her emotions that Dr Cottard (then a promising young practitioner) had once had to reset her jaw, which she had dislocated from laughing too much.

Evening dress was barred, because you were all "good pals" and didn't want to look like the "boring people" who were to be avoided like the plague and only asked to the big evenings, which were given as seldom as possible and then only if it would amuse the painter or make the musician better known. The rest of the time you were quite happy playing charades and having supper in fancy dress, and there was no need to mingle any alien ingredient with the little "clan."

But as the "good pals" came to take a more and more prominent place in Mme Verdurin's life, the "bores," the outcasts, grew to include everybody and everything that kept her friends away from her, that made them sometimes plead "previous engagements," the mother of one, the professional duties of another, the "little place in the country" or the ill-health of a third. If Dr Cottard felt bound to leave as soon as they rose from table, so as to go back to some patient who was seriously ill, "Who knows," Mme Verdurin would say, "it might do him far more good if you didn't go disturbing him again this evening; he'll have a good night without you; to-morrow morning you can go round early and you'll find him cured." From the beginning of December she was sick with anxiety at the thought that the "faithful" might "defect" on Christmas and New Year's Days. The pianist's aunt insisted that he must accompany her, on the latter, to a family dinner at her mother's.

"You don't suppose she'll die, your mother," exclaimed Mme Verdurin bitterly, "if you don't have dinner with her on New Year's Day, like people in the *provinces*!"

Her uneasiness was kindled again in Holy Week: "Now you, Doctor, you're a sensible, broad-minded man; you'll come of course on Good Friday, just like any other day?" she said to Cottard in the first year of the little "nucleus," in a loud and confident voice, as though there could be no doubt of his answer. But she trembled as she waited for it, for if he did not come she might find herself condemned to dine alone.

"I shall come on Good Friday—to say good-bye to you, for we're off to spend the holidays in Auvergne."

"In Auvergne? To be eaten alive by fleas and all sorts of creatures! A fine lot of good that will do you!" And after a solemn pause: "If you'd only told us, we would have tried to get up a party, and all gone there together in comfort."

And so, too, if one of the "faithful" had a friend, or one of the ladies a young man, who was liable, now and then, to make them miss an evening, the Verdurins, who were not in the least afraid of a woman's having a lover, provided that she had him in their company, loved him in their company and did not prefer him to their company, would say: "Very well, then, bring your friend along." And he would be engaged on probation, to see whether he was willing to have no secrets from Mme Verdurin, whether he was susceptible of being enrolled in the "little clan." If he failed to pass, the

faithful one who had introduced him would be taken
on one side, and would be tactfully assisted to break
with the friend or lover or mistress. But if the test
proved satisfactory, the newcomer would in turn be
numbered among the "faithful." And so when, that
year, the *demi-mondaine* told M. Verdurin that she had
made the acquaintance of such a charming man, M.
Swann, and hinted that he would very much like to be
allowed to come, M. Verdurin carried the request at
once to his wife. (He never formed an opinion on any
subject until she had formed hers, it being his special
function to carry out her wishes and those of the "faithful" generally, which he did with boundless ingenuity.)

"My dear, Mme de Crécy has something to say to
you. She would like to bring one of her friends here,
a M. Swann. What do you say?"

"Why, as if anybody could refuse anything to a little
angel like that. Be quiet, no one asked your opinion.
I tell you you're an angel."

"Just as you like," replied Odette, in an affected
tone, and then added: "You know I'm not *fishing for
compliments*."[1]

"Very well; bring your friend, if he's nice."

Now there was nothing whatsoever in common between the "little nucleus" and the society which Swann
frequented, and true socialites would have thought it
hardly worth while to occupy so exceptional a position
in the fashionable world in order to end up with an
introduction to the Verdurins. But Swann was so fond
of women that, once he had got to know more or less
all the women of the aristocracy and they had nothing
more to teach him, he had ceased to regard those na-
turalisation papers, almost a patent of nobility, which
the Faubourg Saint-Germain had bestowed upon him,
save as a sort of negotiable bond, a letter of credit with

no intrinsic value but which enabled him to improvise a status for himself in some out-of-the-way place in the country, or in some obscure quarter of Paris, where the good-looking daughter of a local squire or town clerk had taken his fancy. For at such times desire, or love, would revive in him a feeling of vanity from which he was now quite free in his everyday life (although it was doubtless this feeling which had originally prompted him towards the career as a man of fashion in which he had squandered his intellectual gifts on frivolous amusements and made use of his erudition in matters of art only to advise society ladies what pictures to buy and how to decorate their houses), which made him eager to shine, in the eyes of any fair unknown whom he had fallen for, with an elegance which the name Swann did not in itself imply. And he was most eager when the fair unknown was in humble circumstances. Just as it is not by other men of intelligence that an intelligent man is afraid of being thought a fool, so it is not by a nobleman but by an oaf that a man of fashion is afraid of finding his social value underrated. Three-quarters of the mental ingenuity and the mendacious boasting squandered ever since the world began by people who are only cheapened thereby, have been aimed at inferiors. And Swann, who behaved simply and casually with a duchess, would tremble for fear of being despised, and would instantly begin to pose, when in the presence of a housemaid.

Unlike so many people who, either from lack of energy or else from a resigned sense of the obligation laid upon them by their social grandeur to remain moored like house-boats to a particular point on the shore of life, abstain from the pleasures which are offered to them outside the wordly situation in which they remain confined until the day of their death, and are content, in the end, to describe as pleasures, for want of any better, those mediocre distractions, that just bearable tedium which it encompasses, Swann did not make an effort to find attractive the women with whom he spent his time, but sought to spend his time with women whom he had already found attractive. And as often as not they were women whose beauty was of a distinctly "common" type, for the physical qualities which he instinctively sought were the direct opposite of those he admired in the women painted or sculpted by his favourite masters. Depth of character, or a melancholy expression, would freeze his senses, which were, however, instantly aroused at the sight of healthy, abundant, rosy flesh.

If on his travels he met a family whom it would have been more correct for him to make no attempt to cultivate, but among whom he glimpsed a woman possessed of a special charm that was new to him, to remain on his "high horse" and to stave off the desire she had kindled in him, to substitute a different pleasure for the pleasure which he might have tasted in her company by writing to invite one of his former mistresses to come and join him, would have seemed to him as cowardly an abdication in the face of life, as stupid a renunciation of a new happiness as if, instead of visiting the country where he was, he had shut himself up in his own rooms and looked at views of Paris. He did not immure himself in the edifice of his social relations, but had made of them, so as to be able to set it up afresh upon new foundations wherever a woman might take his fancy, one of those collapsible tents which explorers carry about with them. Any part of it that was not portable or could not be adapted to some fresh pleasure he would have given away for nothing, however enviable it might appear to others. How often had his credit with a duchess, built up over the years by her desire to ingratiate herself with him without having found an opportunity to do so, been squandered in a moment by his calling upon her, in an indiscreetly worded message, for a recommendation by telegraph which would put him in touch at once with one of her stewards whose daughter he had noticed in the country, just as a starving man might barter a diamond for a crust of bread. Indeed he would laugh about it afterwards, for there was in his nature, redeemed by many rare refinements, an element of caddishness. Then he belonged to that class of intelligent men who had led a life of idleness, and who seek a consolation and perhaps an excuse in the notion that their idleness offers to their intelligence objects as worthy of interest as any that might be offered by art or learning, the notion that "Life" contains situations more interesting and more romantic than all the romances ever written. So, at least, he affirmed, and had no difficulty in persuading even the most sharp-witted of his society friends, notably the Baron de Charlus, whom he liked to entertain with accounts of the intriguing adventures that had befallen him, such as when he had met a woman in a train and taken her home with him, before discovering that she was the sister of a reigning monarch in whose hands were gathered at that moment all the threads of European politics, of which Swann was thus kept informed in the most delightful fashion, or when, by a complex freak of circumstance, it depended upon the choice which the Conclave was about to make whether he might or might not become the lover of somebody's cook.

It was not only the brilliant phalanx of virtuous dowagers, generals and academicians with whom he was most intimately associated that Swann so cynically com-

pelled to serve him as panders. All his friends were
accustomed to receive, from time to time, letters calling
on them for a word of recommendation or introduction,
with a diplomatic adroitness which, persisting through-
out all his successive love affairs and varying pretexts,
revealed, more glaringly than the clumsiest indiscre-
tion, a permanent disposition and an identical quest.
I used often to be told, many years later, when I began
to take an interest in his character because of the sim-
ilarities which, in wholly different respects, it offered
to my own, how, when he used to write to my grandfather (who had not yet become my grandfather, for it
was about the time of my birth that Swann's great love
affair began, and it made a long interruption in his
amatory practices), the latter, recognising his friend's
handwriting on the envelope, would exclaim: "Here's
Swann asking for something. On guard!" And, either
from distrust or from the unconscious spirit of devilry
which urges us to offer a thing only to those who do
not want it, my grandparents would offer a blunt refusal
to the most easily satisfied of his requests, as when he
begged them to introduce him to a girl who dined with
them every Sunday, and whom they were obliged,
whenever Swann mentioned her, to pretend that they
no longer saw, although they would be wondering all
through the week whom they could invite with her,
and often ended up with no one, sooner than get in
touch with the man who would so gladly have accepted.

Occasionally a couple of my grandparents' acquaintance, who had been complaining for some time that
they no longer saw Swann, would announce with satisfaction, and perhaps with a slight inclination to make
my grandparents envious of them, that he had suddenly
become as charming as he could possibly be, and was
never out of their house. My grandfather would not

want to shatter their pleasant illusion, but would look at my grandmother as he hummed the air of:

> What is this mystery?
> I cannot understand it.

or of:

> Fugitive vision...

or of:

> In matters such as this
> 'Tis best to close one's eyes.

A few months later, if my grandfather asked Swann's new friend: "What about Swann? Do you still see as much of him as ever?" the other's face would fall: "Never mention his name to me again!"

"But I thought you were such friends..."

He had been intimate in this way for several months with some cousins of my grandmother, dining almost every evening at their house. Suddenly, and without any warning, he ceased to appear. They supposed him to be ill, and the lady of the house was about to send to inquire for him when she found in the pantry a letter in his hand, which her cook had left by accident in the housekeeping book. In this he announced that he was leaving Paris and would not be able to come to the house again. The cook had been his mistress, and on breaking off relations she was the only member of the household whom he had thought it necessary to inform.

But when his mistress of the moment was a woman of rank, or at least one whose birth was not so lowly nor her position so irregular that he was unable to arrange for her reception in "society," then for her sake he would return to it, but only to the particular orbit in which she moved or into which he had drawn her. "No good depending on Swann for this evening," people would say. "Don't you remember, it's his American's night at the Opera?" He would secure invitations for her to the most exclusive salons, to those houses where he himself went regularly for weekly dinners or for poker; every evening, after a slight wave imparted to his stiff red hair had tempered with a certain softness the ardour of his bold green eyes, he would select a flower for his buttonhole and set out to meet his mistress at the house of one or other of the women of his circle; and then, thinking of the affection and admiration which the fashionable people, by whom he was so highly sought-after and whom he would meet again there, would lavish on him in the presence of the woman he loved, he would find a fresh charm in that worldly existence which had begun to pall, but whose substance, pervaded and warmly coloured by the bright flame that now flickered in its midst, seemed to him beautiful and rare since he had incorporated in it a new love.

But, whereas each of these liaisons, or each of these flirtations, had been the realisation, more or less complete, of a dream born of the sight of a face or a body which Swann had spontaneously, without effort on his part, found attractive, on the contrary when, one evening at the theatre, he was introduced to Odette de Crécy by an old friend of his, who had spoken of her as a ravishing creature with whom he might possibly come to an understanding, but had made her out to be harder of conquest than she actually was in order to appear to have done him a bigger favour by the introduction, she had struck Swann not, certainly, as being devoid of beauty, but as endowed with a kind of beauty which left him indifferent, which aroused in him no desire, which gave him, indeed, a sort of physical repulsion, as one of those women of whom all of us can cite examples, different for each of us, who are the converse of the type which our senses demand. Her profile was too sharp, her skin too delicate, her cheek-bones were too prominent, her features too tightly drawn, to be attractive to him. Her eyes were beautiful, but so large they seemed to droop beneath their own weight, strained the rest of her face and always made her appear unwell or in a bad mood. Some time after this introduction at the theatre she had written to ask Swann whether she might see his collections, which would very much interest her, "an ignorant woman with a taste for beautiful things," adding that she felt she would know him better when once she had seen him in his "*home*,"[2] where she imagined him to be "so comfortable with his tea and his books," though she had to admit that she was surprised that he should live in a neighbourhood which must be so depressing, and was "not nearly *smart* enough for such a very *smart* man." And when he allowed her to come she had said to him as she left how sorry she was to have stayed so short a time in a house into which she was so glad to have found her way at last, speaking of him as though he had meant something more to her than the rest of the people she knew, and appearing to establish between their two selves a kind of romantic bond which had made him smile. But at the time of life, tinged already with disenchantment, which Swann was approaching, when a man can content himself with being in love for the pleasure of loving without expecting too much in return, this mutual sympathy, if it is no longer as in early youth the goal towards which love inevitably tends, is nevertheless bound to it by so strong an association of ideas that it may well become the cause of love if it manifests itself first. In his younger days a man dreams of possessing the heart of the woman whom he loves; later, the feeling that he possesses a woman's heart may be enough to make him fall in love with her. And so, at an age when it would appear—since one seeks in love before everything else a subjective pleasure—that the taste for a woman's beauty must play the largest part in it, love may come into being, love of the most physical kind, without any foundation in desire. At this time of life one has already been wounded more than once by the darts of love; it no longer evolves by itself, obeying its own incomprehensible and fatal laws, before our passive and astonished hearts. We come to its aid, we falsify it by memory and by suggestion. Recognising one of its symptoms, we remember and recreate the rest. Since we know its song, which is engraved on our hearts in its entirety, there is no need for a woman to repeat the opening strains—filled with the admiration which beauty inspires—for us to remember what follows. And if she begins in the middle—where hearts are joined and where it sings of our existing, henceforward, for one another only—we are well enough attuned to that music to be able to take it up and follow our partner without hesitation at the appropriate passage.

Odette de Crécy came again to see Swann; her visits grew more frequent, and doubtless each visit revived the sense of disappointment which he felt at the sight of a face whose details he had somewhat forgotten in the interval, not remembering it as either so expressive or, in spite of her youth, so faded; he used to regret, while she was talking to him, that her really considerable beauty was not of the kind which he spontaneously admired. It must be remarked that Odette's face appeared thinner and sharper than it actually was, because the forehead and the upper part of the cheeks, that smooth and almost plane surface, were covered by the masses of hair which women wore at that period drawn forward in a fringe, raised in crimped waves and falling in stray locks over the ears; while as for her figure—and she was admirably built—it was impossible to make out its continuity (on account of the fashion then prevailing, and in spite of her being one of the best-dressed women in Paris) so much did the corsage, jutting out as though over an imaginary stomach and ending in a sharp point, beneath which bulged out the balloon of her double skirts, give a woman the appearance of being composed of different sections badly fitted together; to such an extent did the frills, the flounces, the inner bodice follow quite independently, according to the whim of their designer or the consistency of their material, the line which led them to the bows, the festoons of lace, the fringes of dangling jet beads, or carried them along the busk, but nowhere attached themselves to the living creature, who, according as the architecture of these fripperies drew them towards or away from her own, found herself either strait-laced to suffocation or else completely buried.

But, after Odette had left him, Swann would think with a smile of her telling how the time would drag until he allowed her to come again; he remembered the anxious, timid way in which she had once begged him that it might not be too long, and the way she had gazed at him then, with a look of shy entreaty which gave her a touching air beneath the bunches of white straw, tied with a ribbon of black velvet. "And won't you," she had ventured, "come just once and have tea with me?" He had pleaded pressure of work, an essay— which, in reality, he had abandoned years ago—on Vermeer of Delft. "I know that I'm quite useless," she had replied, "a pitiful creature like me beside a learned great man like you. I should be like the frog in the fable! And yet I should so much like to learn, to know things, to be initiated. What fun it would be to become a regular bookworm, to bury my nose in a lot of old papers!" she had added, with the self-satisfied air which an elegant woman adopts when she insists that her one desire is to undertake, without fear of soiling her fingers, some grubby task, such as cooking the dinner, "really getting down to it" herself. "You'll only laugh at me, but this painter who stops you from seeing me" (she meant Vermeer), "I've never even heard of him; is he alive still? Can I see any of his things in Paris, so as to have some idea of what's going on behind that great brow which works so hard, that head which I feel sure is always puzzling away about things; to be able to say 'There, that's what he's thinking about!' What a joy it would be to be able to help you with your work."

He had excused himself on the grounds of his fear of forming new friendships, which he gallantly described as his fear of being made unhappy. "You're afraid of affection? How odd that is, when I go about seeking nothing else, and would give my soul to find it!" she had said, so naturally and with such an air of conviction that he had been genuinely touched. "Some woman must have made you suffer. And you think that the rest are all like her. She can't have understood you: you're such an exceptional person. That's what I liked about you from the start; I felt that you weren't like everybody else."

"And then, besides, you too," he had said to her, "I know what women are; you must have a whole heap of things to do, and never any time to spare."

"I? Why, I never have anything to do. I'm always free, and I always will be free if you want me. At whatever hour of the day or night it may suit you to see me, just send for me, and I shall be only too delighted to come. Will you do that? Do you know what would be nice—if I were to introduce you to Mme Verdurin, where I go every evening. Just fancy our meeting there, and my thinking that it was a little for my sake that you had come."

And doubtless, in thus remembering their conversations, in thinking about her thus when he was alone, he was simply turning over her image among those of countless other women in his romantic day-dreams; but if, thanks to some accidental circumstance (or even perhaps without that assistance, for the circumstance which presents itself at the moment when a mental state, hitherto latent, makes itself felt, may well have had no influence whatsoever upon that state), the image of Odette de Crécy came to absorb the whole of these day-dreams, if the memory of her could no longer be eliminated from them, then her bodily imperfections would no longer be of the least importance, nor would the conformity of her body, more or less than any other, to the requirements of Swann's taste, since, having become the body of the woman he loved, it must henceforth be the only one capable of causing him joy or anguish.

It so happened that my grandfather had known—which was more than could be said of any of their actual acquaintance—the family of those Verdurins. But he had entirely severed his connection with the "young Verdurin," as he called him, considering him more or less to have fallen—though without losing hold of his millions—among the riff-raff of Bohemia. One day he received a letter from Swann asking whether he could put him in touch with the Verdurins: "On guard! on guard!" my grandfather exclaimed as he read it, "I'm not at all surprised; Swann was bound to finish up like this. A nice lot of people! I cannot do what he asks, because in the first place I no longer know the gentleman in question. Besides, there must be a woman in it somewhere, and I never get mixed up in such matters. Ah, well, we shall see some fun if Swann begins running after the young Verdurins."

And on my grandfather's refusal to act as sponsor, it was Odette herself who had taken Swann to the house.

The Verdurins had had dining with them, on the day when Swann made his first appearance, Dr and Mme Cottard, the young pianist and his aunt, and the painter then in favour, and these were joined, in the course of the evening, by a few more of the "faithful."

Dr Cottard was never quite certain of the tone in which he ought to reply to any observation, or whether the speaker was jesting or in earnest. And so by way of precaution he would embellish all his facial expressions with the offer of a conditional, a provisional smile whose expectant subtlety would exonerate him from the charge of being a simpleton, if the remark addressed to him should turn out to have been facetious. But as he must also be prepared to face the alternative, he dared not allow this smile to assert itself positively on his features, and you would see there a perpetually flickering uncertainty, in which could be deciphered the question that he never dared to ask: "Do you really mean that?" He was no more confident of the manner in which he ought to conduct himself in the street, or indeed in life generally, than he was in a drawing-room; and he might be seen greeting passers-by, carriages, and anything that occurred with a knowing smile which absolved his subsequent behaviour of all impropriety, since it proved, if it should turn out unsuited to the occasion, that he was well aware of that, and that if he had assumed a smile, the jest was a secret of his own.

On all those points, however, where a plain question appeared to him to be permissible, the doctor was unsparing in his endeavours to cultivate the wilderness of his ignorance and uncertainty and to perfect his education.

So it was that, following the advice given him by a wise mother on his first coming up to the capital from his provincial home, he would never let pass either a figure of speech or a proper name that was new to him without an effort to secure the fullest information upon it.

As regards figures of speech, he was insatiable in his thirst for knowledge, for, often imagining them to have a more definite meaning than was actually the case, he would want to know what exactly was meant by those which he most frequently heard used: "devilish pretty," "blue blood," "a cat and dog life," "the day of reckoning," "the glass of fashion," "to give a free hand," "to be absolutely floored," and so forth; and in what particular circumstances he himself might make use of them in conversation. Failing these, he would adorn it with puns and other plays on words which he had learned by rote. As for unfamiliar names which were uttered in his hearing, he used merely to repeat them in a questioning tone, which he thought would suffice to procure him explanations for which he would not ostensibly be seeking.

Since he was completely lacking in the critical faculty on which he prided himself in everything, the refinement of good breeding which consists in assuring someone whom you are obliging, without expecting to be believed, that it is really you who are obliged to him, was wasted on Cottard, who took everything he heard in its literal sense. Blind though she was to his faults,

Mme Verdurin was genuinely irritated, though she continued to regard him as brilliantly clever, when, after she had invited him to see and hear Sarah Bernhardt from a stage box, and had said politely: "It's so good of you to have come, Doctor, especially as I'm sure you must often have heard Sarah Bernhardt; and besides, I'm afraid we're rather too near the stage," the doctor, who had come into the box with a smile which waited before affirming itself or vanishing from his face until some authoritative person should enlighten him as to the merits of the spectacle, replied: "To be sure, we're far too near the stage, and one is beginning to get sick of Sarah Bernhardt. But you expressed a wish that I should come. And your wish is my command. I'm only too glad to be able to do you this little service. What would one not do to please you, you are so kind." And he went on, "Sarah Bernhardt—she's what they call the Golden Voice, isn't she? They say she sets the house on fire. That's an odd expression, ain't it?" in the hope of an enlightening commentary which, however, was not forthcoming.

"D'you know," Mme Verdurin had said to her husband, "I believe we're on the wrong tack when we belittle what we give to the Doctor. He's a scholar who lives in a world of his own; he has no idea what things are worth, and he accepts everything that we say as gospel."

"I never dared to mention it," M. Verdurin had answered, "but I've noticed the same thing myself." And on the following New Year's Day, instead of sending Dr Cottard a ruby that cost three thousand francs and pretending it was a mere trifle, M. Verdurin bought an artificial stone for three hundred, and let it be understood that it was something almost impossible to match.

When Mme Verdurin had announced that they were

to see M. Swann that evening, "Swann!" the doctor had exclaimed in a tone rendered brutal by his astonishment, for the smallest piece of news would always take him utterly unawares though he imagined himself to be prepared for any eventuality. And seeing that no one answered him, "Swann! Who on earth is Swann?" he shouted, in a frenzy of anxiety which subsided as soon as Mme Verdurin had explained, "Why, the friend Odette told us about."

"Ah, good, good; that's all right, then," answered the doctor, at once mollified. As for the painter, he was overjoyed at the prospect of Swann's appearing at the Verdurins', because he supposed him to be in love with Odette, and was always ready to encourage amorous liaisons. "Nothing amuses me more than matchmaking," he confided to Cottard. "I've brought off quite a few, even between women!"

In telling the Verdurins that Swann was extremely "smart," Odette had alarmed them with the prospect of another "bore." When he arrived, however, he made an excellent impression, an indirect cause of which, though they did not know it, was his familiarity with the best society. He had, indeed, one of the advantages which men who have lived and moved in society enjoy over those, however intelligent, who have not, namely that they no longer see it transfigured by the longing or repulsion which it inspires, but regard it as of no importance. Their good nature, freed from all taint of snobbishness and from the fear of seeming too friendly, grown independent, in fact, has the ease, the grace of movement of a trained gymnast each of whose supple limbs will carry out precisely what is required without any clumsy participation by the rest of his body. The simple and elementary gestures of a man of the world as he courteously holds out his hand to the unknown

youth who is introduced to him, or bows discreetly to
the ambassador to whom he is introduced, had gradually
pervaded the whole of Swann's social deportment without his being conscious of it, so that in the company
of people from a lower social sphere, such as the Verdurins and their friends, he displayed an instinctive
alacrity, made amiable overtures, from which in their
view a "bore" would have refrained. He showed a momentary coldness only on meeting Dr Cottard; for,
seeing him wink at him with an ambiguous smile,
before they had yet spoken to one another (a grimace
which Cottard styled "letting 'em all come"), Swann
supposed that the doctor recognised him from having
met him already, probably in some haunt of pleasure,
though these he himself very rarely visited, never having
lived a life of debauchery. Regarding such an allusion
as in bad taste, especially in front of Odette, whose
opinion of himself it might easily alter for the worse,
Swann assumed his most icy manner. But when he
learned that a lady standing near him was Mme Cottard,
he decided that so young a husband would not deliberately have hinted at amusements of that order in his
wife's presence, and so ceased to interpret the doctor's
expression in the sense which he had at first suspected.
The painter at once invited Swann to visit his studio
with Odette; Swann thought him very civil. "Perhaps
you will be more highly favoured than I have been,"
said Mme Verdurin in a tone of mock resentment,
"perhaps you'll be allowed to see Cottard's portrait"
(which she had commissioned from the painter). "Take
care, Master Biche," she reminded the painter, whom
it was a time-honoured pleasantry to address as "Master," "to catch that nice look in his eyes, that witty
little twinkle. You know what I want to have most of
all is his smile; that's what I've asked you to paint—

the portrait of his smile." And since the phrase struck her as noteworthy, she repeated it very loud, so as to make sure that as many as possible of her guests should hear it, and even made use of some vague pretext to draw the circle closer before she uttered it again. Swann begged to be introduced to everyone, even to an old friend of the Verdurins called Saniette, whose shyness, simplicity and goodnature had lost him most of the consideration he had earned for his skill in palaeography, his large fortune, and the distinguished family to which he belonged. When he spoke, his words came out in a burble which was delightful to hear because one felt that it indicated not so much a defect of speech as a quality of the soul, as it were a survival from the age of innocence which he had never wholly outgrown. All the consonants which he was unable to pronounce seemed like harsh utterances of which his gentle lips were incapable. In asking to be introduced to M. Saniette, Swann gave Mme Verdurin the impression of reversing roles (so much so that she replied, with emphasis on the distinction: "M. Swann, pray allow me to introduce our friend Saniette to you") but aroused in Saniette himself a warmth of devotion, which, however, the Verdurins never disclosed to Swann, since Saniette rather irritated them, and they did not feel inclined to provide him with friends. On the other hand the Verdurins were extremely touched by Swann's next request, for he felt that he must ask to meet the pianist's aunt. She wore a black dress, as was her invariable custom, for she believed that a woman always looked well in black and that nothing could be more distinguished; but her face was exceedingly red, as it always was for some time after a meal. She bowed to Swann with deference, but drew herself up again with great dignity. As she was entirely uneducated, and was afraid of making mistakes in grammar and pronunciation, she used purposely to speak in an indistinct and garbling manner, thinking that if she should make a slip it would be so buried in the surrounding confusion that no one could be certain whether she had actually made it or not; with the result that her talk was a sort of continuous, blurred expectoration, out of which would emerge, at rare intervals, the few sounds and syllables of which she felt sure. Swann supposed himself entitled to poke a little mild fun at her in conversation with M. Verdurin, who, however, was rather put out.

"She's such an excellent woman!" he rejoined. "I grant you that she's not exactly brilliant; but I assure you that she can be most agreeable when you chat with her alone."

"I'm sure she can," Swann hastened to concede. "All I meant was that she hardly struck me as 'distinguished,'" he went on, isolating the epithet in the inverted commas of his tone, "and that, on the whole, is something of a compliment."

"For instance," said M. Verdurin, "now this will surprise you: she writes quite delightfully. You've never heard her nephew play? It's admirable, eh, Doctor? Would you like me to ask him to play something, M. Swann?"

"Why, it would be a joy..." Swann was beginning to reply, when the doctor broke in derisively. Having once heard it said, and never having forgotten, that in general conversation over-emphasis and the use of formal expressions were out of date, whenever he heard a solemn word used seriously, as the word "joy" had just been used by Swann, he felt that the speaker had been guilty of pomposity. And if, moreover, the word in question happened to occur also in what he called an old "tag," however common it might still be in current usage, the doctor jumped to the conclusion that the remark which was about to be made was ridiculous, and completed it ironically with the cliché he assumed the speaker was about to perpetrate, although in reality it had never entered his mind.

"A joy for ever!" he exclaimed mischievously, throwing up his arms in a grandiloquent gesture.

M. Verdurin could not help laughing.

"What are all those good people laughing at over there? There's no sign of brooding melancholy down in your corner," shouted Mme Verdurin. "You don't suppose I find it very amusing to be stuck up here by myself on the stool of repentance," she went on with mock peevishness, in a babyish tone of voice.

Mme Verdurin was seated on a high Swedish chair of waxed pinewood, which a violinist from that country had given her, and which she kept in her drawing-room although in appearance it suggested a work-stand and clashed with the really good antique furniture which she had besides; but she made a point of keeping on view the presents which her "faithful" were in the habit of making her from time to time, so that the donors might have the pleasure of seeing them there when they came to the house. She tried to persuade them to confine their tributes to flowers and sweets, which had at least the merit of mortality; but she never succeeded, and the house was gradually filled with a collection of footwarmers, cushions, clocks, screens, barometers and vases, a constant repetition and a boundless incongruity of useless but indestructible objects.

From this lofty perch she would take a spirited part in the conversation of the "faithful," and would revel in all their "drollery"; but, since the accident to her jaw, she had abandoned the effort involved in wholehearted laughter, and had substituted a kind

of symbolical dumb-show which signified, without
endangering or fatiguing her in any way, that she was
"splitting her sides." At the least witticism aimed by
a member of the circle against a "bore," or against a
former member who was now relegated to the limbo
of "bores"—and to the utter despair of M. Verdurin,
who had always made out that he was just as affable as
his wife, but who, since his laughter was the "real
thing," was out of breath in a moment and so was
overtaken and vanquished by her device of a feigned
but continuous hilarity—she would utter a shrill cry,
shut tight her little bird-like eyes, which were beginning to be clouded over by a cataract, and quickly, as
though she had only just time to avoid some indecent
sight or to parry a mortal blow, burying her face in her
hands, which completely engulfed it and hid it from
view, would appear to be struggling to suppress, to
annihilate, a laugh which, had she succumbed to it,
must inevitably have left her inanimate. So, stupefied
with the gaiety of the "faithful," drunk with good-
fellowship, scandal and asseveration, Mme Verdurin,
perched on her high seat like a cage-bird whose biscuit
has been steeped in mulled wine, would sit aloft and
sob with affability.

Meanwhile M. Verdurin, after first asking Swann's
permission to light his pipe ("No ceremony here, you
understand; we're all pals!"), went and asked the young
musician to sit down at the piano.

"Leave him alone; don't bother him; he hasn't come
here to be tormented," cried Mme Verdurin. "I won't
have him tormented."

"But why on earth should it bother him?" rejoined
M. Verdurin. "I'm sure M. Swann has never heard the
sonata in F sharp which we discovered. He's going to
play us the pianoforte arrangement."

"No, no, no, not my sonata!" she screamed, "I don't want to be made to cry until I get a cold in the head, and neuralgia all down my face, like last time. You're all so very kind and considerate, it's easy to see that none of you will have to stay in bed for a week."

This little scene, which was re-enacted as often as the young pianist sat down to play, never failed to delight her friends as much as if they were witnessing it for the first time, as a proof of the seductive originality of the "Mistress" and of the acute sensitiveness of her musical "ear." Those nearest to her would attract the attention of the rest, who were smoking or playing cards at the other end of the room, by their cries of "Hear, hear!" which, as in Parliamentary debates, showed that something worth listening to was being said. And next day they would commiserate with those who had been prevented from coming that evening, assuring them that the "little scene" had been even more amusing than usual.

"Well, all right, then," said M. Verdurin, "he can play just the *andante*."

"Just the *andante*! That really is a bit rich!" cried his wife. "As if it weren't precisely the *andante* that breaks every bone in my body. The Master is really too priceless! Just as though, in the Ninth, he said 'we'll just hear the *finale*,' or 'just the overture' of the *Mastersingers*."

The doctor, however, urged Mme Verdurin to let the pianist play, not because he supposed her to be feigning when she spoke of the distressing effects that music always had upon her—for he recognised certain neurasthenic symptoms therein—but from the habit, common to many doctors, of at once relaxing the strict letter of a prescription as soon as it jeopardises something they regard as more important, such as the success of a social gathering at which they are present, and of which the patient whom they urge for once to forget his dyspepsia or his flu is one of the essential ingredients.

"You won't be ill this time, you'll find," he told her, seeking at the same time to influence her with a hypnotic stare. "And if you are ill, we'll look after you."

"Will you really?" Mme Verdurin spoke as though, with so great a favour in store for her, there was nothing for it but to capitulate. Perhaps, too, by dint of saying that she was going to be ill, she had worked herself into a state in which she occasionally forgot that it was all a fabrication and adopted the attitude of a genuine invalid. And it may often be remarked that invalids, weary of having to make the infrequency of their attacks depend on their own prudence, like to persuade themselves that they can do everything that they enjoy, and that does them harm, with impunity, provided that they place themselves in the hands of a higher authority who, without putting them to the least inconvenience, can and will, by uttering a word or by administering a pill, set them once again on their feet.

Odette had gone to sit on a tapestry-covered settee near the piano, saying to Mme Verdurin, "I have my own little corner, haven't I?"

And Mme Verdurin, seeing Swann by himself on a chair, made him get up: "You're not at all comfortable there. Go along and sit by Odette. You can make room for M. Swann there, can't you, Odette?"

"What charming Beauvais!" said Swann politely, stopping to admire the settee before he sat down on it.

"Ah! I'm glad you appreciate my settee," replied Mme Verdurin, "and I warn you that if you expect ever to see another like it you may as well abandon the idea at once. They've never made anything else like it. And these little chairs, too, are perfect marvels. You can look at them in a moment. The emblems in each of the bronze mouldings correspond to the subject of the tapestry on the chair; you know, you'll have a great deal to enjoy if you want to look at them—I can promise you a delightful time, I assure you. Just look at the little friezes round the edges; here, look, the little vine on a red background in this one, the Bear and the Grapes. Isn't it well drawn? What do you say? I think they knew a thing or two about drawing! Doesn't it make your mouth water, that vine? My husband makes out that I'm not fond of fruit, because I eat less of them than he does. But not a bit of it, I'm greedier than any of you, but I have no need to fill my mouth with them when I can feed on them with my eyes. What are you all laughing at now, pray? Ask the doctor; he'll tell you that those grapes act on me like a regular purge. Some people go to Fontainebleau for cures; I take my own little Beauvais cure here. But, M. Swann, you mustn't run away without feeling the little bronze mouldings on the backs. Isn't it an exquisite patina? No, no, you must feel them properly, with your whole hand!"

"If Mme Verdurin is going to start fingering her bronzes," said the painter, "we shan't get any music to-night."

"Be quiet, you wretch! And yet we poor women," she went on, turning towards Swann, "are forbidden pleasures far less voluptuous than this. There is no flesh in the world to compare with it. None. When M. Verdurin did me the honour of being madly jeal-ous... Come, you might at least be polite—don't say that you've never been jealous!"

"But, my dear, I've said absolutely nothing. Look

here, Doctor, I call you as a witness. Did I utter a word?"

Swann had begun, out of politeness, to finger the bronzes, and did not like to stop.

"Come along; you can caress them later. Now it's you who are going to be caressed, caressed aurally. You'll like that, I think. Here's the young gentleman who will tke charge of that."

After the pianist had played, Swann was even more affable towards him than towards any of the other guests, for the following reason:

The year before, at an evening party, he had heard a piece of music played on the piano and violin. At first he had appreciated only the material quality of the sounds which those instruments secreted. And it had been a source of keen pleasure when, below the delicate line of the violin-part, slender but robust, compact and commanding, he had suddenly become aware of the mass of the piano-part beginning to surge upward in plashing waves of sound, multiform but indivisible, smooth yet restless, like the deep blue tumult of the sea, silvered and charmed into a minor key by the moonlight. But then at a certain moment, without being able to distinguish any clear outline, or to give a name to what was pleasing him, suddenly enraptured, he had tried to grasp the phrase or harmony—he did not know which—that had just been played and that had opened and expanded his soul, as the fragrance of certain roses, wafted upon the moist air of evening, has the power of dilating one's nostrils. Perhaps it was owing to his ignorance of music that he had received so confused an impression, one of those that are nonetheless the only purely musical impressions, limited in their extent, entirely original, and irreducible to any other kind. An impression of this order, vanishing in an instant, is, so to speak, *sine materia*. Doubtless the notes which we hear at such moments tend, according to their pitch and volume, to spread out before our eyes over surfaces of varying dimensions, to trace arabesques, to give us the sensation of breadth or tenuity, stability or caprice. But the notes themselves have vanished before these sensations have developed sufficiently to escape submersion under those which the succeeding or even simultaneous notes have already begun to awaken in us. And this impression would continue to envelop in its liquidity, its ceaseless overlapping, the *motifs* which from time to time emerge, barely discernible, to plunge again and disappear and drown, recognised only by the particular kind of pleasure which they instil, impossible to describe, to recollect, to name, ineffable—did not our memory, like a labourer who toils at the laying down of firm foundations beneath the tumult of the waves, by fashioning for us facsimiles of those fugitive phrases, enable us to compare and to contrast them with those that follow. And so, scarcely had the exquisite sensation which Swann had experienced died away, before his memory had furnished him with an immediate transcript, sketchy, it is true, and provisional, which he had been able to glance at while the piece continued, so that, when the same impression suddenly returned, it was no longer impossible to grasp. He could picture to himself its extent, its symmetrical arrangement, its notation, its expressive value; he had before him something that was no longer pure music, but rather design, architecture, thought, and which allowed the actual music to be recalled. This time he had distinguished quite clearly a phrase which emerged for a few moments above the waves of sound. It had at once suggested to him a world of inexpressible delights, of whose existence, before hearing it, he had never dreamed, into which he felt that nothing else could initiate him; and he had been filled with love for it, as with a new and strange desire.

With a slow and rhythmical movement it led him first this way, then that, towards a state of happiness that was noble, unintelligible, and yet precise. And then suddenly, having reached a certain point from which he was preparing to follow it, after a momentary pause, abruptly it changed direction, and in a fresh movement, more rapid, fragile, melancholy, incessant, sweet, it bore him off with it towards new vistas. Then it vanished. He hoped, with a passionate longing, that he might find it again, a third time. And reappear it did, though without speaking to him more clearly, bringing him, indeed, a pleasure less profound. But when he returned home he felt the need of it: he was like a man into whose life a woman he has seen for a moment passing by has brought the image of a new beauty which deepens his own sensibility, although he does not even know her name or whether he will ever see her again.

Indeed this passion for a phrase of music seemed, for a time, to open up before Swann the possibility of a sort of rejuvenation. He had so long ceased to direct his life towards any ideal goal, confining himself to the pursuit of ephemeral satisfactions, that he had come to believe, without ever admitting it to himself in so many words, that he would remain in that condition for the rest of his days. More than this, since his mind no longer entertained any lofty ideas, he had ceased to believe in (although he could not have expressly denied) their reality. Thus he had grown into the habit of taking refuge in trivial considerations, which enabled him to disregard matters of fundamental importance. Just as he never stopped to ask himself whether he would not have done better by not going into society, but on the other hand knew for certain that if he had accepted an invitation he must put in an appearance, and that afterwards, if he did not actually call, he must at least leave cards upon his hostess, so in his conversation he took care never to express with any warmth a personal opinion about anything, but instead would supply facts and details which were valid enough in themselves and excused him from showing his real capacities. He would be extremely precise about the recipe for a dish, the dates of a painter's birth and death, and the titles of his works. Sometimes, in spite of himself, he would let himself go so far as to express an opinion on a work of art, or on someone's interpretation of life, but then he would cloak his words in a tone of irony, as though he did not altogether associate himself with what he was saying. But now, like a confirmed invalid in whom, all of a sudden, a change of air and surroundings, or a new course of treatment, or sometimes an organic change in himself, spontaneous and unaccountable, seems to have brought about such an improvement in his health that he begins to envisage the possibility, hitherto beyond all hope, of starting to lead belatedly a wholly different life, Swann found in himself, in the memory of the phrase that he had heard, in certain other sonatas which he had made people play to him to see whether he might not perhaps discover his phrase therein, the presence of one of those invisible realities in which he had ceased to believe and to which, as though the music had had upon the moral barrenness from which he was suffering a sort of recreative influence, he was conscious once again of the desire and almost the strength to consecrate his life. But, never having managed to find out whose work it was that he had heard played that

evening, he had been unable to procure a copy and had
finally forgotten the quest. He had indeed, in the course
of that week, encountered several of the people who
had been at the party with him, and had questioned
them; but most of them had either arrived after or left
before the piece was played; some had indeed been there
at the time but had gone into another room to talk,
and those who had stayed to listen had no clearer
impression than the rest. As for his hosts, they knew
that it was a recent work which the musicians whom
they had engaged for the evening had asked to be allowed to play; but, as these last had gone away on tour,
Swann could learn nothing further. He had, of course,
a number of musical friends, but, vividly as he could
recall the exquisite and inexpressible pleasure which the
little phrase had given him, and could see in his mind's
eye the forms that it had traced, he was quite incapable
of humming it to them. And so, at last, he ceased to
think of it.

But that night, at Mme Verdurin's, scarcely had the
young pianist begun to play than suddenly, after a high
note sustained through two whole bars, Swann sensed
its approach, stealing forth from beneath that long-
drawn sonority, stretched like a curtain of sound to veil
the mystery of its incubation, and recognised, secret,
murmuring, detached, the airy and perfumed phrase
that he had loved. And it was so peculiarly itself, it
had so individual, so irreplaceable a charm, that Swann
felt as though he had met, in a friend's drawing-room,
a woman whom he had seen and admired in the street
and had despaired of ever seeing again. Finally the
phrase receded, diligently guiding its successors through
the ramifications of its fragrance, leaving on Swann's
features the reflection of its smile. But now, at last, he
could ask the name of his fair unknown (and was told

that it was the *andante* of Vinteuil's sonata for piano and violin); he held it safe, could have it again to himself, at home, as often as he wished, could study its language and acquire its secret.

And so, when the pianist had finished, Swann crossed the room and thanked him with a vivacity which delighted Mme Verdurin.

"Isn't he a charmer?" she asked Swann, "doesn't he just understand his sonata, the little wretch? You never dreamed, did you, that a piano could be made to express all that? Upon my word, you'd think it was everything but the piano! I'm caught out every time I hear it; I think I'm listening to an orchestra. Though it's better, really, than an orchestra, more complete."

The young pianist bowed as he answered, smiling and underlining each of his words as though he were making an epigram: "You are most generous to me."

And while Mme Verdurin was saying to her husband, "Run and fetch him a glass of orangeade; he's earned it," Swann began to tell Odette how he had fallen in love with that little phrase. When their hostess, who was some way off, called out, "Well! It looks to me as though someone was saying nice things to you, Odette!" she replied, "Yes, very nice," and he found her simplicity delightful. Then he asked for information about this Vinteuil: what else he had done, at what period in his life he had composed the sonata, and what meaning the little phrase could have had for him—that was what Swann wanted most to know.

But none of these people who professed to admire this musician (when Swann had said that the sonata was really beautiful Mme Verdurin had exclaimed, "Of course it's beautiful! But you don't dare to confess that you don't know Vinteuil's sonata; you have no right not to know it!"—and the painter had added, "Ah, yes, it's a very fine bit of work, isn't it? Not, of course, if you want something 'obvious,' something 'popular,' but, I mean to say, it makes a very great impression on us artists"), none of them seemed ever to have asked himself these questions, for none of them was able to answer them.

Even to one or two particular remarks made by Swann about his favourite phrase: "D'you know, that's a funny thing; I had never noticed it. I may as well tell you that I don't much care about peering at things through a microscope, and pricking myself on pin-points of difference. No, we don't waste time splitting hairs in this house," Mme Verdurin replied, while Dr Cottard gazed at her with open-mouthed admiration and studious zeal as she skipped lightly from one stepping-stone to another of her stock of ready-made phrases. Both he, however, and Mme Cottard, with a kind of common sense which is shared by many people of humble origin, were careful not to express an opinion, or to pretend to admire a piece of music which they confessed to each other, once they were back at home, that they no more understood than they could understand the art of "Master" Biche. Inasmuch as the public cannot recognise the charm, the beauty, even the outlines of nature save in the stereotyped impressions of an art which they have gradually assimilated, while an original artist starts by rejecting those stereotypes, so M. and Mme Cottard, typical, in this respect, of the public, were incapable of finding, either in Vinteuil's sonata or in Biche's portraits, what constituted for them harmony in music or beauty in painting. It appeared to them, when the pianist played his sonata, as though he were striking at random from the piano a medley of notes which bore no relation to the musical forms to which they themselves were accustomed, and that the painter simply flung the colours at random on his canvases. When, in one of these, they were able to distinguish a human form, they always found it coarsened and vulgarised (that is to say lacking in the elegance of the school of painting through whose spectacles they were in the habit of seeing even the real, living people who passed them in the street) and devoid of truth, as though M. Biche had not known how the human shoulder was constructed, or that a woman's hair was not ordinarily purple.

However, when the "faithful" were scattered out of earshot, the doctor felt that the opportunity was too good to be missed, and so (while Mme Verdurin was adding a final word of commendation of Vinteuil's sonata), like a would-be swimmer who jumps into the water so as to learn, but chooses a moment when there are not too many people looking on: "Yes, indeed; he's what they call a musician *di primo cartello*!" he exclaimed with sudden determination.

Swann discovered no more than that the recent appearance of Vinteuil's sonata had caused a great stir among the most advanced school of musicians, but that it was still unknown to the general public.

"I know someone called Vinteuil," said Swann, thinking of the old piano-teacher at Combray who had taught my grandmother's sisters.

"Perhaps he's the man," cried Mme Verdurin.

"Oh, no, if you'd ever set eyes on him you wouldn't entertain the idea."

"Then to entertain the idea is to affirm it?" the doctor suggested.

"But it may well be some relation," Swann went on. "That would be bad enough; but, after all, there's no reason why a genius shouldn't have a cousin who's a silly old fool. And if that should be so, I swear there's no known or unknown form of torture I wouldn't undergo to get the old fool to introduce me to the man who composed the sonata; starting with the torture of the old fool's company, which would be ghastly."

The painter understood that Vinteuil was seriously ill at the moment, and that Dr Potain despaired of his life.

"What!" cried Mme Verdurin, "Do people still call in Potain?"

"Ah! Mme Verdurin," Cottard simpered, "you forget that you are speaking of one of my colleagues—I should say one of my masters."

The painter had heard it said that Vinteuil was threatened with the loss of his reason. And he insisted that signs of this could be detected in certain passages in the sonata. This remark did not strike Swann as ridiculous; but it disturbed him, for, since a work of pure music contains none of the logical sequences whose deformation, in spoken or written language, is a proof of insanity, so insanity diagnosed in a sonata seemed to him as mysterious a thing as the insanity of a dog or a horse, although instances may be observed of these.

"Don't speak to me about your masters; you know ten times as much as he does!" Mme Verdurin answered Dr Cottard, in the tone of a woman who has the courage of her convictions and is quite ready to stand up to anyone who disagrees with her. "At least you don't kill your patients!"

"But, Madame, he is in the Academy," replied the doctor with heavy irony. "If a patient prefers to die at the hands of one of the princes of science. . . . It's much smarter to be able to say, 'Yes, I have Potain.'"

"Oh, indeed! Smarter, is it?" said Mme Verdurin. "So there are fashions, nowadays, in illness, are there? I didn't know that. . . . Oh, you do make me laugh!"

she screamed suddenly, burying her face in her hands. "And here was I, poor thing, talking quite seriously and never realising that you were pulling my leg."

As for M. Verdurin, finding it rather a strain to raise a laugh for so little, he was content with puffing out a cloud of smoke from his pipe, reflecting sadly that he could never hope to keep pace with his wife in her Atalanta-flights across the field of mirth.

"D'you know, we like your friend very much," said Mme Verdurin when Odette was bidding her good night. "He's so unaffected, quite charming. If they're all like that, the friends you want to introduce to us, by all means bring them."

M. Verdurin remarked that Swann had failed, all the same, to appreciate the pianist's aunt.

"I dare say he felt a little out of his depth, poor man," suggested Mme Verdurin. "You can't expect him to have caught the tone of the house already, like Cottard, who has been one of our little clan now for years. The first time doesn't count; it's just for breaking the ice. Odette, it's agreed that he's to join us to-morrow at the Châtelet. Perhaps you might call for him?"

"No, he doesn't want that."

"Oh, very well; just as you like. Provided he doesn't fail us at the last moment."

Greatly to Mme Verdurin's surprise, he never failed them. He would go to meet them no matter where, sometimes at restaurants on the outskirts of Paris which were little frequented as yet, since the season had not yet begun, more often at the theatre, of which Mme Verdurin was particularly fond. One evening at her house he heard her remark how useful it would be to have a special pass for first nights and gala performances, and what a nuisance it had been not having one on the day of Gambetta's funeral. Swann, who never spoke of his brilliant connections, but only of those not highly thought of in the Faubourg Saint-Germain whom he would have considered it snobbish to conceal, and among whom he had come to include his connections in the official world, broke in: "I'll see to that. You shall have it in time for the *Danicheff* revival. I happen to be lunching with the Prefect of Police to-morrow at the Elysée."

"What's that? The Elysée?" Dr Cottard roared in a voice of thunder.

"Yes, at M. Grévy's," replied Swann, a little embarrassed at the effect which his announcement had produced.

"Are you often taken like that?" the painter asked Cottard with mock-seriousness.

As a rule, once an explanation had been given, Cottard would say: "Ah, good, good; that's all right, then," after which he would show not the least trace of emotion. But this time Swann's last words, instead of the usual calming effect, had that of raising to fever-pitch his astonishment at the discovery that a man with whom he himself was actually sitting at table, a man who had no official position, no honours or distinction of any sort, was on visiting terms with the Head of State.

"What's that you say? M. Grévy? You know M. Grévy?" he demanded of Swann, in the stupid and incredulous tone of a constable on duty at the palace who, when a stranger asks to see the President of the Republic, realising at once "the sort of man he is dealing with," as the newspapers say, assures the poor lunatic that he will be admitted at once, and directs him to the reception ward of the police infirmary.

"I know him slightly; we have some friends in common" (Swann dared not add that one of these friends was the Prince of Wales). "Besides, he is very free with his invitations, and I assure you his luncheon-parties are not the least bit amusing. They're very simple affairs, too, you know—never more than eight at table," he went on, trying desperately to cut out everything that seemed to show off his relations with the President in a light too dazzling for the doctor's eyes.

Whereupon Cottard, at once conforming in his mind to the literal interpretation of what Swann was saying, decided that invitations from M. Grévy were very little sought after, were sent out, in fact, into the highways and byways. And from that moment he was no longer surprised to hear that Swann, or anyone else, was "always at the Elysée"; he even felt a little sorry for a man who had to go to luncheon-parties which he himself admitted were a bore.

"Ah, good, good; that's quite all right, then," he said, in the tone of a suspicious customs official who, after hearing your explanations, stamps your passport and lets you proceed on your journey without troubling to examine your luggage.

"I can well believe you don't find them amusing, those luncheons. Indeed, it's very good of you to go to them," said Mme Verdurin, who regarded the President of the Republic as a "bore" to be especially dreaded, since he had at his disposal means of seduction, and even of compulsion, which, if employed to captivate her "faithful," might easily make them default. "It seems he's as deaf as a post and eats with his fingers."

"Upon my word! Then it can't be much fun for you, going there." A note of pity sounded in the doctor's voice; and then struck by the number—only eight at table—"Are these luncheons what you would describe as 'intimate'?" he inquired briskly, not so much out of idle curiosity as from linguistic zeal.

But so great was the prestige of the President of the

Republic in the eyes of Dr Cottard that neither the modesty of Swann nor the malevolence of Mme Verdurin could wholly efface it, and he never sat down to dinner with the Verdurins without asking anxiously, "D'you think we shall see M. Swann here this evening? He's a personal friend of M. Grévy's. I suppose that means he's what you'd call a 'gentleman'?" He even went to the length of offering Swann a card of invitation to the Dental Exhibition.

"This will let you in, and anyone you take with you," he explained, "but dogs are not admitted. I'm just warning you, you understand, because some friends of mine went there once without knowing, and bitterly regretted it."

As for M. Verdurin, he did not fail to observe the distressing effect upon his wife of the discovery that Swann had influential friends of whom he had never spoken.

If no arrangement had been made to go out, it was at the Verdurins' that Swann would find the "little nucleus" assembled, but he never appeared there except in the evenings, and rarely accepted their invitations to dinner, in spite of Odette's entreaties.

"I could dine with you alone somewhere, if you'd rather," she suggested.

"But what about Mme Verdurin?"

"Oh, that's quite simple. I need only say that my dress wasn't ready, or that my cab came late. There's always some excuse."

"How sweet of you."

But Swann told himself that if he could make Odette feel (by consenting to meet her only after dinner) that there were other pleasures which he preferred to that of her company, then the desire that she felt for his would be all the longer in reaching the point of satiety.

Besides, as he infinitely preferred to Odette's style of beauty that of a young seamstress, as fresh and plump as a rose, with whom he was smitten, he preferred to spend the first part of the evening with her, knowing that he was sure to see Odette later on. It was for the same reason that he never allowed Odette to call for him at his house, to take him on to the Verdurins'. The little seamstress would wait for him at a street corner which Rémi, his coachman, knew; she would jump in beside him, and remain in his arms until the carriage drew up at the Verdurins'. He would enter the drawing-room; and there, while Mme Verdurin, pointing to the roses which he had sent her that morning, said: "I'm furious with you," and sent him to the place kept for him beside Odette, the pianist would play to them—for their two selves—the little phrase by Vinteuil which was, so to speak, the national anthem of their love. He began, always, with the sustained tremolos of the violin part which for several bars was heard alone, filling the whole foreground; until suddenly it seemed to draw aside, and—as in those interiors by Pieter de Hooch which are deepened by the narrow frame of a half-opened door, in the far distance, of a different colour, velvety with the radiance of some intervening light—the little phrase appeared, dancing, pastoral, interpolated, episodic, belonging to another world. It rippled past, simple and immortal, scattering on every side the bounties of its grace, with the same ineffable smile; but Swann thought that he could now discern in it some disenchantment. It seemed to be aware how vain, how hollow was the happiness to which it showed the way. In its airy grace there was the sense of something over and done with, like the mood of philosophic detachment which follows an outburst of vain regret. But all this mattered little to him; he

contemplated the little phrase less in its own light—
in what it might express to a musician who knew nothing of the existence of him and Odette when he had
composed it, and to all those who would hear it in
centuries to come—than as a pledge, a token of his
love, which made even the Verdurins and their young
pianist think of Odette at the same time as himself—
which bound her to him by a lasting tie; so much so
that (whimsically entreated by Odette) he had abandoned the idea of getting some "professional" to play
over to him the whole sonata, of which he still knew
no more than this one passage. "Why do you want the
rest?" she had asked him. "Our little bit; that's all we
need." Indeed, agonised by the reflection, as it floated
by, so near and yet so infinitely remote, that while it
was speaking to them it did not know them, he almost
regretted that it had a meaning of its own, an intrinsic
and unalterable beauty, extraneous to themselves, just
as in the jewels given to us, or even in the letters written
to us by a woman we love, we find fault with the "water"
of the stone, or with the words of the message, because
they are not fashioned exclusively from the essence of
a transitory relationship and a particular person.

Often it would happen that he had stayed so long
with the young seamstress before going to the Verdurins' that, as soon as the little phrase had been rendered by the pianist, Swann realised that it was almost
time for Odette to go home. He used to take her back
as far as the door of her little house in the Rue La
Pérouse, behind the Arc de Triomphe. And it was
perhaps on this account, and so as not to demand the
monopoly of her favours, that he sacrificed the pleasure
(not so essential to his well-being) of seeing her earlier
in the evening, of arriving with her at the Verdurins',
to the exercise of this other privilege which she accorded

him of their leaving together; a privilege he valued all the more because it gave him the feeling that no one else would see her, no one would thrust himself between them, no one could prevent him from remaining with her in spirit, after he had left her for the night.

And so, night after night, she would return home in Swann's carriage. Once, after she had got down, and while he stood at the gate murmuring "Till to-morrow, then," she turned impulsively from him, plucked a last lingering chrysanthemum from the little garden in front of the house, and gave it to him before he left. He held it pressed to his lips during the drive home, and when in due course the flower withered, he put it away carefully in a drawer of his desk.

But he never went into her house. Twice only, in the daytime, had he done so, to take part in the ceremony—of such vital importance in her life—of "afternoon tea." The loneliness and emptiness of those short streets (consisting almost entirely of low-roofed houses, self-contained but not detached, their monotony interrupted here and there by the dark intrusion of some sinister workshop, at once an historical witness to and a sordid survival from the days when the district was still one of ill repute), the snow which still clung to the garden-beds and the branches of the trees, the unkemptness of the season, the proximity of nature, had all combined to add an element of mystery to the warmth, the flowers, the luxury which he had found inside.

From the ground floor, somewhat raised above street level, leaving on the left Odette's bedroom, which looked out to the back over another little street running parallel with her own, he had climbed a staircase that went straight up between dark painted walls hung with Oriental draperies, strings of Turkish beads, and a huge

Japanese lantern suspended by a silken cord (which last, however, so that her visitors should not be deprived of the latest comforts of Western civilisation, was lighted by a gas-jet inside), to the two drawing-rooms, large and small. These were entered through a narrow vestibule, the wall of which, chequered with the lozenges of a wooden trellis such as you see on garden walls, only gilded, was lined from end to end by a long rectangular box in which bloomed, as in a hothouse, a row of large chrysanthemums, at that time still uncommon though by no means so large as the mammoth specimens which horticulturists have since succeeded in producing. Swann was irritated, as a rule, by the sight of these flowers, which had then been "the rage" in Paris for about a year, but it had pleased him, on this occasion, to see the gloom of the vestibule shot with rays of pink and gold and white by the fragrant petals of these ephemeral stars, which kindle their cold fires in the murky atmosphere of winter afternoons. Odette had received him in a pink silk dressing-gown, which left her neck and arms bare. She had made him sit down beside her in one of the many mysterious little alcoves which had been contrived in the various recesses of the room, sheltered by enormous palms growing out of pots of Chinese porcelain, or by screens upon which were fastened photographs and fans and bows of ribbon. She had said at once, "You're not comfortable there; wait a minute, I'll arrange things for you," and with a little simpering laugh which implied that some special invention of her own was being brought into play, she had installed behind his head and beneath his feet great cushions of Japanese silk which she pummelled and buffeted as though to prove that she was prodigal of these riches, regardless of their value. But when her footman came into the room bringing, one after another, the innumerable lamps which (contained, mostly, in porcelain vases) burned singly or in pairs upon the different pieces of furniture as upon so many altars, rekindling in the twilight, already almost nocturnal, of this winter afternoon the glow of a sunset more lasting, more roseate, more human—filling, perhaps, with romantic wonder the thoughts of some solitary lover wandering in the street below and brought to a standstill before the mystery of the human presence which those lighted windows at once revealed and screened from sight—she had kept a sharp eye on the servant, to see that he set them down in their appointed places. She felt that if he were to put even one of them where it ought not to be the general effect of her drawing-room would be destroyed, and her portrait, which rested upon a sloping easel draped with plush, inadequately lit. And so she followed the man's clumsy movements with feverish impatience, scolding him severely when he passed too close to a pair of jardinières, which she made a point of always cleaning herself for fear that they might be damaged, and went across to examine now to make sure he had not chipped them. She found something "quaint" in the shape of each of her Chinese ornaments, and also in her orchids, the cattleyas especially—these being, with chrysanthemums, her favourite flowers, because they had the supreme merit of not looking like flowers, but of being made, apparently, of silk or satin. "This one looks just as though it had been cut out of the lining of my cloak," she said to Swann, pointing to an orchid, with a shade of respect in her voice for so "chic" a flower, for this elegant, unexpected sister whom nature had bestowed upon her, so far removed from her in the scale of existence, and yet so delicate, so refined, so much more worthy than many real women of admission to her drawing-room.

As she drew his attention, now to the fiery-tongued dragons painted on a bowl or stitched on a screen, now to a fleshy cluster of orchids, now to a dromedary of inlaid silver-work with ruby eyes which kept company, upon her mantel-piece, with a toad carved in jade, she would pretend now to be shrinking from the ferocity of the monsters or laughing at their absurdity, now blushing at the indecency of the flowers, now carried away by an irresistible desire to run across and kiss the toad and dromedary, calling them "darlings." And these affectations were in sharp contrast to the sincerity of some of her attitudes, notably her devotion to Our Lady of Laghet, who had once, when Odette was living at Nice, cured her of a mortal illness, and whose medal, in gold, she always carried on her person, attributing to it unlimited powers. She poured out Swann's tea, inquired "Lemon or cream?" and, on his answering "Cream, please," said to him with a laugh: "A cloud!" And as he pronounced it excellent, "You see, I know just how you like it." This tea had indeed seemed to Swann, just as it seemed to her, something precious, and love has such a need to find some justification for itself, some guarantee of duration, in pleasures which without it would have no existence and must cease with its passing, that when he left her at seven o'clock to go and dress for the evening, all the way home in his brougham, unable to repress the happiness with which the afternoon's adventure had filled him, he kept repeating to himself: "How nice it would be to have a little woman like that in whose house one could always be certain of finding, what one never can be certain of finding, a really good cup of tea." An hour or so later he received a note from Odette, and at once recognised that large handwriting in which an affectation of British stiffness imposed an apparent discipline upon ill-formed characters, suggestive, perhaps, to less biassed eyes than his, of an untidiness of mind, a fragmentary education, a want of sincerity and will-power. Swann had left his cigarette-case at her house. "If only," she wrote, "you had also forgotten your heart! I should never have let you have that back."

More important, perhaps, was a second visit which he paid her a little later. On his way to the house, as always when he knew that they were to meet, he formed a picture of her in his mind; and the necessity, if he was to find any beauty in her face, of concentrating on the fresh and rosy cheekbones to the exclusion of the rest of her cheeks which were so often drawn and sallow, and sometimes mottled with little red spots, distressed him as proving that the ideal is unattainable and happiness mediocre. He was bringing her an engraving which she had asked to see. She was not very well, and received him in a dressing-gown of mauve *crêpe de Chine*, drawing its richly embroidered material over her bosom like a cloak. Standing there beside him, her loosened hair flowing down her cheeks, bending one knee in a slightly balletic pose in order to be able to lean without effort over the picture at which she was gazing, her head on one side, with those great eyes of hers which seemed so tired and sullen when there was nothing to animate her, she struck Swann by her resemblance to the figure of Zipporah, Jethro's daughter, which is to be seen in one of the Sistine frescoes. He had always found a peculiar fascination in tracing in the paintings of the old masters not merely the general characteristics of the people whom he encountered in his daily life, but rather what seems least susceptible of generalisation, the individual features of men and women whom he knew: as, for instance, in a bust of the Doge Loredan by Antonio Rizzo, the prominent cheekbones, the slant-

ing eyebrows, in short, a speaking likeness to his own
coachman Rémi; in the colouring of a Ghirlandaio, the
nose of M. de Palancy; in a portrait by Tintoretto, the
invasion of the cheek by an outcrop of whisker, the
broken nose, the penetrating stare, the swollen eyelids
of Dr du Boulbon. Perhaps, having always regretted,
in his heart, that he had confined his attention to the
social side of life, had talked, always, rather than acted,
he imagined a sort of indulgence bestowed upon him
by those great artists in the fact that they also had
regarded with pleasure and had introduced into their
works such types of physiognomy as give those works
the strongest possible certificate of reality and truth to
life, a modern, almost a topical savour; perhaps, also,
he had so far succumbed to the prevailing frivolity of
the world of fashion that he felt the need to find in an
old masterpiece some such anticipatory and rejuven-
ating allusion to personalities of to-day. Perhaps, on
the other hand, he had retained enough of the artistic
temperament to be able to find a genuine satisfaction
in watching these individual characteristics take on a
more general significance when he saw them, uprooted
and disembodied, in the resemblance between an historic portrait and a modern original whom it was not
intended to represent. However that might be—and
perhaps because the abundance of impressions which he
had been receiving for some time past, even though
they had come to him rather through the channel of
his appreciation of music, had enriched his appetite for
painting as well—it was with an unusual intensity of
pleasure, a pleasure destined to have a lasting effect
upon him, that Swann remarked Odette's resemblance
to the Zipporah of that Alessandro de Mariano to whom
one shrinks from giving his more popular surname,
Botticelli, now that it suggests not so much the actual

work of the Master as that false and banal conception
of it which has of late obtained common currency. He
no longer based his estimate of the merit of Odette's
face on the doubtful quality of her cheeks and the purely
fleshy softness which he supposed would greet his lips
there should he ever hazard a kiss, but regarded it rather
as a skein of beautiful, delicate lines which his eyes
unravelled, following their curves and convolutions,
relating the rhythm of the neck to the effusion of the
hair and the droop of the eyelids, as though in a portrait
of her in which her type was made clearly intelligible.

He stood gazing at her; traces of the old fresco were
apparent in her face and her body, and these he tried
incessantly to recapture thereafter, both when he was
with Odette and when he was only thinking of her in
her absence; and, although his admiration for the Florentine masterpiece was doubtless based upon his discovery that it had been reproduced in her, the similarity
enhanced her beauty also, and made her more precious.
Swann reproached himself with his failure, hitherto, to
estimate at her true worth a creature whom the great
Sandro would have adored, and was gratified that his
pleasure in seeing Odette should have found a justification in his own aesthetic culture. He told himself
that in associating the thought of Odette with his dreams
of ideal happiness he had not resigned himself to a
stopgap as inadequate as he had hitherto supposed, since
she satisfied his most refined predilections in matters
of art. He failed to observe that this quality would not
naturally avail to bring Odette into the category of
women whom he found desirable, since, as it happened,
his desires had always run counter to his aesthetic taste.
The words "Florentine painting" were invaluable to
Swann. They enabled him, like a title, to introduce the
image of Odette into a world of dreams and fancies

which, until then, she had been debarred from entering, and where she assumed a new and nobler form. And whereas the mere sight of her in the flesh, by perpetually reviving his misgivings as to the quality of her face, her body, the whole of her beauty, cooled the ardour of his love, those misgivings were swept away and that love confirmed now that he could re-erect his estimate of her on the sure foundations of aesthetic principle; while the kiss, the physical possession which would have seemed natural and but moderately attractive had they been granted him by a creature of somewhat blemished flesh and sluggish blood, coming, as they now came, to crown his adoration of a masterpiece in a gallery, must, it seemed, prove supernaturally delicious.

And when he was tempted to regret that, for months past, he had done nothing but see Odette, he would assure himself that he was not unreasonable in giving up much of his time to an inestimably precious work of art, cast for once in a new, a different, an especially delectable metal, in an unmatched exemplar which he would contemplate at one moment with the humble, spiritual, disinterested mind of an artist, at another with the pride, the selfishness, the sensual thrill of a collector.

He placed on his study table, as if it were a photograph of Odette, a reproduction of Jethro's daughter. He would gaze in admiration at the large eyes, the delicate features in which the imperfection of the skin might be surmised, the marvellous locks of hair that fell along the tired cheeks; and, adapting to the idea of a living woman what he had until then felt to be beautiful on aesthetic grounds, he converted it into a series of physical merits which he was gratified to find assembled in the person of one whom he might ulti-

mately possess. The vague feeling of sympathy which
attracts one to a work of art, now that he knew the
original in flesh and blood of Jethro's daughter, became
a desire which more than compensated, thenceforward,
for the desire which Odette's physical charms had at
first failed to inspire in him. When he had sat for a
long time gazing at the Botticelli, he would think of
his own living Botticelli, who seemed even lovelier still,
and as he drew towards him the photograph of Zipporah
he would imagine that he was holding Odette against
his heart.

It was not only Odette's lassitude, however, that he
must take pains to circumvent; it was also, not infre-
quently, his own. Feeling that, since Odette had had
every facility for seeing him, she seemed no longer to
have very much to say to him, he was afraid lest the
manner—at once trivial, monotonous, and seemingly
unalterable—which she now adopted when they were
together should ultimately destroy in him that romantic
hope, which alone had aroused and sustained his love,
that a day might come when she would declare her
passion. And so, in an attempt to revitalise Odette's
too fixed and unvarying attitude towards him, of which
he was afraid of growing weary, he would write to her,
suddenly, a letter full of feigned disappointment and
simulated anger, which he sent off so that it should
reach her before dinner. He knew that she would be
alarmed, and that she would reply, and he hoped that,
when the fear of losing him clutched at her heart, it
would force from her words such as he had never yet
heard her utter; and indeed, it was by this device that
he had won from her the most affectionate letters she
had so far written him. One of them, which she had
sent round to him at midday from the Maison Dorée
(it was the day of the Paris-Murcie Fête given for the

victims of the recent floods in Murcia) began: "My dear, my hand trembles so that I can scarcely write," and had been put in the same drawer as the withered chrysanthemum. Or else, if she had not had time to write to him, when he arrived at the Verdurins' she would come running up to him with an "I've something to say to you!" and he would gaze curiously at the revelation in her face and speech of what she had hitherto kept concealed from him of her heart.

Even before he reached the Verdurins' door, when he caught sight of the great lamp-lit spaces of the drawing-room windows, whose shutters were never closed, he would begin to melt at the thought of the charming creature he would see as he entered the room, basking in that golden light. Here and there the figures of the guests stood out in silhouette, slender and black, between lamp and window, like those little pictures which one sees at regular intervals round a translucent lampshade, the other panels of which are simply naked light. He would try to distinguish Odette's silhouette. And then, when he was once inside, without his being aware of it, his eyes would sparkle suddenly with such radiant happiness that M. Verdurin said to the painter: "Hm. Seems to be warming up." And indeed her presence gave the house what none of the other houses that he visited seemed to possess: a sort of nervous system, a sensory network which ramified into each of its rooms and sent a constant stimulus to his heart.

Thus the simple and regular manifestations of this social organism, the "little clan," automatically provided Swann with a daily rendezvous with Odette, and enabled him to feign indifference to the prospect of seeing her, or even a desire not to see her; in doing which he incurred no very great risk since, even though he had written to her during the day, he would of necessity see her in the evening and accompany her home.

But one evening, when, depressed by the thought of that inevitable dark drive together, he had taken his young seamstress all the way to the Bois, so as to delay as long as possible the moment of his appearance at the Verdurins', he arrived at the house so late that Odette, supposing that he did not intend to come, had already left. Seeing the room bare of her, Swann felt a sudden stab at the heart; he trembled at the thought of being deprived of a pleasure whose intensity he was able for the first time to gauge, having always, hitherto, had that certainty of finding it whenever he wished which (as in the case of all our pleasures) reduced if it did not altogether blind him to its dimensions.

"Did you notice the face he pulled when he saw that she wasn't here?" M. Verdurin asked his wife. "I think we may say that he's hooked."

"The face he pulled?" exploded Dr Cottard who, having left the house for a moment to visit a patient, had just returned to fetch his wife and did not know whom they were discussing.

"D'you mean to say you didn't meet him on the doorstep—the loveliest of Swanns?"

"No. M. Swann has been here?"

"Just for a moment. We had a glimpse of a Swann tremendously agitated. In a state of nerves. You see, Odette had left."

"You mean to say that she has gone the 'whole hog' with him; that she has 'burned her boats'?" inquired the doctor, cautiously trying out the meaning of these phrases.

"Why, of course not, there's absolutely nothing in it; in fact, between you and me, I think she's making a great mistake, and behaving like a silly little fool, which is what she is, in fact."

"Come, come, come!" said M. Verdurin, "How on earth do you know that there's 'nothing in it'? We haven't been there to see, have we now?"

"She would have told me," answered Mme Verdurin with dignity. "I may say that she tells me everything. As she has no one else at present, I told her that she ought to sleep with him. She makes out that she can't, that she did in fact have a crush on him at first, but he's always shy with her, and that makes her shy with him. Besides, she doesn't care for him in that way, she says; it's an ideal love, 'Platonic,' you know; she's afraid of rubbing the bloom off—oh, I don't know half the things she says, how should I? And yet it's just what she needs."

"I beg to differ from you," M. Verdurin courteously interrupted. "I don't entirely care for the gentleman. I feel he puts on airs."

Mme Verdurin's whole body stiffened, and her eyes stared blankly as though she had suddenly been turned into a statue; a device which enabled her to appear not to have caught the sound of that unutterable phrase which seemed to imply that it was possible for people to "put on airs" in their house, in other words consider themselves "superior" to them.

"Anyhow, if there's nothing in it, I don't suppose it's because our friend believes she's *virtuous*," M. Verdurin went on sarcastically. "And yet, you never know; he seems to think she's intelligent. I don't know whether you heard the way he lectured her the other evening about Vinteuil's sonata. I'm devoted to Odette, but really—to expound theories of aesthetics to her—the man must be a prize idiot."

"Look here, I won't have you saying nasty things about Odette," broke in Mme Verdurin in her "little girl" manner. "She's sweet."

"But that doesn't prevent her from being sweet. We're not saying anything nasty about her, only that she isn't exactly the embodiment of virtue or intellect. After all," he turned to the painter, "does it matter so very much whether she's virtuous or not? She might be a great deal less charming if she were."

On the landing Swann had run into the Verdurins' butler, who had been somewhere else a moment earlier when he arrived, and who had been asked by Odette to tell Swann in case he still turned up (but that was at least an hour ago) that she would probably stop for a cup of chocolate at Prévost's on her way home. Swann set off at once for Prévost's, but every few yards his carriage was held up by others, or by people crossing the street, loathsome obstacles that he would gladly have crushed beneath his wheels, were it not that a policeman fumbling with a note-book would delay him even longer than the actual passage of the pedestrian. He counted the minutes feverishly, adding a few seconds to each so as to be quite certain that he had not given himself short measure and so, possibly, exaggerated whatever chance there might actually be of his arriving at Prévost's in time, and of finding her still there. And then, in a moment-of illumination, like a man in a fever who awakes from sleep and is conscious of the absurdity of the dream-shapes among which his mind has been wandering without any clear distinction between himself and them, Swann suddenly perceived how foreign to his nature were the thoughts which had been revolving in his mind ever since he had heard at the Verdurins' that Odette had left, how novel the heartache from which he was suffering, but of which he was only now conscious, as though he had just woken up. What! all this agitation simply because he would not see Odette till to-morrow, exactly what he had been hoping, not an hour before, as he drove towards Mme Verdurin's. He was obliged to acknowledge that now, as he sat in that same carriage and drove to Prévost's, he was no longer the same man, was no longer alone even—that a new person was there beside him, adhering to him, amalgamated with him, a person whom he might, perhaps, be unable to shake off, whom he might have to treat with circumspection, like a master or an illness. And yet, from the moment he had begun to feel that another, a fresh personality was thus conjoined with his own, life had seemed somehow more interesting.

He gave scarcely a thought to the likelihood that this possible meeting at Prévost's (the tension of waiting for which so ravished and stripped bare the intervening moments that he could find nothing, not one idea, not one memory in his mind behind which his troubled spirit might take shelter and repose) would after all, should it take place, be much the same as all their meetings, of no great significance. As on every other evening, once he was in Odette's company, casting furtive glances at her changing countenance and instantly withdrawing his eyes lest she should read in them the first signs of desire and believe no more in his indifference, he would cease to be able even to think of her, so busy would he be in the search for pretexts which would enable him not to leave her immediately and to ensure, without betraying his concern, that he would find her again next evening at the Verdurins'; pretexts, that is to say, which would enable him to prolong for the time being, and to renew for one day more, the disappointment and the torture engendered by the vain presence of this woman whom he pursued yet never dared embrace.

She was not at Prévost's; he must search for her, then, in every restaurant along the boulevards. To save time, while he went in one direction, he sent in the other his coachman Rémi (Rizzo's Doge Loredan) for whom he presently—after a fruitless search—found himself waiting at the spot where the carriage was to meet him. It did not appear, and Swann tantalised himself with alternate pictures of the approaching moment, as one in which Rémi would say to him: "Sir, the lady is there," or as one in which Rémi would say to him: "Sir, the lady was not in any of the cafés." And so he saw the remainder of the evening stretching out in front of him, single and yet alternative, preceded either by the meeting with Odette which would put an end to his agony, or by the abandonment of all hope of finding her that evening, the acceptance of the necessity of returning home without having seen her.

The coachman returned; but, as he drew up opposite him, Swann asked, not "Did you find the lady?" but "Remind me, to-morrow, to order in some more firewood. I'm sure we must be running short." Perhaps he had persuaded himself that, if Rémi had at last found Odette in some café where she was waiting for him, then the baleful alternative was already obliterated by the realisation, begun already in his mind, of the happy one, and that there was no need for him to hasten towards the attainment of a joy already captured and held in a safe place, which would not escape his grasp again. But it was also from the force of inertia; there was in his soul that want of adaptability that afflicts the bodies of certain people who, when the moment comes to avoid a collision, to snatch their clothes out of reach of a flame, or to perform any other such nec-

essary movement, take their time, begin by remaining
for a moment in their original position, as though seeking to find in it a starting-point, a source of strength
and motion. And no doubt, if the coachman had interrupted him with, "I have found the lady," he would
have answered, "Oh, yes, of course; that's what I told
you to do. I'd quite forgotten," and would have continued to discuss his supply of firewood, so as to hide
from his servant the emotion he had felt, and to give
himself time to break away from the thraldom of his
anxieties and devote himself to happiness.

The coachman came back, however, with the report
that he could not find her anywhere, and added the
advice, as an old and privileged servant: "I think, sir,
that all we can do now is to go home."

But the air of indifference which Swann could so
lightly assume when Rémi uttered his final, unalterable
response, fell from him like a cast-off cloak when he
saw Rémi attempt to make him abandon hope and retire
from the quest.

"Certainly not!" he exclaimed. "We must find the
lady. It's most important. She would be extremely put
out—it's a business matter—and vexed with me if she
didn't see me."

"But I don't see how the lady can be vexed," answered
Rémi, "since it was she who left without waiting for
you, sir, and said she was going to Prévost's, and then
wasn't there."

Meanwhile the restaurants were closing and their
lights began to go out. Under the trees of the boulevards
there were still a few people strolling to and fro, barely
distinguishable in the gathering darkness. From time
to time the shadowy figure of a woman gliding up to
Swann, murmuring a few words in his ear, asking him
to take her home, would make him start. Anxiously he

brushed past all these dim forms, as though among the phantoms of the dead, in the realms of darkness, he had been searching for a lost Eurydice.

Among all the methods by which love is brought into being, among all the agents which disseminate that blessed bane, there are few so efficacious as this gust of feverish agitation that sweeps over us from time to time. For then the die is cast, the person whose company we enjoy at that moment is the person we shall henceforward love. It is not even necessary for that person to have attracted us, up till then, more than or even as much as others. All that was needed was that our predilection should become exclusive. And that condition is fulfilled when—in this moment of deprivation—the quest for the pleasures we enjoyed in his or her company is suddenly replaced by an anxious, torturing need, whose object is the person alone, an absurd, irrational need which the laws of this world make it impossible to satisfy and difficult to assuage—the insensate, agonising need to possess exclusively.

Swann made Rémi drive him to such restaurants as were still open; it was the sole hypothesis, now, of that happiness which he had contemplated so calmly; he no longer concealed his agitation, the price he set upon their meeting, and promised in case of success to reward his coachman, as though, by inspiring in him a will to succeed which would reinforce his own, he could bring it to pass, by a miracle, that Odette—assuming that she had long since gone home to bed—might yet be found seated in some restaurant on the boulevards. He pursued the search as far as the Maison Dorée, burst twice into Tortoni's and, still without catching sight of her, was emerging from the Café Anglais, striding with haggard gaze towards his carriage, which was waiting for him at the corner of the Boulevard des Italiens, when he collided with a person coming in the opposite direction: it was Odette. She explained, later, that there had been no room at Prévost's, that she had gone, instead, to sup at the Maison Dorée, in an alcove where he must have failed to see her, and that she was going back to her carriage.

She had so little expected to see him that she started back in alarm. As for him, he had ransacked the streets of Paris not because he supposed it possible that he should find her, but because it was too painful for him to abandon the attempt. But this happiness which his reason had never ceased to regard as unattainable, that evening at least, now seemed doubly real; for, since he himself had contributed nothing to it by anticipating probabilities, it remained external to himself; there was no need for him to think it into existence—it was from itself that there emanated, it was itself that projected towards him, that truth whose radiance dispelled like a bad dream the loneliness he had so dreaded, that truth on which his happy musings now dwelt unthinkingly. So will a traveller, arriving in glorious weather at the Mediterranean shore, no longer certain of the existence of the lands he has left behind, let his eyes be dazzled by the radiance streaming towards him from the luminous and unfading azure of the sea.

He climbed after her into the carriage which she had kept waiting, and ordered his own to follow.

She was holding in her hand a bunch of cattleyas, and Swann could see, beneath the film of lace that covered her head, more of the same flowers fastened to a swansdown plume. She was dressed, beneath her cloak, in a flowing gown of black velvet, caught up on one side to reveal a large triangle of white silk skirt, and with a yoke, also of white silk, in the cleft of the low-necked bodice, in which were fastened a few more cattleyas. She had scarcely recovered from the shock which the sight of Swann had given her, when some obstacle made the horse start to one side. They were thrown forward in their seats; she uttered a cry, and fell back quivering and breathless.

"It's all right," he assured her, "don't be frightened." And he slipped his arm round her shoulder, supporting her body against his own. Then he went on: "Whatever you do, don't utter a word; just make a sign, yes or no, or you'll be out of breath again. You won't mind if I straighten the flowers on your bodice? The jolt has disarranged them. I'm afraid of their dropping out, so I'd just like to fasten them a little more securely."

She was not used to being made so much fuss of by men, and she smiled as she answered: "No, not at all; I don't mind in the least."

But he, daunted a little by her answer, and also, perhaps, to bear out the pretence that he had been sincere in adopting the stratagem, or even because he was already beginning to believe that he had been, exclaimed, "No, no, you mustn't speak. You'll get out of breath again. You can easily answer in signs; I shall understand. Really and truly now, you don't mind my doing this? Look, there's a little—I think it must be pollen, spilt over your dress. Do you mind if brush it off with my hand? That's not too hard? I'm not hurting you, am I? Perhaps I'm tickling you a bit? I don't want to touch the velvet in case I crease it. But you see, I really had to fasten the flowers; they would have fallen out if I hadn't. Like that, now; if I just tuck them a little farther down .... Seriously, I'm not annoying you, am I? And if I just sniff them to see whether they've really got no scent? I don't believe I ever smelt any before. May I? Tell the truth, now."

Still smiling, she shrugged her shoulders ever so

slightly, as who should say, "You're quite mad; you know very well that I like it."

He ran his other hand upwards along Odette's cheek; she gazed at him fixedly, with that languishing and solemn air which marks the women of the Florentine master in whose faces he had found a resemblance with hers; swimming at the brink of her fringed lids, her brilliant eyes, wide and slender like theirs, seemed on the verge of welling out like two great tears. She bent her neck, as all their necks may be seen to bend, in the pagan scenes as well as in the religious pictures. And in an attitude that was doubtless habitual to her, one which she knew to be appropriate to such moments and was careful not to forget to assume, she seemed to need all her strength to hold her face back, as though some invisible force were drawing it towards Swann's. And it was Swann who, before she allowed it, as though in spite of herself, to fall upon his lips, held it back for a moment longer, at a little distance, between his hands. He had wanted to leave time for his mind to catch up with him, to recognise the dream which it had so long cherished and to assist at its realisation, like a relative invited as a spectator when a prize is given to a child of whom she has been especially fond. Perhaps, too, he was fixing upon the face of an Odette not yet possessed, nor even kissed by him, which he was seeing for the last time, the comprehensive gaze with which, on the day of his departure, a traveller hopes to bear away with him in memory a landscape he is leaving forever.

But he was so shy in approaching her that, after this evening which had begun by his arranging her cattleyas and had ended in her complete surrender, whether from fear of offending her, or from reluctance to appear retrospectively to have lied, or perhaps because he lacked the audacity to formulate a more urgent requirement

than this (which could always be repeated, since it had
not annoyed her on the first occasion), he resorted to
the same pretext on the following days. If she had
cattleyas pinned to her bodice, he would say: "It's most
unfortunate; the cattleyas don't need tucking in this
evening; they've not been disturbed as they were the
other night. I think, though, that this one isn't quite
straight. May I see if they have more scent than the
others?" Or else, if she had none: "Oh! no cattleyas this
evening; then there's no chance of my indulging in my
little rearrangements." So that for some time there was
no change in the procedure which he had followed on
that first evening, starting with fumblings with fingers
and lips at Odette's bosom, and it was thus that his
caresses still began. And long afterwards, when the
rearrangement (or, rather, the ritual pretence of a rearrangement) of her cattleyas had quite fallen into de-
suetude, the metaphor "Do a cattleya," transmuted into
a simple verb which they would employ without thinking when they wished to refer to the act of physical
possession (in which, paradoxically, the possessor possesses nothing), survived to commemorate in their vocabulary the long forgotten custom from which it sprang.
And perhaps this particular manner of saying "to make
love" did not mean exactly the same thing as its syn-
onyms. However jaded we may be about women, however much we may regard the possession of the most
divergent types as a repetitive and predictable experience, it none the less becomes a fresh and stimulating
pleasure if the women concerned are—or are thought
by us to be—so difficult as to oblige us to make it
spring from some unrehearsed incident in our relations
with them, as had originally been for Swann the arrangement of the cattleyas. He tremblingly hoped, that
evening (but Odette, he told himself, if she was de-

ceived by his stratagem, could not guess his intention), that it was the possession of this woman that would emerge for him from their large mauve petals; and the pleasure which he had already felt and which Odette tolerated, he thought, perhaps only because she had not recognised it, seemed to him for that reason—as it might have seemed to the first man when he enjoyed it amid the flowers of the earthly paradise—a pleasure which had never before existed, which he was striving now to create, a pleasure—as the special name he gave it was to certify—entirely individual and new.

Now, every evening, when he had taken her home, he had to go in with her; and often she would come out again in her dressing-gown and escort him to his carriage, and would kiss him in front of his coachman, saying: "What do I care what other people think?" And on evenings when he did not go to the Verdurins' (which happened occasionally now that he had opportunities of seeing Odette elsewhere), when—more and more rarely—he went into society, she would ask him to come to her on his way home, however late he might be. It was spring, and the nights were clear and frosty. Coming away from a party, he would climb into his victoria, spread a rug over his knees, tell the friends who were leaving at the same time and who wanted him to join them, that he couldn't, that he wasn't going in their direction; and the coachman would set off at a fast trot without further orders, knowing where he had to go. His friends would be left wondering, and indeed Swann was no longer the same man. No one ever received a letter from him now demanding an introduction to a woman. He had ceased to pay any attention to women, and kept away from the places in which they were ordinarily to be met. In a restaurant, or in the country, his attitude was the opposite of the one

by which, only yesterday, his friends would have recognized him, and which had seemed inevitably and
permanently his. To such an extent does passion manifest itself in us as a temporary and distinct character
which not only takes the place of our normal character
but obliterates the invariable signs by which it has
hitherto been discernible! What was invariable now was
that wherever Swann might be, he never failed to go
on afterwards to Odette. The interval of space separating
her from him was one which he must traverse as inevitably as though it were the irresistible and rapid slope
of life itself. Truth to tell, as often as not, when he
had stayed late at a party, he would have preferred to
return home at once, without going so far out of his
way, and to postpone their meeting until the morrow;
but the very fact of his putting himself to such inconvenience at an abnormal hour in order to visit her, while
he guessed that his friends, as he left them, were saying
to one another: "He's tied hand and foot; there must
certainly be a woman somewhere who insists on his
going to her at all hours," made him feel that he was
leading the life of the class of men whose existence is
coloured by a love-affair, and in whom the perpetual
sacrifice they make of their comfort and of their practical
interests engenders a sort of inner charm. Then, though
he may not consciously have taken this into consideration, the certainty that she was waiting for him, that
she was not elsewhere with others, that he would see
her before he went home, drew the sting from that
anguish, forgotten but latent and ever ready to be reawakened, which he had felt on the evening when Odette
had left the Verdurins' before his arrival, an anguish
the present assuagement of which was so agreeable that
it might almost be called happiness. Perhaps it was to
that hour of anguish that he owed the importance which

Odette had since assumed in his life. Other people as a rule mean so little to us that, when we have invested one of them with the power to cause us so much suffering or happiness, that person seems at once to belong to a different universe, is surrounded with poetry, makes of one's life a sort of stirring arena in which he or she will be more or less close to one. Swann could not ask himself with equanimity what Odette would mean to him in the years that were to come. Sometimes, as he looked up from his victoria on those fine and frosty nights and saw the bright moonbeams fall between his eyes and the deserted street, he would think of that other face, gleaming and faintly roseate like the moon's, which had, one day, risen on the horizon of his mind, and since then had shed upon the world the mysterious light in which he saw it bathed. If he arrived after the hour at which Odette sent her servants to bed, before ringing the bell at the gate of her little garden he would go round first into the other street, over which, on the ground-floor, among the windows (all exactly alike, but darkened) of the adjoining houses, shone the solitary lighted window of her room. He would rap on the pane, and she would hear the signal, and answer, before going to meet him at the front door. He would find, lying open on the piano, some of her favourite music, the *Valse des Roses*, the *Pauvre Fou* of Tagliafico (which, according to the instructions embodied in her will, was to be played at her funeral); but he would ask her, instead, to give him the little phrase from Vinteuil's sonata. It was true that Odette played vilely, but often the most memorable impression of a piece of music is one that has arisen out of a jumble of wrong notes struck by unskilful fingers upon a tuneless piano. The little phrase continued to be associated in Swann's mind with his love for Odette. He was well aware that his love was something that did not correspond to anything outside itself, verifiable by others besides him; he realised that Odette's qualities were not such as to justify his setting so high a value on the hours he spent in her company. And often, when the cold government of reason stood unchallenged in his mind, he would readily have ceased to sacrifice so many of his intellectual and social interests to this imaginary pleasure. But the little phrase, as soon as it struck his ear, had the power to liberate in him the room that was needed to contain it; the proportions of Swann's soul were altered; a margin was left for an enjoyment that corresponded no more than his love for Odette to any external object and yet was not, like his enjoyment of that love, purely individual, but assumed for him a sort of reality superior to that of concrete things. This thirst for an unknown delight was awakened in him by the little phrase, but without bringing him any precise gratification to assuage it. With the result that those parts of Swann's soul in which the little phrase had obliterated all concern for material interests, those human considerations which affect all men alike, were left vacant by it, blank pages on which he was at liberty to inscribe the name of Odette. Moreover, in so far as Odette's affection might seem a little abrupt and disappointing, the little phrase would come to supplement it, to blend with it, its own mysterious essence. Watching Swann's face while he listened to the phrase, one would have said that he was inhaling an anaesthetic which allowed him to breathe more freely. And the pleasure which the music gave him, which was shortly to create in him a real need, was in fact akin at such moments to the pleasure which he would have derived from experimenting with perfumes, from entering into contact with a world for which we men were not made, which appears to us formless because our eyes cannot perceive it, meaning-less because it eludes our understanding, to which we may attain by way of one sense only. There was a deep repose, a mysterious refreshment for Swann,—whose eyes, although delicate interpreters of painting, whose mind, although an acute observer of manners, must bear for ever the indelible imprint of the barrenness of his life,—in feeling himself transformed into a creature estranged from humanity, blinded, deprived of his log-ical faculty, almost a fantastic unicorn, a chimaera-like creature conscious of the world through his hearing alone. And since he sought in the little phrase for a meaning to which his intelligence could not descend, with what a strange frenzy of intoxication did he strip bare his innermost soul of the whole armour of reason and make it pass unattended through the dark filter of sound! He began to realise how much that was painful, perhaps even how much secret and unappeased sorrow underlay the sweetness of the phrase; and yet to him it brought no suffering. What matter though the phrase repeated that love is frail and fleeting, when his love was so strong! He played with the melancholy which the music diffused, and he felt it stealing over him, but like a caress which only deepened and sweetened his sense of his own happiness. He would make Odette play it over to him again and again, ten, twenty times on end, insisting that, as she did so, she must never stop kissing him. Every kiss provokes another. Ah, in those earliest days of love how naturally the kisses spring into life! So closely, in their profusion, do they crowd together that lovers would find it as hard to count the kisses exchanged in an hour as to count the flowers in a meadow in May. Then she would pretend to stop, saying: "How do you expect me to play when you keep on holding me? I can't do everything at once. Make up your mind what you want: am I to play the phrase or do you want to play with me?" and he would get angry, and she would burst out laughing, a laugh that was soon transformed and descended upon him in a shower of kisses. Or else she would look at him sulkily, and he would see once again a face worthy to figure in Botticelli's "Life of Moses;" he would place it there, giving to Odette's neck the necessary inclination; and when he had finished her portrait in tempera, in the fifteenth century, on the wall of the Sistine, the idea that she was none the less in the room with him still, by the piano, at that very moment, ready to be kissed and enjoyed, the idea of her material existence would sweep over him with so violent an intoxication that, with eyes starting from his head and jaws tensed as though to devour her, he would fling himself upon this Botticelli maiden and kiss and bite her cheeks. And then, once he had left her, not without returning to kiss her again because he had forgotten to take away with him the memory of some detail of her fragrance or of her features, as he drove home in his victoria he blessed Odette for allowing him those daily visits which could not, he felt, bring any great joy to her, but which, by keeping him immune from the fever of jealousy— by removing from him any possibility of a fresh outbreak of the heart-sickness which had afflicted him on the evening when he had failed to find her at the Verdurins'—would help him to arrive, without any recurrence of those crises of which the first had been so painful that it must also be the last, at the end of this strange period of his life, of these hours, enchanted almost, like those in which he drove through Paris by moonlight. And, noticing as he drove home that the moon had now changed its position relatively to his own and was almost touching the horizon, feeling that his love, too, was obedient to these immutable natural laws, he asked himself whether this period upon which he had entered would last much longer, whether presently his mind's eye would cease to behold that beloved face save as occupying a distant and diminished position, and on the verge of ceasing to shed on him the radiance of its charm. For Swann was once more finding in things, since he had fallen in love, the charm that he had found when, in his adolescence, he had fancied himself an artist; with this difference, that the charm that lay in them now was conferred by Odette alone. He felt the inspirations of his youth, which had been dissipated by a frivolous life, stirring again in him, but they all bore now the reflection, the stamp of a particular being; and during the long hours which he now found a subtle pleasure in spending at home, alone with his convalescent soul, he became gradually himself again, but himself in thraldom to another.

He went to her only in the evenings, and knew nothing of how she spent her time during the day, any more than her past; so little, indeed, that he had not even the tiny, initial clue which, by allowing us to imagine what we do not know, stimulates a desire for knowledge. And so he never asked himself what she might be doing, or what her life had been. Only he smiled sometimes at the thought of how, some years earlier, when he did not yet know her, people had spoken to him of a woman who, if he remembered rightly, must certainly have been Odette, as of a "tart," a "kept" woman, one of those women to whom he still attributed (having lived but little in their company) the wilful, fundamentally perverse character with which they had so long been endowed by the imagination of certain novelists. He told himself that as often as not one has only to take the opposite view to the reputation created by the world in order to judge a person accurately, when with such a character he contrasted that of Odette, so kind, so simple, so enthusiastic in the pursuit of ideals, so incapable, almost, of not telling the truth that, when he had once begged her, so that they might dine together alone, to write to Mme Verdurin saying that she was unwell, the next day he had seen her, face to face with Mme Verdurin who asked whether she had recovered, blushing, stammering and in spite of herself revealing in every feature how painful, what a torture it was to her to act a lie and, as in her answer she multiplied the fictitious details of her alleged indisposition, seeming to ask forgiveness, by her suppliant look and her stricken accents, for the obvious falsehood of her words.

On certain days, however, though these were rare, she would call upon him in the afternoon, interrupting his musings or the essay on Vermeer to which he had latterly returned. His servant would come in to say that Mme de Crécy was in the small drawing-room. He would go and join her, and when he opened the door, on Odette's rosy face, as soon as she caught sight of Swann, would appear—changing the curve of her lips, the look in her eyes, the moulding of her cheeks—an all-absorbing smile. Once he was alone he would see that smile again, and also her smile of the day before, and another with which she had greeted him sometime else, and the smile which had been her answer, in the carriage that night, when he had asked her whether she objected to his rearranging her cattleyas; and the life of Odette at all other times, since he knew nothing of it, appeared to him, with its neutral and colourless background, like those sheets of sketches by Watteau upon which one sees here, there, at every corner and at various angles, traced in three colours upon the buff paper, innumerable smiles. But once in a while, illuminating a chink of that existence which Swann still saw as a complete blank, even if his mind assured him that it was not, because he was unable to visualise it, some friend who knew them both and, suspecting that they were in love, would not have dared to tell him anything about her that was of the least importance, would describe how he had glimpsed Odette that very morning walking up the Rue Abbattucci, in a cape trimmed with skunk, a Rembrandt hat, and a bunch of violets in her bosom. Swann would be bowled over by this simple sketch because it suddenly made him realise that Odette had an existence that was not wholly subordinated to his own; he longed to know whom she had been seeking to impress by this costume in which he had never seen her, and he made up his mind to ask her where she had been going at that intercepted moment, as though, in all the colourless life of his mistress—a life almost non-existent, since it was invisible to him—there had been but a single incident apart from all those smiles directed towards himself: namely, her walking abroad beneath a Rembrandt hat, with a bunch of violets in her bosom.

Except when he asked her for Vinteuil's little phrase instead of the *Valse des Roses*, Swann made no effort to induce her to play the things that he himself preferred, or, in literature any more than in music, to correct the manifold errors of her taste. He fully realised that she was not intelligent. When she said how much she would like him to tell her about the great poets, she had imagined that she would immediately get to know whole pages of romantic and heroic verse, in the style of the Vicomte de Borelli, only even more moving. As for Vermeer of Delft, she asked whether he had been made to suffer by a woman, if it was a woman who had inspired him, and once Swann had told her that no one knew, she had lost all interest in that painter. She would often say: "Poetry, you know—well, of course, there'd be nothing like it if it was all true, if the poets really believed what they say. But as often as not you'll find there's no one so mean and calculating as those fellows. I know something about it: I had a friend, once, who was in love with a poet of sorts. In his verses he never spoke of anything but love and the sky and the stars. Oh! she was properly taken in! He had more than three hundred thousand francs out of her before he'd finished."

If, then, Swann tried to show her what artistic beauty consisted in, how one ought to appreciate poetry or painting, after a minute or two she would cease to listen, saying: "Yes . . . I never thought it would be like that." And he felt that her disappointment was so great that he preferred to lie to her, assuring her that what he had said was nothing, that he had only touched the surface, that he had no time to go into it all properly, that there was more in it than that. Then she would interrupt sharply: "More in it? What? . . . Do tell me!", but he did not tell her, knowing how feeble it would appear to her, how different from what she had expected, less sensational and less touching, and fearing lest, disillusioned with art, she might at the same time be disillusioned with love.

With the result that she found Swann inferior, intellectually, to what she had supposed. "You're always so reserved; I can't make you out." She was more impressed by his indifference to money, by his kindness to everyone, by his courtesy and tact. And indeed it happens, often enough, to greater men than Swann, to a scientist or an artist, when he is not misunderstood by the people among whom he lives, that the feeling

on their part which proves that they have been convinced of the superiority of his intellect is not their
admiration for his ideas — for these are beyond them —
but their respect for his kindness. Swann's position in
society also inspired Odette with respect, but she had
no desire that he should attempt to secure invitations
for herself. Perhaps she felt that such attempts would
be bound to fail; perhaps she even feared that, merely
by speaking of her to his friends, he might provoke
disclosures of an unwelcome kind. At all events she had
made him promise never to mention her name. Her
reason for not wishing to go into society was, she had
told him, a quarrel she had once had with a friend who
had avenged herself subsequently by speaking ill of her.
"But surely," Swann objected, "not everyone knew your
friend." "Yes, but don't you see, it spreads like wildfire;
people are so horrid." Swann found this story frankly
incomprehensible; on the other hand, he knew that such
generalisations as "People are so horrid," and "A word
of scandal spreads like wildfire," were generally accepted as true; there must be cases to which they were
applicable. Could Odette's be one of these? He teased
himself with the question, though not for long, for he
too was subject to that mental torpor that had so weighed
upon his father, whenever he was faced by a difficult
problem. In any event, that world of society which so
frightened Odette did not, perhaps, inspire her with
any great longings, since it was too far removed from
the world she knew for her to be able to form any clear
conception of it. At the same time, while in certain
aspects she had retained a genuine simplicity (she had,
for instance, kept up a friendship with a little dressmaker, now retired from business, up whose steep and
dark and fetid staircase she clambered almost every day),
she still thirsted to be in the fashion, though her idea

of it was not altogether the same as that of society people. For the latter, it emanates from a comparatively small number of individuals, who project it to a considerable distance—more and more faintly the further one is from their intimate centre—within the circle of their friends and the friends of their friends, whose names form a sort of tabulated index. People "in society" know this index by heart; they are gifted in such matters with an erudition from which they have extracted a sort of taste, of tact, so automatic in its operation that Swann, for example, without needing to draw upon his knowledge of the world, if he read in a newspaper the names of the people who had been at a dinner-party, could tell at once its exact degree of smartness, just as a man of letters, simply by reading a sentence, can estimate exactly the literary merit of its author. But Odette was one of those persons (an extremely numerous category, whatever the fashionable world may think, and to be found in every class of society) who do not share these notions, but imagine smartness to be something quite other, which assumes different aspects according to the circle to which they themselves belong, but has the special characteristic—common alike to the fashion of which Odette dreamed and to that before which Mme Cottard bowed—of being directly accessible to all. The other kind, the smartness of society people, is, it must be admitted, accessible also; but there is a time-lag. Odette would say of someone: "He only goes to really smart places."

And if Swann asked her what she meant by that, she would answer with a touch of contempt: "Smart places! Why, good heavens, just fancy, at your age, having to be told what the smart places are in Paris! Well, on Sunday mornings there's the Avenue de l'Impératrice, and round the lake at five o'clock, and on Thursdays, the Eden-Théâtre, and the Races on Fridays; then there are the balls . . ."

"What balls?"

"Why, silly, the balls people give in Paris; the smart ones, I mean. For instance, Herbinger, you know who I mean, the fellow who's in one of the jobbers' offices. Yes, of course you must know him, he's one of the best-known men in Paris, that great big fair-haired boy who wears such swagger clothes—always has a flower in his buttonhole and a light-coloured overcoat with a stripe down the back. He goes about with that old frump, takes her to all the first-nights. Well, he gave a ball the other night, and all the smart people in Paris were there. I should have loved to go! But you had to show your invitation at the door, and I couldn't get one anywhere. Still, I'm just as glad, now, that I didn't go; I should have been killed in the crush, and seen nothing. It's really just to be able to say you've been to Herbinger's ball. You know what a braggart I am! However, you may be quite certain that half the people who tell you they were there are lying. . . . But I'm surprised you weren't there, a regular 'tip-topper' like you."

Swann made no attempt, however, to modify his conception of fasionable life; feeling that his own came no nearer to the truth, was just as fatuous and trivial, he saw no point in imparting it to his mistress, with the result that, after a few months, she ceased to take any interest in the people to whose houses he went, except as a means of obtaining tickets for the paddock at racemeetings or first-nights at the theatre. She hoped that he would continue to cultivate such profitable acquaintances, but in other respects she was inclined to regard them as anything but smart, ever since she had passed the Marquise de Villeparisis in the street, wearing a black woollen dress and a bonnet with strings.

"But she looks like a lavatory attendant, like an old charwoman, darling! A marquise, her! Goodness knows I'm not a marquise, but you'd have to pay me a lot of money before you'd get me to go round Paris rigged out like that!"

Nor could she understand Swann's continuing to live in his house on the Quai d'Orléans, which, though she dared not tell him so, she considered unworthy of him.

It was true that she claimed to be fond of "antiques," and used to assume a rapturous and knowing air when she confessed how she loved to spend the whole day "rummaging" in curio shops, hunting for "bric-à-brac" and "period" things. Although it was a point of honour to which she obstinately clung, as though obeying some old family precept, that she should never answer questions or "account for" how she spent her days, she spoke to Swann once about a friend to whose house she had been invited, and had found that everything in it was "of the period." Swann could not get her to tell him what "period" it was. But after thinking the matter over she replied that it was "mediaeval"; by which she meant that the walls were panelled. Some time later she spoke to him again of her friend, and added, in the hesitant tone and with the knowing air one adopts in referring to a person one has met at dinner the night before and of whom one had never heard until then, but whom one's hosts seemed to regard as someone so celebrated and important that one hopes that one's listener will know who is meant and be duly impressed: "Her dining-room . . . is . . . eighteenth century!" She herself had thought it hideous, all bare, as though the house were still unfinished; women looked frightful in it, and it would never become the fashion. She mentioned it again, a third time, when she showed Swann a card with the name and address of the man who had designed the dining-room, and whom she wanted to send for when she had enough money, to see whether he couldn't do one for her too; not one like that, of course, but one of the sort she used to dream of and which unfortunately her little house wasn't large enough to contain, with tall sideboards, Renaissance furniture and fireplaces like the château at Blois. It was on this occasion that she blurted out to Swann what she really thought of his abode on the Quai d'Orléans; he having ventured the criticism that her friend had indulged, not in the Louis XVI style, for although that was not, of course, done, still it might be made charming, but in the "sham-antique."

"You wouldn't have her live like you among a lot of broken-down chairs and threadbare carpets!" she exclaimed, the innate respectability of the bourgeois housewife getting the better of the acquired dilettantism of the courtesan.

People who enjoyed picking up antiques, who liked poetry, despised sordid calculations of profit and loss, and nourished ideals of honour and love, she placed in a class by themselves, superior to the rest of humanity. There was no need actually to have those tastes, as long as one proclaimed them; when a man had told her at dinner that he loved to wander about and get his hands covered with dust in old furniture shops, that he would never be really appreciated in this commerical age since he was not interested in its concerns, and that he belonged to another generation altogether, she would come home saying: "Why, he's an adorable creature, so sensitive, I had no idea," and she would conceive for him an immediate bond of friendship. But on the other hand, men who, like Swann, had these tastes but did not speak of them, left her cold. She was obliged, of course, to admit that Swann was not interested in money, but she would add sulkily: "It's not the same thing, you see, with him," and, as a matter of fact, what appealed to her imagination was not the practice of disinterestedness, but its vocabulary.

Feeling that, often, he could not give her in reality the pleasures of which she dreamed, he tried at least to ensure that she should be happy in his company, tried not to counteract those vulgar ideas, that bad taste which she displayed on every possible occasion, and which in fact he loved, as he could not help loving everything that came from her, which enchanted him even, for were they not so many characteristic features by virtue of which the essence of this woman revealed itself to him? And so, when she was in a happy mood because she was going to see the *Reine Topaze*,[3] or when her expression grew serious, worried, petulant because she was afraid of missing the flower-show, or merely of not being in time for tea, with muffins and toast, at the Rue Royale tea-rooms, where she believed that regular attendance was indispensable in order to set the seal upon a woman's certificate of elegance, Swann, enraptured as we all are at times by the naturalness of a child or the verisimilitude of a portrait which appears to be on the point of speaking, would feel so distinctly the soul of his mistress rising to the surface of her face that he could not refrain from touching it with his lips. "Ah, so little Odette wants us to take her to the flower-show, does she? She wants to be admired, does she? Very well, we'll take her there, we can but obey her wishes." As Swann was a little short-sighted, he had to resign himself to wearing spectacles at home when working, while to face the world he adopted a monocle as being less disfiguring. The first time that she saw it in his eye, she could not contain her joy: "I really do think—for a man, that is to say—it's tremendously smart! How nice you look with it! Every inch a gentleman. All you want now is a title!" she concluded with a tinge of regret. He liked Odette to say these things, just as if he had been in love with a Breton girl, he would have enjoyed seeing her in her coif and hearing her say that she believed in ghosts. Always until then, as is common among men whose taste for the arts develops independently of their sensuality, a weird disparity had existed between the satisfactions which he would accord to both simultaneously; yielding to the seductions of more and more rarefied works of art in the company of more and more vulgar women, taking a little servant-girl to a screened box at the theatre for the performance of a decadent piece he particularly wanted to see, or to an exhibition of impressionist painting, convinced, moreover, that a cultivated "society" woman would have understood them no better, but would not have managed to remain so prettily silent. But, now that he was in love with Odette, all this was changed; to share her sympathies, to strive to be one with her in spirit, was a task so attractive that he tried to find enjoyment in the things that she liked, and did find a pleasure, not only in imitating her habits but in adopting her opinions, which was all the deeper because, as those habits and opinions had no roots in his own intelligence they reminded him only of his love, for the sake of which he had preferred them to his own. If he went again to *Serge Panine*, if he looked out for opportunities of going to see Olivier Métra conduct,[4] it was for the pleasure of being initiated into every one of Odette's ideas and fancies, of feeling that he had an equal share in all her tastes. This charm, which her favourite plays and pictures and places possessed, of drawing him closer to her, struck him as being more mysterious than the intrinsic charm of more beautiful things and places with which she had no connection. Besides, having allowed the intellectual beliefs of his youth to languish, and his man-of-the-world scepticism having permeated them without his being aware of it, he felt (or at least he had felt for so long that he had fallen into the habit of saying) that the objects we admire have no absolute value in themselves, that the whole thing is a matter of period and class, is no more than a series of fashions, the most vulgar of which are worth just as much as those which are regarded as the most refined. And as he considered that the importance Odette attached to receiving an invitation to a private view was not in itself any more ridiculous than the pleasure he himself had at one time felt in lunching with the Prince of Wales, so he did not think that the admiration she professed for Monte-Carlo or for the Righi was any more unreasonable than his own liking for Holland (which she imagined to be ugly) and for Versailles (which bored her to tears). And so he denied himself the pleasure of visiting those places, delighted to be able to tell himself that it was for her sake, that he wished only to feel, to enjoy things with her.

Like everything else that formed part of Odette's environment, and was no more, in a sense, than the means whereby he might see and talk to her more often, he enjoyed the society of the Verdurins. There, since at the heart of all their entertainments, dinners, musical evenings, games, suppers in fancy dress, excursions to the country, theatre outings, even the infrequent "gala evenings" when they entertained the "bores," there was the presence of Odette, the sight of Odette, conversations with Odette, an inestimable boon which the Verdurins bestowed on Swann by inviting him to their house, he was happier in the little "nucleus" than anywhere else, and tried to find some genuine merit in each of its members, imagining that this would lead him to frequent their society from choice for the rest of his life. Not daring to tell himself, lest he should doubt the truth of the suggestion, that he would always love Odette, at least in supposing that he would go on visiting the Verdurins (a proposition which, *a priori*, raised fewer fundamental objections on the part of his intelligence) he saw himself in the future continuing to meet Odette every evening; that did not, perhaps, come quite to the same thing as loving her for ever, but for the moment, while he loved her, to feel that he would not eventually cease to see her was all that he asked. "What a charming atmosphere!" he said to himself. "How entirely genuine is the life these people lead! How much more intelligent, more artistic they are, than the people one knows! And Mme Verdurin, in spite of a few trifling exaggerations which are rather absurd, what a sincere love of painting and music she has, what a passion for works of art, what anxiety to give pleasure to artists! Her ideas about some of the people one knows are not quite right, but then their ideas about artistic circles are altogether wrong! Possibly I make no great intellectual demands in conversation, but I'm perfectly happy talking to Cottard, although he does trot out those idiotic puns. And as for the painter, if he is rather disagreeably pretentious when he tries to shock, still he has one of the finest brains that I've ever come across. Besides, what is most important, one feels quite free there, one does what one likes without constraint or fuss. What a flow of good humour there is every day in that drawing-room! No question about it, with a few rare exceptions I never want to go anywhere else again. It will become more and more of a habit, and I shall spend the rest of my life among them."

And as the qualities which he supposed to be intrinsic to the Verdurins were no more than the superficial reflection of pleasures which he had enjoyed in their society through his love for Odette, those qualities became more serious, more profound, more vital, when those pleasures were too. Since Mme Verdurin often gave Swann what alone could constitute his happiness—since, on an evening when he felt anxious because Odette had talked rather more to one of the party than to another, and, irritated by this, would not take the initiative of asking her whether she was coming home with him, Mme Verdurin brought peace and joy to his troubled spirit by saying spontaneously: "Odette, you'll see M. Swann home, won't you?"; and since, when the summer holidays were impending and he had asked himself uneasily whether Odette might not leave Paris without him, whether he would still be able to see her every day, Mme Verdurin had invited them both to spend the summer with her in the country— Swann, unconsciously allowing gratitude and self-interest to infiltrate his intelligence and to influence his ideas, went so far as to proclaim that Mme Verdurin was "a great and noble soul." Should one of his old fellow-students from the Ecole du Louvre speak to him of some delightful or eminent people he had come across, "I'd a hundred times rather have the Verdurins" he would reply. And, with a solemnity of diction that was new in him: "They are magnanimous creatures, and magnanimity is, after all, the one thing that matters, the one thing that gives us distinction here on earth. You see, there are only two classes of people, the magnanimous, and the rest; and I have reached an age when one has to take sides, to decide once and for all whom one is going to like and dislike, to stick to the people one likes, and, to make up for the time one has wasted with the others, never to leave them again as long as one lives. And so," he went on, with the slight thrill of emotion which a man feels when, even without being fully aware of it, he says something not because it is true but because he enjoys saying it, and listens to his own voice uttering the words as though they came from someone else, "the die is now cast. I have elected to love none but magnanimous souls, and to live only in an atmosphere of magnanimity. You ask me whether Mme Verdurin is really intelligent. I can assure you that she has given me proofs of a nobility of heart, of a loftiness of soul, to which no one could possibly attain without a corresponding loftiness of mind. Without question, she has a profound understanding of art. But it is not, perhaps, in that that she is most admirable; every little action, ingeniously, exquisitely kind, which she has performed for my sake, every thoughtful attention, every little gesture, quite domestic and yet quite sublime, reveals a more profound comprehension of existence than all your text-books of philosophy."

He might have reminded himself that there were various old friends of his family who were just as simple as the Verdurins, companions of his youth who were just as fond of art, that he knew other "great-hearted" people, and that nevertheless, since he had opted in favour of simplicity, the arts, and magnanimity, he had entirely ceased to see them. But these people did not know Odette, and, if they had known her, would never have thought of introducing her to him.

And so, in the whole of the Verdurin circle, there was probably not a single one of the "faithful" who loved them, or believed that he loved them, as dearly as did Swann. And yet, when M. Verdurin had said that he did not take to Swann, he had not only expressed his own sentiments, he had divined those of his wife. Doubtless Swann had too exclusive an affection for Odette, of which he had neglected to make Mme Verdurin his regular confidante; doubtless the very discretion with which he availed himself of the Verdurins' hospitality, often refraining from coming to dine with them for a reason which they never suspected and in place of which they saw only an anxiety on his part not to have to decline an invitation to the house of some "bore" or other, and doubtless, too, despite all the precautions which he had taken to keep it from them, the gradual discovery which they were making of his brilliant position in society—doubtless all this contributed to their growing irritation with Swann. But the real, the fundamental reason was quite different. The fact was that they had very quickly sensed in him a locked door, a reserved, impenetrable chamber in which he still professed silently to himself that the Princesse de Sagan was not grotesque and that Cottard's jokes were not amusing, in a word, for all that he never deviated from his affability or revolted against their dogmas, an impermeability to those dogmas, a resistance to complete conversion, the like of which they had never come across in anyone before. They would have forgiven him for associating with "bores" (to whom, as it happened, in his heart of hearts he infinitely preferred the Verdurins and all the little "nucleus") had he consented to set a good example by openly renouncing those "bores" in the presence of the "faithful." But that was an abjuration which they realised they were powerless to extort from him.

How different he was from a "newcomer" whom Odette had asked them to invite, although she herself had met him only a few times, and on whom they were building great hopes—the Comte de Forcheville! (It turned out that he was Saniette's brother-in-law, a discovery which filled all the faithful with amazement: the manners of the old palaeographer were so humble that they had always supposed him to be socially inferior to themselves, and had never expected to learn that he came from a rich and relatively aristocratic background.) Of course, Forcheville was a colossal snob, which Swann was not; of course he would never dream of placing, as Swann now did, the Verdurin circle above all others. But he lacked that natural refinement which prevented Swann from associating himself with the more obviously false accusations that Mme Verdurin levelled at people he knew. As for the vulgar and pretentious tirades in which the painter sometimes indulged, the commercial traveller's pleasantries which Cottard used to hazard, and for which Swann, who liked both men sincerely, could easily find excuses without having either the heart or the hypocrisy to applaud them, Forcheville by contrast was of an intellectual calibre to be dumbfounded, awestruck by the first (without in the least understanding them) and to revel in the second. And as it happened, the very first dinner at the Verdurins' at which Forcheville was present threw a glaring light upon all these differences, brought out his qualities and precipitated Swann's fall from grace.

There was at this dinner, besides the usual party, a professor from the Sorbonne, one Brichot, who had met M. and Mme Verdurin at a watering-place somewhere and who, if his university duties and scholarly labours had not left him with very little time to spare, would gladly have come to them more often. For he had the sort of curiosity and superstitious worship of life which, combined with a certain scepticism with regard to the famous Brichot? Why, he's celebrated all over Europe."

"Oh, that's Bréchot, is it?" exclaimed Forcheville, who had not quite caught the name. "You must tell me all about him," he went on, fastening a pair of goggle eyes on the celebrity. "It's always interesting to dine with prominent people. But, I say, you ask one to very select parties here. No dull evenings in this house, I'm sure."

"Well, you know what it is really," said Mme Verdurin modestly, "they feel at ease here. They can talk about whatever they like, and the conversation goes off like fireworks. Now Brichot, this evening, is nothing. I've seen him, don't you know, when he's been in my house, simply dazzling; you'd want to go on your knees to him. Well, anywhere else he's not the same man, he's not in the least witty, you have to drag the words out of him, he's even boring."

"That's strange," remarked Forcheville with fitting astonishment.

A sort of wit like Brichot's would have been regarded as out-and-out stupidity by the people among whom Swann had spent his early life, for all that it is quite compatible with real intelligence. And the intelligence of the Professor's vigorous and well-nourished brain might easily have been envied by many of the people in society who seemed witty enough to Swann. But these last had so thoroughly inculcated into him their likes and dislikes, at least in everything that pertained to social life, including that adjunct to social life which belongs, strictly speaking, to the domain of intelligence, namely, conversation, that Swann could not but find Brichot's pleasantries pedantic, vulgar and naueseating. He was shocked, too, being accustomed to good manners, by the rude, almost barrack-room tone the pugnacious academic adopted no matter to whom he was speaking. Finally, perhaps, he had lost some of his tolerance that evening when he saw the cordiality displayed by Mme Verdurin towards this Forcheville fellow whom it had been Odette's unaccountable idea to bring to the house. Somewhat embarrassed vis-à-vis Swann, she asked him on her arrival: "What do you think of my guest?"

And he, suddenly realising for the first time that Forcheville, whom he had known for years, could actually attract a woman and was quite a good-looking man, replied: "Unspeakable!" It did not occur to him to be jealous of Odette, but he did not feel quite so happy as usual, and when Brichot, having begun to tell them the story of Blanche of Castile's mother who, according to him, "had been with Henry Plantagenet for years before they were married," tried to prompt Swann to beg him to continue the story by interjecting "Isn't that so, M. Swann?" in the martial accents people use in order to put themselves on a level with a country bumpkin or to put the fear of God into a trooper, Swann cut his story short, to the intense fury of their hostess, by begging to be excused for taking so little interest in Blanche of Castile, as he had something that he wished to ask the painter. The latter, it appeared, had been that afternoon to an exhibition of the work of another artist, also a friend of Mme Verdurin, who had recently died, and Swann wished to find out from him (for he valued his discrimination) whether there had really been anything more in these last works than the virtuosity which had struck people so forcibly in his earlier exhibitions.

"From that point of view it was remarkable, but it did not seem to me to be a form of art which you could call 'elevated,'" said Swann with a smile.

"Elevated . . . to the purple," interrupted Cottard,

object of their studies, earns for some intelligent men of whatever profession, doctors who do not believe in medicine, schoolmasters who do not believe in Latin exercises, the reputation of having broad, brilliant and indeed superior minds. He affected, when at Mme Verdurin's, to choose his illustrations from among the most topical subjects of the day when he spoke of philosophy or history, principally because he regarded those sciences as no more than a preparation for life, and imagined that he was seeing put into practice by the "little clan" what hitherto he had known only from books, and perhaps also because, having had instilled into him as a boy, and having unconsciously preserved, a reverence for certain subjects, he thought that he was casting aside the scholar's gown when he ventured to treat those subjects with a conversational licence which in fact seemed daring to him only because the folds of the gown still clung.

Early in the course of the dinner, when M. de Forcheville, seated on the right of Mme Verdurin who in the "newcomer's" honour had taken great pains with her toilet, observed to her: "Quite original, that white dress," the doctor, who had never taken his eyes off him so curious was he to learn the nature and attributes of what he called a "de," and who was on the lookout for an opportunity of attracting his attention and coming into closer contact with him, caught in its flight the adjective "*blanche*" and, his eyes still glued to his plate, snapped out, "*Blanche*? Blanche of Castile?" then, without moving his head, shot a furtive glance to right and left of him, smiling uncertainly. While Swann, by the painful and futile effort which he made to smile, showed that he thought the pun absurd, Forcheville had shown at one and the same time that he could appreciate its subtlety and that he was a man of the world, by keeping within its proper limits a mirth the spontaneity of which had charmed Mme Verdurin.

"What do you make of a scientist like that?" she asked Forcheville. "You can't talk seriously to him for two minutes on end. Is that the sort of thing you tell them at your hospital?" she went on, turning to the doctor. "They must have some pretty lively times there, if that's the case. I can see that I shall have to get taken in as a patient!"

"I think I heard the Doctor speak of that old termagant, Blanche of Castile, if I may so express myself. Am I not right, Madame?" Brichot appealed to Mme Verdurin, who, swooning with merriment, her eyes tightly closed, had buried her face in her hands, from behind which muffled screams could be heard.

"Good gracious, Madame, I would not dream of shocking the reverent-minded, if there are any such around this table, *sub rosa* . . . I recognise, moreover, that our ineffable and Athenian—oh, how infinitely Athenian—republic is capable of honouring, in the person of that obscurantist old she-Capet, the first of our strong-arm chiefs of police. Yes, indeed, my dear host, yes indeed, yes indeed!" he repeated in his ringing voice, which sounded a separate note for each syllable, in reply to a protest from M. Verdurin. "The Chronicle of Saint Denis, and the authenticity of its information is beyond question, leaves us no room for doubt on that point. No one could be more fitly chosen as patron by a secularised proletariat than that mother of a saint, to whom, incidentally, she gave a pretty rough time, according to Suger and other great St Bernards of the sort; for with her everyone got hauled over the coals."

"Who is that gentleman?" Forcheville asked Mme Verdurin. "He seems first-rate."

"What! Do you mean to say you don't know the

raising his arms with mock solemnity. The whole table burst out laughing.

"What did I tell you?" said Mme Verdurin to Forcheville. "It's simply impossible to be serious with him. When you least expect it, out he comes with some piece of foolery."

But she observed that Swann alone had not unbent. For one thing he was none too pleased with Cottard for having secured a laugh at his expense in front of Forcheville. But the painter, instead of replying in a way that might have interested Swann, as he would probably have done had they been alone together, preferred to win the easy admiration of the rest with a witty dissertation on the talent of the deceased master.

"I went up to one of them," he began, "just to see how it was done. I stuck my nose into it. Well, it's just not true! Impossible to say whether it was done with glue, with soap, with sealing-wax, with sunshine, with leaven, with caca!"

"And one makes twelve!" shouted the doctor, but just too late, for no one saw the point of his interruption.

"It looks as though it was done with nothing at all," resumed the painter. "No more chance of discovering the trick than there is in the 'Night Watch' or the 'Regents,' and technically it's even better than either Rembrandt or Hals. It's all there—but really, I swear it."

Then, just as singers who have reached the highest note in their compass continue in a head voice, *piano*, he proceeded to murmur, laughing the while, as if, after all, there had been something irresistibly absurd in the sheer beauty of the painting: "It smells good, it makes your head whirl; it takes your breath away; you feel ticklish all over—and not the faintest clue to how it's done. The man's a sorcerer; the thing's a conjuring-trick, a miracle," bursting into outright laughter, "it's almost dishonest!" And stopping, solemnly raising his head, pitching his voice on a *basso profundo* note which he struggled to bring into harmony, he concluded, "And it's so sincere!"

Except at the moment when he had called it "better than the 'Night Watch,'" a blasphemy which had called forth an instant protest from Mme Verdurin, who regarded the "Night Watch" as the supreme masterpiece of the universe (conjointly with the "Ninth" and the "Winged Victory"), and at the word "caca," which had made Forcheville throw a sweeping glance round the table to see whether it was "all right," before he allowed his lips to curve in a prudish and conciliatory smile, all the guests (save Swann) had kept their fascinated and adoring eyes fixed upon the painter.

"I do so love him when he gets carried away like that!" cried Mme Verdurin the moment he had finished, enraptured that the table-talk should have proved so entertaining on the very night that Forcheville was dining with them for the first time. "Hallo, you!" she turned to her husband, "What's the matter with you, sitting there gaping like a great animal? You know he talks well. Anybody would think it was the first time he had ever listened to you," she added to the painter. "If you had only seen him while you were speaking; he was just drinking it all in. And to-morrow he'll tell us everything you said, without missing a word."

"No, really, I'm not joking!" protested the painter, enchanted by the success of his speech. "You all look as if you thought I was pulling your legs, that it's all eyewash. I'll take you to see the show, and then you can say whether I've been exaggerating; I'll bet you anything you like, you'll come away even more enthusiastic than I am!"

"But we don't suppose for a moment that you're exaggerating. We only want you to go on with your dinner, and my husband too. Give M. Biche some more sole, can't you see his has got cold? We're not in any hurry; you're dashing round as if the house was on fire. Wait a little; don't serve the salad just yet."

Mme Cottard, who was a modest woman and spoke but seldom, was not however lacking in self-assurance when a happy inspiration put the right word in her mouth. She felt that it would be well received, and this gave her confidence, but what she did with it was with the object not so much of shining herself as of helping her husband on in his career. And so she did not allow the word "salad," which Mme Verdurin had just uttered, to pass unchallenged.

"It's not a Japanese salad, is it?" she said in a loud undertone, turning towards Odette.

And then, in her joy and confusion at the aptness and daring of making so discreet and yet so unmistakable an allusion to the new and brilliantly successful play by Dumas, she broke into a charming, girlish laugh, not very loud, but so irresistible that it was some time before she could control it.

"Who is that lady? She seems devilish clever," said Forcheville.

"No, it is not. But we'll make one for you if you'll all come to dinner on Friday."

"You will think me dreadfully provincial," said Mme Cottard to Swann, "but I haven't yet seen this famous *Francillon* that everybody's talking about. The Doctor has been (I remember now, he told me he had the great pleasure of spending the evening with you) and I must confess I didn't think it very sensible for him to spend money on seats in order to see it again with me. Of course an evening at the Théâtre-Français is never really wasted; the acting's so good there always; but we have some very nice friends" (Mme Cottard rarely uttered a proper name, but restricted herself to "some friends of ours" or "one of my friends," as being more "distinguished," speaking in an affected tone and with the self-importance of a person who need give names only when she chooses) "who often have a box, and are kind enough to take us to all the new pieces that are worth going to, and so I'm certain to see *Francillon* sooner or later, and then I shall know what to think. But I do feel such a fool about it, I must confess, for wherever I go I naturally find everybody talking about that wretched Japanese salad. In fact one's beginning to get just a little tired of hearing about it," she went on, seeing that Swann seemed less interested than she had hoped in so burning a topic. "I must admit, though, that it provides an excuse for some quite amusing notions. I've got a friend, now, who is most original, though she's a very pretty woman, very popular in society, very sought-after, and she tells me that she got her cook to make one of those Japanese salads, putting in everything that young M. Dumas says you're to in the play. Then she asked a few friends to come and taste it. I was not among the favoured few, I'm sorry to say. But she told us all about it at her next 'at home'; it seems it was quite horrible, she made us all laugh till we cried. But of course it's all in the telling," Mme Cottard added, seeing that Swann still looked grave.

And imagining that it was perhaps because he had not liked *Francillon*: "Well, I daresay I shall be disappointed with it, after all. I don't suppose it's as good as the piece Mme de Crécy worships, *Serge Panine*. There's a play, if you like; really deep, makes you think! But just fancy giving a recipe for a salad on the stage of the Théâtre-Français! Now, *Serge Panine*! But then, it's like everything that comes from the pen of M. Georges Ohnet, it's always so well written. I wonder if you know the *Maître des Forges*, which I like even better than *Serge Panine*."

"Forgive me," said Swann with polite irony, "but I must confess that my want of admiration is almost equally divided between those masterpieces."

"Really, and what don't you like about them? Are you sure you aren't prejudiced? Perhaps you think he's a little too sad. Well, well, what I always say is, one should never argue about plays or novels. Everyone has his own way of looking at things, and what you find detestable may be just what I like best."

She was interrupted by Forcheville addressing Swann. While Mme Cottard was discussing *Francillon*, Forcheville had been expressing to Mme Verdurin his admiration for what he called the painter's "little speech": "Your friend has such a flow of language, such a memory!" he said to her when the painter had come to a standstill. "I've seldom come across anything like it. He'd make a first-rate preacher. By Jove, I wish I was like that. What with him and M. Bréchot you've got a couple of real characters, though as regards the gift of the gab, I'm not so sure that this one doesn't knock a few spots off the Professor. It comes more naturally with him, it's less studied. Although now and then he does use some words that are a bit realistic, but that's quite the thing nowadays. Anyhow, it's not often I've seen a man hold the floor as cleverly as that—'hold the spittoon' as we used to say in the regiment, where, by the way, we had a man he rather reminds me of. You could take anything you liked—I don't know what—

this glass, say, and he'd rattle on about it for hours; no, not this glass, that's a silly thing to say, but something like the battle of Waterloo, or anything of that sort, he'd spin you such a yarn you simply wouldn't believe it. Why, Swann was in the same regiment; he must have known him."

"Do you see much of M. Swann?" asked Mme Verdurin.

"Oh dear, no!" he answered, and then, thinking that if he made himself pleasant to Swann he might find favour with Odette, he decided to take this opportunity of flattering him by speaking of his fashionable friends, but to do so as a man of the world himself, in a tone of good-natured criticism, and not as though he were congratulating Swann upon some unexpected success. "Isn't that so, Swann? I never see anything of you, do I?—But then, where on earth is one to see him? The fellow spends all his time ensconced with the La Trémoïlles, the Laumes and all that lot!" The imputation would have been false at any time, and was all the more so now that for at least a year Swann scarcely went anywhere except to the Verdurins'. But the mere name of a person whom the Verdurins did not know was greeted by them with a disapproving silence. M. Verdurin, dreading the painful impression which the names of these "bores," especially when flung at her in this tactless fashion in front of all the "faithful," were bound to make on his wife, cast a covert glance at her, instinct with anxious solicitude. He saw then that in her determination not to take cognizance of, not to have been affected by the news which had just been imparted to her, not merely to remain dumb, but to have been deaf as well, as we pretend to be when a friend who has offended us attempts to slip into his conversation some excuse which we might appear to be accepting if we heard it without protesting, or when someone utters the name of an enemy the very mention of whom in our presence is forbidden, Mme Verdurin, so that her silence should have the appearance not of consent but of the unconscious silence of inanimate objects, had suddenly emptied her face of all life, of all mobility; her domed forehead was no more than an exquisite piece of sculpture in the round, which the name of those La Trémoïlles with whom Swann was always "ensconced" had failed to penetrate; her nose, just perceptibly wrinkled in a frown, exposed to view two dark cavities that seemed modelled from life. You would have said that her half-opened lips were just about to speak. She was no more than a wax cast, a plaster mask, a maquette for a monument, a bust for the Palace of Industry, in front of which the public would most certainly gather and marvel to see how the sculptor, in expressing the unchallengeable dignity of the Verdurins as opposed to that of the La Trémoïlles or Laumes, whose equals (if not indeed their betters) they were, and the equals and betters of all other "bores" upon the face of the earth, had contrived to impart an almost papal majesty to the whiteness and rigidity of the stone. But the marble at last came to life and let it be understood that it didn't do to be at all squeamish if one went to that house, since the wife was always drunk and the husband so uneducated that he called a corridor a "collidor"!

"You'd need to pay me a lot of money before I'd let any of that lot set food inside my house," Mme Verdurin concluded, gazing imperially down on Swann.

She could scarcely have expected him to capitulate so completely as to echo the holy simplicity of the pianist's aunt, who at once exclaimed: "To think of that, now! What surprises me is that they can get anybody to go near them. I'm sure I should be afraid;

one can't be too careful. How can people be so common as to go running after them?" But he might at least have replied, like Forcheville: "Gad, she's a duchess; there are still plenty of people who are impressed by that sort of thing," which would at least have permitted Mme Verdurin the retort, "And a lot of good may it do them!" Instead of which, Swann merely smiled, in a manner which intimated that he could not, of course, take such an outrageous statement seriously. M. Verdurin, who was still casting furtive glances at his wife, saw with regret and understood only too well that she was now inflamed with the passion of a Grand Inquisitor who has failed to stamp out heresy; and so, in the hope of bringing Swann round to a recantation (for the courage of one's opinions is always a form of calculating cowardice in the eyes of the "other side"), challenged him: "Tell us frankly, now, what you think of them yourself. We shan't repeat it to them, you may be sure."

To which Swann answered: "Why, I'm not in the least afraid of the Duchess (if it's the La Trémoïlles you're speaking of). I can assure you that everyone likes going to her house. I wouldn't go so far as to say that she's at all 'profound'" (he pronounced "profound" as if it was a ridiculous word, for his speech kept the traces of certain mental habits which the recent change in his life, a rejuvenation illustrated by his passion for music, had inclined him temporarily to discard, so that at times he would actually state his views with considerable warmth) "but I'm quite sincere when I say that she's intelligent, while her husband is positively a man of letters. They're charming people."

Whereupon Mme Verdurin, realising that this one infidel would prevent her "little nucleus" from achieving complete unanimity, was unable to restrain herself, in her fury at the obstinacy of this wretch who could not see what anguish his words were causing her, from screaming at him from the depths of her tortured heart: "You may think so if you wish, but at least you needn't say so to us."

"It all depends on what you call intelligence." Forcheville felt that it was his turn to be brilliant. "Come now, Swann, tell us what you mean by intelligence."

"There," cried Odette, "that's the sort of big subject I'm always asking him to talk to me about, and he never will."

"Oh, but..." protested Swann.

"Oh, but nonsense!" said Odette.

"A water-butt?" asked the doctor.

"In your opinion," pursued Forcheville, "does intelligence mean the gift of the gab—you know, glib society talk?"

"Finish your sweet, so that they can take your plate away," said Mme Verdurin sourly to Saniette, who was lost in thought and had stopped eating. And then, perhaps a little ashamed of her rudeness, "It doesn't matter, you can take your time about it. I only reminded you because of the others, you know; it keeps the servants back."

"There is," began Brichot, hammering out each syllable, "a rather curious definition of intelligence by that gentle old anarchist Fénelon..."

"Just listen to this!" Mme Verdurin rallied Forcheville and the doctor. "He's going to give us Fénelon's definition of intelligence. Most interesting. It's not often you get a chance of hearing that!"

But Brichot was keeping Fénelon's definition until Swann had given his. Swann remained silent, and, by this fresh act of recreancy, spoiled the brilliant dialectical contest which Mme Verdurin was rejoicing at being able to offer to Forcheville.

"You see, it's just the same with me!" said Odette peevishly. "I'm not at all sorry to see that I'm not the only one he doesn't find quite up to his level."

"Are these de La Trémouailles whom Mme Verdurin has shown us to be so undesirable," inquired Brichot, articulating vigorously, "descended from the couple whom that worthy old snob Mme de Sévigné said she was delighted to know because it was so good for her peasants? True, the Marquise had another reason, which in her case probably came first, for she was a thorough journalist at heart, and always on the look-out for 'copy.' And in the journal which she used to send regularly to her daughter, it was Mme de La Trémouaille, kept well-informed through all her grand connections, who supplied the foreign politics."

"No, no, I don't think they're the same family," hazarded Mme Verdurin.

Saniette, who ever since he had surrendered his untouched plate to the butler had been plunged once more in silent meditation, emerged finally to tell them, with a nervous laugh, the story of a dinner he had once had with the Duc de La Trémoïlle, from which it transpired that the Duke did not know that George Sand was the pseudonym of a woman. Swann, who was fond of Saniette, felt bound to supply him with a few facts illustrative of the Duke's culture proving that such ignorance on his part was literally impossible; but suddenly he stopped short, realising that Saniette needed no proof, but knew already that the story was untrue for the simple reason that he had just invented it. The worthy man suffered acutely from the Verdurins' always finding him so boring; and as he was conscious of having been more than ordinarily dull this evening, he had made up his mind that he would succeed in being amusing at least once before the end of dinner. He capitulated so quickly, looked so wretched at the sight of his castle in ruins, and replied in so craven a tone to Swann, appealing to him not to persist in a refutation which was now superfluous—"All right; all right; anyhow, even if I'm mistaken it's not a crime, I hope"—that Swann longed to be able to console him by insisting that the story was indubitably true and exquisitely funny. The doctor, who had been listening, had an idea that it was the right moment to interject "*Se non è vero,*" but he was not quite certain of the words, and was afraid of getting them wrong.

After dinner, Forcheville went up to the doctor.

"She can't have been at all bad looking, Mme Verdurin; and besides, she's a woman you can really talk to, which is the main thing. Of course she's getting a bit broad in the beam. But Mme de Crécy! There's a little woman who knows what's what, all right. Upon my word and soul, you can see at a glance she's got her wits about her, that girl. We're speaking of Mme de Crécy," he explained, as M. Verdurin joined them, his pipe in his mouth. "I should say that, as a specimen of the female form . . ."

"I'd rather have it in my bed than a slap with a wet fish," the words came tumbling from Cottard, who had for some time been waiting in vain for Forcheville to pause for breath so that he might get in this hoary old joke for which there might not be another cue if the conversation should take a different turn and which he now produced with that excessive spontaneity and confidence that seeks to cover up the coldness and the anxiety inseparable from a prepared recitation. Forcheville knew and saw the joke, and was thoroughly amused.

As for M. Verdurin, he was unsparing of his merriment, having recently discovered a way of expressing it by a convention that was different from his wife's but equally simple and obvious. Scarcely had he begun the movement of head and shoulders of a man "shaking with laughter" than he would begin at once to cough, as though, in laughing too violently, he had swallowed a mouthful of pipe-smoke. And by keeping the pipe firmly in his mouth he could prolong indefinitely the dumb-show of suffocation and hilarity. Thus he and Mme Verdurin (who, at the other side of the room, where the painter was telling her a story, was shutting her eyes preparatory to flinging her face into her hands) resembled two masks in a theatre each representing Comedy in a different way.

M. Verdurin had been wiser than he knew in not taking his pipe out of his mouth, for Cottard, having occasion to leave the room for a moment, murmured a witty euphemism which he had recently acquired and repeated now whenever he had to go to the place in question: "I must just go and see the Duc d'Aumale for a minute," so drolly that M. Verdurin's cough began all over again.

"Do take your pipe out of your mouth. Can't you see that you'll choke if you try to bottle up your laughter like that," counselled Mme Verdurin as she came round with a tray of liqueurs.

"What a delightful man your husband is; he's dev-ilish witty," declared Forcheville to Mme Cottard. "Thank you, thank you, an old soldier like me can never say no to a drink."

"M. de Forcheville thinks Odette charming," M. Verdurin told his wife.

"Ah, as a matter of fact she'd like to have lunch with you one day. We must arrange it, but don't on any account let Swann hear about it. He spoils everything, don't you know. I don't mean to say that you're not to come to dinner too, of course; we hope to see you very often. Now that the warm weather's coming, we're going to dine out of doors whenever we can. It won't bore you will it, a quiet little dinner now and then in the Bois? Splendid, splendid, it will be so nice. . . .

"I say, aren't you going to do any work this evening?" she screamed suddenly to the young pianist, seeing an opportunity for displaying, before a "newcomer" of Forcheville's importance, at once her unfailing wit and her despotic power over the "faithful."

"M. de Forcheville has been saying dreadful things about you," Mme Cottard told her husband as he reappeared in the room. And he, still following up the idea of Forcheville's noble birth, which had obsessed him all through dinner, said to him: "I'm treating a Baroness just now, Baroness Putbus. Weren't there some Putbuses in the Crusades? Anyhow they've got a lake in Pomerania that's ten times the size of the Place de la Concorde. I'm treating her for rheumatoid arthritis; she's a charming woman. Mme Verdurin knows her too, I believe."

Which enabled Forcheville, a moment later, finding himself alone again with Mme Cottard, to complete his favourable verdict on her husband with: "He's an interesting man, too; you can see that he knows a few people. Gad! they do get to know a lot of things, those doctors."

"I'm going to play the phrase from the sonata for M. Swann," said the pianist.

"What the devil's that? Not the sonata-snake, I hope!" shouted M. de Forcheville, hoping to create an effect. But Dr Cottard, who had never heard this pun, missed the point of it, and imagined that M. de Forche-ville had made a mistake. He dashed in boldly to correct him: "No, no. The word isn't *serpent-à-sonates*, it's *serpent-à-sonnettes*!" he explained in a tone at once zealous, impatient, and triumphant.[5]

Forcheville explained the joke to him. The doctor blushed.

"You'll admit it's not bad, eh, Doctor?"

"Oh! I've known it for ages."

Then they were silent; beneath the restless tremolos of the violin part which protected it with their throbbing *sostenuto* two octaves above it—and as in a mountainous country, behind the seeming immmobility of a vertiginous waterfall, one descries, two hundred feet below, the tiny form of a woman walking in the valley—the little phrase had just appeared, distant, graceful, protected by the long, gradual unfurling of its transparent, incessant and sonorous curtain. And Swann, in his heart of hearts, turned to it as to a confidant of his love, as to a friend of Odette who would surely tell her to pay no attention to this Forcheville.

"Ah! you've come too late!" Mme Verdurin greeted one of the faithful whose invitation had been only "to look in after dinner." "We've been having a simply incomparable Brichot! You never heard such eloquence! But he's gone. Isn't that so, M. Swann? I believe it's the first time you've met him," she went on, to emphasise the fact that it was to her that Swann owed the introduction. "Wasn't he delicious, our Brichot?"

Swann bowed politely.

"No? You weren't interested?" she asked dryly.

"Oh, but I assure you, I was quite enthralled. He's perhaps a little too peremptory, a little too jovial for my taste. I should like to see him a little less confident at times, a little more tolerant, but one feels that he knows a great deal, and on the whole he seems a very sound fellow."

The party broke up very late. Cottard's first words to his wife were: "I've rarely seen Mme Verdurin in such form as she was to-night."

"What exactly is your Mme Verdurin? A bit of a demirep, eh?" said Forcheville to the painter, to whom he had offered a lift.

Odette watched his departure with regret; she dared not refuse to let Swann take her home, but she was moody and irritable in the carriage, and when he asked whether he might come in, replied, "I suppose so," with an impatient shrug of her shoulders.

When all the guests had gone, Mme Verdurin said to her husband: "Did you notice the way Swann laughed, such an idiotic laugh, when we spoke about Mme La Trémoïlle?"

She had remarked, more than once, how Swann and Forcheville suppressed the particle "de" before that lady's name. Never doubting that it was done on purpose, to show that they were not afraid of a title, she had made up her mind to imitate their arrogance, but had not quite grasped what grammatical form it ought to take. And so, the natural corruptness of her speech overcoming her implacable republicanism, she still said instinctively "the de La Trémoïlles," or rather (by an abbreviation sanctified by usage in music hall lyrics and cartoon captions, where the 'de' is elided), "the d'La Trémoïlles," but redeemed herself by saying "Madame La Trémoïlle.—The *Duchess*, as Swann calls her," she added ironically, with a smile which proved that she was merely quoting and would not, herself, accept the least responsibility for a classification so puerile and absurd.

"I don't mind saying that I thought him extremely stupid."

M. Verdurin took it up: "He's not sincere. He's a crafty customer, always sitting on the fence, always trying to run with the hare and hunt with the hounds. What a difference between him and Forcheville. There at least you have a man who tells you straight out what he thinks. Either you agree with him or you don't. Not like the other fellow, who's never definitely fish or fowl. Did you notice, by the way, that Odette seemed all out for Forcheville, and I don't blame her, either. And besides, if Swann wants to come the man of fashion over us, the champion of distressed duchesses, at any rate the other man has got a title—he's always Comte de Forcheville," he concluded with an air of discrimination, as though, familiar with every page of the history of that dignity, he were making a scrupulously exact estimate of its value in relation to others of the sort.

"I may tell you," Mme Verdurin went on, "that he saw fit to utter some venomous and quite absurd insinuations against Brichot. Naturally, once he saw that Brichot was popular in this house, it was a way of hitting back at us, of spoiling our party. I know his sort, the dear, good friend of the family who runs you down behind your back."

"Didn't I say so?" retorted her husband. "He's simply a failure, one of those small-minded individuals who are envious of anything that's at all big."

In reality there was not one of the "faithful" who was not infinitely more malicious than Swann; but they all took the precaution of tempering their calumnies with obvious pleasantries, with little sparks of emotion and cordiality; while the slightest reservation on Swann's part, undraped in any such conventional formula of "Of course, I don't mean to be unkind," to which he would not have deigned to stoop, appeared to them a deliberate act of treachery. There are certain original and distinguished authors in whom the least outspokenness is thought shocking because they have not begun by flattering the tastes of the public and serving up to it the commonplaces to which it is accustomed; it was by the same process that Swann infuriated M. Verdurin. In his case as in theirs it was the novelty of his language which led his audience to suspect the blackness of his designs.

Swann was still unconscious of the disgrace that threatened him at the Verdurins', and continued to regard all their absurdities in the most rosy light, through the admiring eyes of love.

As a rule he met Odette only in the evenings; he was afraid of her growing tired of him if he visited her during the day as well, but, being reluctant to forfeit the place that he held in her thoughts, he was constantly looking out for opportunities of claiming her attention in ways that would not be displeasing to her. If, in a florist's or a jeweller's window, a plant or an ornament caught his eye, he would at once think of sending them to Odette, imagining that the pleasure which the casual sight of them had given him would instinctively be felt also by her, and would increase her affection for him; and he would order them to be taken at once to the Rue La Pérouse, so as to accelerate the moment when, as she received an offering from him, he might feel himself somehow transported into her presence. He was particularly anxious, always, that she should receive these presents before she went out for the evening, so that her gratitude towards him might give additional tenderness to her welcome when he arrived at the Verdurins', might even—for all he knew—if the shop-

keeper made haste, bring him a letter from her before
dinner, or herself in person upon his doorstep, come
on a little supplementary visit of thanks. As in an earlier
phase, when he had tested the reactions of chagrin on
Odette's nature, he now sought by those of gratitude
to elicit from her intimate scraps of feeling which she
had not yet revealed to him.

Often she was plagued with money troubles, and
under pressure from a creditor would appeal to him for
assistance. He was pleased by this, as he was pleased
by anything that might impress Odette with his love
for her, or merely with his influence, with the extent
to which he could be of use to her. If anyone had said
to him at the beginning, "It's your position that attracts
her," or at this stage, "It's your money that she's really
in love with," he would probably not have believed the
suggestion; nor, on the other hand, would he have been
greatly distressed by the thought that people supposed
her to be attached to him—that people felt them to
be united—by ties so binding as those of snobbishness
or wealth. But even if he had believed it to be true, it
might not have caused him any suffering to discover
that Odette's love for him was based on a foundation
more lasting than the charms or the qualities which she
might see in him: namely, self-interest, a self-interest
which would postpone for ever the fatal day when she
might be tempted to bring their relations to an end.
For the moment, by heaping presents on her, by doing
her all manner of favours, he could fall back on advantages extraneous to his person, or to his intellect, as a
relief from the endless, killing effort to make himself
attractive to her. And the pleasure of being a lover, of
living by love alone, the reality of which he was sometimes inclined to doubt, was enhanced in his eyes, as
a dilettante of intangible sensations, by the price he

was paying for it—as one sees people who are doubtful whether the sight of the sea and the sound of its waves are really enjoyable become convinced that they are— and convinced also of the rare quality and absolute detachment of their own taste—when they have agreed to pay several pounds a day for a room in an hotel from which that sight and that sound may be enjoyed.

One day, when reflections of this sort had brought him back to the memory of the time when someone had spoken to him of Odette as of a "kept woman," and he was amusing himself once again with contrasting that strange personification, the "kept woman"—an iridescent mixture of unknown and demoniacal qualities embroidered, as in some fantasy of Gustave Moreau, with poison-dripping flowers interwoven with precious jewels—with the Odette on whose face he had seen the same expressions of pity for a sufferer, revolt against an act of injustice, gratitude for an act of kindness, which he had seen in earlier days on his own mother's face and on the faces of his friends, the Odette whose con- versation so frequently turned on the things that he himself knew better than anyone, his collections, his room, his old servant, the banker who kept all his securities, it happened that the thought of the banker reminded him that he must call on him shortly to draw some money. The fact was that if, during the current month, he were to come less liberally to the aid of Odette in her financial difficulties than in the month before, when he had given her five thousand francs, if he refrained from offering her a diamond necklace for which she longed, he would be allowing her admiration for his generosity, her heart-warming gratitude, to de- cline, and would even run the risk of giving her to believe that his love for her (as she saw its visible man- ifestations grow smaller) had itself diminished. And then, suddenly, he wondered whether that was not precisely what was implied by "keeping" a woman (as if, in fact, that notion of "keeping" could be derived from elements not at all mysterious or perverse but belonging to the intimate routine of his daily life; such as that thousand-franc note, a familiar and domestic object, torn in places and stuck together again, which his valet, after paying the household accounts and the rent, had locked up in a drawer in the old writing-desk whence he had extracted it to send it, with four others, to Odette) and whether it might not be possible to apply to Odette, since he had known her (for he never suspected for a moment that she could ever have taken money from anyone before him), that title, which he had believed so wholly inapplicable to her, of "kept woman." He could not explore the idea further, for a sudden access of that mental lethargy which was, with him, congenital, intermittent and providential, happened at that moment to extinguish every particle of light in his brain, as instantaneously as, at a later period, when electric lighting had been everywhere installed, it became possible to cut off the supply of light from a house. His mind fumbled for a moment in the darkness, he took off his spectacles, wiped the glasses, drew his hand across his eyes, and only saw light again when he found himself face to face with a wholly different idea, to wit, that he must endeavour, in the coming month, to send Odette six or seven thousand francs instead of five because of the surprise and pleasure it would cause her.

In the evening, when he did not stay at home until it was time to meet Odette at the Verdurins', or rather at one of the open-air restaurants which they patronised in the Bois and especially at Saint-Cloud, he would go to dine in one of those fashionable houses in which at one time he had been a constant guest. He did not wish to lose touch with people who, for all that he knew, might some day be of use to Odette, and thanks to whom he was often, in the meantime, able to procure for her some privilege or pleasure. Besides, his long inurement to luxury and high society had given him a need as well as a contempt for them, with the result that by the time he had come to regard the humblest lodgings as precisely on a par with the most princely mansions, his senses were so thoroughly accustomed to the latter that he could not enter the former without a feeling of acute discomfort. He had the same regard— to a degree of identity which they would never have suspected—for the little families with small incomes who asked him to dances in their flats ("straight upstairs to the fifth floor, and the door on the left") as for the Princesse de Parme who gave the most splendid parties in Paris; but he did not have the feeling of being actually at a party when he found himself herded with the fathers of families in the bedroom of the lady of the house, while the spectacle of wash-hand-stands covered over with towels, and of beds converted into cloak-rooms, with a mass of hats and greatcoats sprawling over their counterpanes, gave him the same stifling sensation that, nowadays, people who have been used for half a lifetime to electric light derive from a smoking lamp or a candle that needs to be snuffed.

If he was dining out, he would order his carriage for half-past seven. While he changed his clothes, he would be thinking all the time about Odette, and in this way was never alone, for the constant thought of Odette gave the moments during which he was separated from her the same peculiar charm as those in which she was at his side. He would get into his carriage and drive off, but he knew that this thought had jumped in after

114

him and had settled down on his lap, like a pet animal
which he might take everywhere, and would keep with
him at the dinner-table unbeknownst to his fellow-
guests. He would stroke and fondle it, warm himself
with it, and, overcome with a sort of languor, would
give way to a slight shuddering which contracted his
throat and nostrils—a new experience, this,—as he
fastened the bunch of columbines in his buttonhole.
He had for some time been feeling depressed and unwell, especially since Odette had introduced Forcheville
to the Verdurins, and he would have liked to go away
for a while to rest in the country. But he could never
summon up the courage to leave Paris, even for a day,
while Odette was there. The air was warm; it was
beautiful spring weather. And for all that he was driving
through a city of stone to immure himself in a house
without grass or garden, what was incessantly before
his eyes was a park which he owned near Combray,
where, at four in the afternoon, before coming to the
asparagus-bed, thanks to the breeze that was wafted
across the fields from Méséglise, one could enjoy the
fragrant coolness of the air beneath an arbour in the
garden as much as by the edge of the pond fringed with
forget-me-nots and iris, and where, when he sat down
to dinner, the table ran riot with the roses and the
flowering currant trained and twined by his gardener's
skilful hand.

After dinner, if he had an early appointment in the
Bois or at Saint-Cloud, he would rise from table and
leave the house so abruptly—especially if it threatened
to rain, and thus to scatter the "faithful" before their
normal time—that on one occasion the Princesse des
Laumes (at whose house dinner had been so late that
Swann had left before the coffee was served to join the
Verdurins on the Island in the Bois) observed: "Really,

if Swann were thirty years older and had bladder trouble, there might be some excuse for his running away like that. I must say it's pretty cool of him."

He persuaded himself that the charm of spring which he could not go down to Combray to enjoy might at least be found on the Ile des Cygnes or at Saint-Cloud. But as he could think only of Odette, he did not even know whether he had smelt the fragrance of the young leaves, or if the moon had been shining. He would be greeted by the little phrase from the sonata, played in the garden on the restaurant piano. If there was no piano in the garden, the Verdurins would have taken immense pains to have one brought down either from one of the rooms or from the dining-room. Not that Swann was now restored to favour; far from it. But the idea of arranging an ingenious form of entertainment for someone, even for someone they disliked, would stimulate them, during the time spent in its preparation, to a momentary sense of cordiality and affection. From time to time he would remind himself that another fine spring evening was drawing to a close, and would force himself to notice the trees and the sky. But the state of agitation into which Odette's presence never failed to throw him, added to a feverish ailment which had persisted for some time now, robbed him of that calm and well-being which are the indispensable background to the impressions we derive from nature.

One evening, when Swann had consented to dine with the Verdurins, and had mentioned during dinner that he had to attend next day the annual banquet of an old comrades' association, Odette had exclaimed across the table, in front of Forcheville, who was now one of the "faithful," in front of the painter, in front of Cottard:

"Yes, I know you have your banquet to-morrow; I

shan't see you, then, till I get home; don't be too late."

And although Swann had never yet taken serious
offence at Odette's friendship for one or other of the
"faithful," he felt an exquisite pleasure on hearing her
thus avow in front of them all, with that calm im-
modesty, the fact that they saw each other regularly
every evening, his privileged position in her house and
the preference for him which it implied. It was true
that Swann had often reflected that Odette was in no
way a remarkable woman, and there was nothing especially flattering in seeing the supremacy he wielded
over someone so inferior to himself proclaimed to all
the "faithful"; but since he had observed that to many
other men besides himself Odette seemed a fascinating
and desirable woman, the attraction which her body
held for them had aroused in him a painful longing to
secure the absolute mastery of even the tiniest particles
of her heart. And he had begun to attach an incalculable
value to those moments spent in her house in the evenings, when he held her upon his knee, made her tell
him what she thought about this or that, and counted
over the only possessions on earth to which he still
clung. And so, drawing her aside after this dinner, he
took care to thank her effusively, seeking to indicate
to her by the extent of his gratitude the corresponding
intensity of the pleasures which it was in her power to
bestow on him, the supreme pleasure being to guarantee
him immunity, for so long as his love should last and
he remain vulnerable, from the assaults of jealousy.

When he came away from his banquet, the next
evening, it was pouring with rain, and he had nothing
but his victoria. A friend offered to take him home in
a closed carriage, and as Odette, by the fact of her
having invited him to come, had given him an assurance
that she was expecting no one else, he could have gone

home to bed with a quiet mind and an untroubled heart, rather than set off thus in the rain. But perhaps, if she saw that he seemed not to adhere to his resolution to spend the late evening always, without exception, in her company, she might not bother to keep it free for him on the one occasion when he particularly desired it.

It was after eleven when he reached her door, and as he made his apology for having been unable to come away earlier, she complained that it was indeed very late, that the storm had made her feel unwell and her head ached, and warned him that she would not let him stay more than half an hour, that at midnight she would send him away; a little while later she felt tired and wished to sleep.

"No cattleya, then, to-night?" he asked, "and I've been so looking forward to a nice little cattleya."

She seemed peevish and on edge, and replied: "No, dear, no cattleya to-night. Can't you see I'm not well?"

"It might have done you good, but I won't bother you."

She asked him to put out the light before he went; he drew the curtains round her bed and left. But, when he was back in his own house, the idea suddenly struck him that perhaps Odette was expecting someone else that evening, that she had merely pretended to be tired, so that she had asked him to put the light out only so that he should suppose that she was going to sleep, that the moment he had left the house she had put it on again and had opened her door to the man who was to spend the night with her. He looked at his watch. It was about an hour and a half since he had left her. He went out, took a cab, and stopped it close to her house, in a little street running at right angles to that other street which lay at the back of her house and along which he used sometimes to go, to tap upon her bed-room window, for her to let him in. He left his cab; the streets were deserted and dark; he walked a few yards and came out almost opposite her house. Amid the glimmering blackness of the row of windows in which the lights had long since been put out, he saw one, and only one, from which percolated—between the slats of its shutters, closed like a wine-press over its mysterious golden juice—the light that filled the room within, a light which on so many other evenings, as soon as he saw it from afar as he turned into the street, had rejoiced his heart with its message: "She is there—expecting you," and which now tortured him, saying: "She is there with the man she was expecting." He must know who; he tiptoed along the wall until he reached the window, but between the slanting bars of the shutters he could see nothing, could only hear, in the silence of the night, the murmur of conversation.

Certainly he suffered as he watched that light, in whose golden atmosphere, behind the closed sash, stirred the unseen and detested pair, as he listened to that murmur which revealed the presence of the man who had crept in after his own departure, the perfidy of Odette, and the pleasures which she was at that moment enjoying with the stranger. And yet he was not sorry he had come; the torment which had forced him to leave his own house had become less acute now that it had become less vague, now that Odette's other life, of which he had had, at that first moment, a sudden helpless suspicion, was definitely there, in the full glare of the lamp-light, almost within his grasp, an unwit-ting prisoner in that room into which, when he chose, he would force his way to seize it unawares; or rather he would knock on the shutters, as he often did when he came very late, and by that signal Odette would at

least learn that he knew, that he had seen the light and
had heard the voices, and he himself, who a moment
ago had been picturing her as laughing with the other
at his illusions, now it was he who saw them, confident
in their error, tricked by none other than himself, whom
they believed to be far away but who was there, in
person, there with a plan, there with the knowledge
that he was going, in another minute, to knock on the
shutter. And perhaps the almost pleasurable sensation
he felt at that moment was something more than the
assuagement of a doubt, and of a pain: was an intellectual pleasure. If, since he had fallen in love, things
had recovered a little of the delightful interest that they
had had for him long ago—though only in so far as
they were illuminated by the thought or the memory
of Odette—now it was another of the faculties of his
studious youth that his jealousy revived, the passion
for truth, but for a truth which, too, was interposed
between himself and his mistress, receiving its light
from her alone, a private and personal truth the sole
object of which (an infinitely precious object, and one
almost disinterested in its beauty) was Odette's life, her
actions, her environment, her plans, her past. At every
other period in his life, the little everyday activities of
another person had always seemed meaningless to Swann;
if gossip about such things was repeated to him, he
would dismiss it as insignificant, and while he listened
it was only the lowest, the most commonplace part of
his mind that was engaged; these were the moments
when he felt at his most inglorious. But in this strange
phase of love the personality of another person becomes
so enlarged, so deepened, that the curiosity which he
now felt stirring inside him with regard to the smallest
details of a woman's daily life, was the same thirst for
knowledge with which he had once studied history.

And all manner of actions from which hitherto he would have recoiled in shame, such as spying, to-night, outside a window, to-morrow perhaps, for all he knew, putting adroitly provocative questions to casual witnesses, bribing servants, listening at doors, seemed to him now to be precisely on a level with the deciphering of manuscripts, the weighing of evidence, the interpretation of old monuments—so many different methods of scientific investigation with a genuine intellectual value and legitimately employable in the search for truth.

On the point of knocking on the shutters, he felt a pang of shame at the thought that Odette would now know that he had suspected her, that he had returned, that he had posted himself outside her window. She had often told him what a horror she had of jealous men, of lovers who spied. What he was about to do was singularly inept, and she would detest him for ever after, whereas now, for the moment, for so long as he refrained from knocking, even in the act of infidelity, perhaps she loved him still. How often the prospect of future happiness is thus sacrificed to one's impatient insistence upon an immediate gratification! But his desire to know the truth was stronger, and seemed to him nobler. He knew that the reality of certain circumstances which he would have given his life to be able to reconstruct accurately and in full, was to be read behind that window, streaked with bars of light, as within the illuminated, golden boards of one of those precious manuscripts by whose artistic wealth itself the scholar who consults them cannot remain unmoved. He felt a voluptuous pleasure in learning the truth which he passionately sought in that unique, ephemeral and precious transcript, on that translucent page, so warm, so beautiful. And moreover, the advantage which he felt—which he so desperately wanted to feel—that he had over them lay perhaps not so much in knowing as in being able to show them that he knew. He raised himself on tiptoe. He knocked. They had not heard; he knocked again, louder, and the conversation ceased. A man's voice—he strained his ears to distinguish whose, among such of Odette's friends as he knew, it might be—asked:

"Who's there?"

He could not be certain of the voice. He knocked once again. The window first, then the shutters were thrown open. It was too late, now, to draw back, and since she was about to know all, in order not to seem too miserable, too jealous and inquisitive, he called out in a cheerful, casual tone of voice:

"Please don't bother; I just happened to be passing, and saw the light. I wanted to know if you were feeling better."

He looked up. Two old gentleman stood facing him at the window, one of them with a lamp in his hand; and beyond them he could see into the room, a room that he had never seen before. Having fallen into the habit, when he came late to Odette, of identifying her window by the fact that it was the only one still lit up in a row of windows otherwise all alike, he had been misled this time by the light, and had knocked at the window beyond hers, which belonged to the adjoining house. He made what apology he could and hurried home, glad that the satisfaction of his curiosity had preserved their love intact, and that, having feigned for so long a sort of indifference towards Odette, he had not now, by his jealousy, given her the proof that he loved her too much, which, between a pair of lovers, forever dispenses the recipient from the obligation to love enough.

He never spoke to her of this misadventure, and ceased even to think of it himself. But now and then his thoughts in their wandering course would come upon this memory where it lay unobserved, would startle it into life, thrust it forward into his consciousness, and leave him aching with a sharp, deep-rooted pain. As though it were a bodily pain, Swann's mind was powerless to alleviate it; but at least, in the case of bodily pain, since it is independent of the mind, the mind can dwell upon it, can note that it has diminished, that it has momentarily ceased. But in this case the mind, merely by recalling the pain, created it afresh. To determine not to think of it was to think of it still, to suffer from it still. And when, in conversation with his friends, he forgot about it, suddenly a word casually uttered would make him change countenance like a wounded man when a clumsy hand has touched his aching limb. When he came away from Odette he was happy, he felt calm, he recalled her smiles, of gentle mockery when speaking of this or that other person, of tenderness for himself; he recalled the gravity of her head which she seemed to have lifted from its axis to let it droop and fall, as though in spite of herself, upon his lips, as she had done on the first evening in the carriage, the languishing looks she had given him as she lay in his arms, nestling her head against her shoulder as though shrinking from the cold.

But then at once his jealousy, as though it were the shadow of his love, presented him with the complement, with the converse of that new smile with which she had greeted him that very evening—and which now, perversely, mocked Swann and shone with love for another—of that droop of the head, now sinking on to other lips, of all the marks of affection (now given to another) that she had shown to him. And all the voluptuous memories which he bore away from her house were, so to speak, but so many sketches, rough plans like those which a decorator submits to one, enabling Swann to form an idea of the various attitudes, aflame or faint with passion, which she might adopt for others. With the result that he came to regret every pleasure that he tasted in her company, every new caress of which he had been so imprudent as to point out to her the delights, every fresh charm that he found in her, for he knew that, a moment later, they would go to enrich the collection of instruments in his secret torture-chamber.

A fresh turn was given to the screw when Swann recalled a sudden expression which he had intercepted, a few days earlier, and for the first time, in Odette's eyes. It was after dinner at the Verdurins'. Whether it was because Forcheville, aware that Saniette, his brother-in-law, was not in favour with them, had decided to make a butt of him and to shine at his expense, or because he had been annoyed by some awkward remark which Saniette had made to him, although it had passed unnoticed by the rest of the party who knew nothing of whatever offensive allusion it might quite unintentionally have concealed, or possibly because he had been for some time looking for an opportunity of securing the expulsion from the house of a fellow-guest who knew rather too much about him, and whom he knew to be so sensitive that he himself could not help feeling embarrassed at times merely by his presence in the room, Forcheville replied to Saniette's tactless utterance with such a volley of abuse, going out of his way to insult him, emboldened, the louder he shouted, by the fear, the pain, the entreaties of his victim, that the poor creature, after asking Mme Verdurin whether he should stay and receiving no answer, had left the house in stammering confusion, and with tears in his eyes. Odette had watched this scene impassively, but when the door had closed behind Saniette, she had forced the normal expression of her face down, so to speak, by several pegs, in order to bring herself on to the same level of baseness as Forcheville, her eyes had sparkled with a malicious smile of congratulation upon his audacity, of ironical pity for the poor wretch who had been its victim, she had darted at him a look of complicity in the crime which so clearly implied: "That's finished him off, or I'm very much mistaken. Did you see how pathetic he looked? He was actually crying," that Forcheville, when his eyes met hers, sobered instantaneously from the anger, or simulated anger, with which he was still flushed, smiled as he explained: "He need only have made himself pleasant and he'd have been here still; a good dressing-down does a man no harm, at any age."

One day when Swann had gone out early in the afternoon to pay a call, and had failed to find the person he wished to see, it occurred to him to go to see Odette instead, at an hour when, although he never called on her then as a rule, he knew that she was always at home resting or writing letters until tea-time, and would enjoy seeing her for a moment without disturbing her. The porter told him that he believed Odette to be in; Swann rang the bell, thought he heard the sound of footsteps, but no one came to the door. Anxious and irritated, he went round to the other little street at the back of her house and stood beneath her bedroom window: the curtains were drawn and he could see nothing; he knocked loudly upon the pane, and called out; no one opened. He could see that the neighbours were staring at him. He turned away, thinking that after all he had perhaps been mistaken in believing that he heard footsteps; but he remained so preoccupied with the suspicion that he could not think of anything else. After waiting for an hour, he returned. He found her at home; she told him that she had been in the house when he rang, but had been asleep; the bell had awakened her, she had guessed that it must be Swann, and had run to meet him, but he had already gone. She had, of course, heard him knocking at the window. Swann could at once detect in this story one of those fragments of literal truth which liars, when caught off guard, console themselves by introducing into the composition of the falsehood which they have to invent, thinking that it can be safely incorporated and will lend the whole story an air of verisimilitude. It was true that when Odette had just done something she did not wish to disclose, she would take pains to bury it deep down inside herself. But as soon as she found herself face to face with the man to whom she was obliged to lie, she became uneasy, all her ideas melted like wax before a flame, her inventive and her reasoning faculties were paralysed, she might ransack her brain but could find only a void; yet she must say something, and there lay within her reach precisely the fact which she had wished to conceal and which, being the truth, was the one thing that had remained. She broke off from it a tiny fragment, of no importance in itself, assuring herself that, after all, it was the best thing to do, since it was a verifiable detail and less dangerous, therefore, than a fictitious one. "At any rate, that's true," she said to herself, "which is something to the good. He may make inquiries, and he'll see that it's true, so at least it won't be that that gives me away." But she was wrong; it *was* what gave her away; she had failed to realise that this fragmentary detail of the truth had sharp edges which could not be made to fit in, except with those contiguous fragments of the truth from which she had arbitrarily detached it, edges which, whatever the fictitious details in which she might embed it, would continue to show, by their overlapping angles and by the gaps she had forgotten to fill in, that its proper place was elsewhere.

"She admits that she heard me ring and then knock, that she knew it was me, and that she wanted to see me," Swann thought to himself. "But that doesn't fit in with the fact that she didn't let me in."

He did not, however, draw her attention to this inconsistency, for he thought that if left to herself Odette might perhaps produce some falsehood which would give him a faint indication of the truth. She went on speaking, and he did not interrupt her, but gathered up, with an eager and sorrowful piety, the words that fell from her lips, feeling (and rightly feeling, since she was hiding the truth behind them as she spoke) that, like the sacred veil, they retained a vague imprint, traced a faint outline, of that infinitely precious and, alas, undiscoverable reality—what she had been doing that afternoon at three o'clock when he had called—of which he would never possess any more than these falsifications, illegible and divine traces, and which would exist henceforward only in the secretive memory of this woman who could contemplate it in utter ignorance of its value but would never yield it up to him. Of course it occurred to him from time to time that Odette's daily activities were not in themselves passionately interesting, and that such relations as she might have with other men did not exhale naturally, universally and for every rational being a spirit of morbid gloom capable of infecting with fever or of inciting to suicide. He realised at such moments that that interest, that gloom, existed in him alone, like a disease, and that once he was cured of this disease, the actions of Odette, the kisses that she might have bestowed, would become once again as innocuous as those of countless other women. But the consciousness that the painful curiosity which he now brought to them had its origin only in himself was not enough to make Swann decide that it was unreasonable to regard that curiosity as important and to take every possible step to satisfy it. The fact was that Swann had reached an age whose philosophy—encouraged, in his case, by the current philosophy of the day, as well as by that of the circle in which he had spent much of his life, the group that surrounded the Princesse des Laumes, where it was agreed that intelligence was in direct ratio to the degree of scepticism and nothing was considered real and incontestable except the individual tastes of each person—is no longer that of youth, but a positive, almost a medical philosophy, the philosophy of men who, instead of exteriorising the objects of their aspirations, endeavour to extract from the accumulation of the years already spent a fixed residue of habits and passions which they can regard as characteristic and permanent, and with which they will deliberately arrange, before anything else, that the kind of existence they choose to adopt shall not prove inharmonious. Swann deemed it wise to make allowance in his life for the suffering which he derived from not knowing what Odette had done, just as he made allowance for the impetus which a damp climate always gave to his eczema; to anticipate in his budget the expenditure of a considerable sum on procuring, with regard to the daily occupations of Odette, information the lack of which would make him unhappy, just as he reserved a margin for the gratification of other tastes from which he knew that pleasure was to be expected (at least, before he had fallen in love), such as his taste for collecting or for good cooking.

When he proposed to take leave of Odette and return home, she begged him to stay a little longer and even detained him forcibly, seizing him by the arm as he was opening the door to go. But he paid no heed to this, for among the multiplicity of gestures, remarks, little incidents that go to make up a conversation, it is inevitable that we should pass (without noticing anything that attracts our attention) close by those that hide a truth for which our suspicions are blindly searching, whereas we stop to examine others beneath which nothing lies concealed. She kept on saying: "What a dreadful pity—you never come in the afternoon, and the one time you do come I miss you." He knew very well that she was not sufficiently in love with him to be so keenly distressed merely at having missed his visit, but since she was good-natured, anxious to make him happy, and often grieved when she had offended him, he found it quite natural that she should be sorry on this occasion for having deprived him of the pleasure of spending an hour in her company, which was so very great, if not for her, at any rate for him. All the same, it was a matter of so little importance that her air of unrelieved sorrow began at length to astonish him. She reminded him, even more than usual, of the faces of some of the women created by the painter of the "Primavera." She had at this moment their downcast, heartbroken expression, which seems ready to succumb beneath the burden of a grief too heavy to be borne when they are merely allowing the Infant Jesus to play with a pomegranate or watching Moses pour water into a trough. He had seen the same sorrow once before on her face, but when, he could no longer say. Then, suddenly, he remembered: it was when Odette had lied in apologising to Mme Verdurin on the evening after the dinner from which she had stayed away on a pretext of illness, but really so that she might be alone with Swann. Surely, even had she been the most scrupulous of women, she could hardly have felt remorse for so innocent a lie. But the lies which Odette ordinarily told were less innocent, and served to prevent discoveries which might have involved her in the most terrible difficulties with one or another of her friends. And so when she lied, smitten with fear, feeling herself to be but feebly armed for her defence, unconfident of success, she felt like weeping from sheer exhaustion, as children weep sometimes when they have not slept. Moreover she knew that her lie was usually wounding to the man to whom she was telling it, and that she might find herself at his mercy if she told it badly. Therefore she felt at once humble and guilty in his presence. And when she had to tell an insignificant social lie its hazardous associations, and the memories which it recalled, would leave her weak with a sense of exhaustion and penitent with a consciousness of wrongdoing.

What depressing lie was she now concocting for Swann's benefit, to give her that doleful expression, that plaintive voice, which seemed to falter beneath the effort she was forcing herself to make, and to plead for mercy? He had an idea that it was not merely the truth about what had occurred that afternoon that she was endeavouring to hide from him, but something more immediate, something, possibly, that had not yet happened, that was imminent, and that would throw light upon that earlier event. At that moment, he heard the front-door bell ring. Odette went on talking, but her words dwindled into an inarticulate moan. Her regret at not having seen Swann that afternoon, at not having opened the door to him, had become a veritable cry of despair.

He could hear the front door being closed, and the sound of a carriage, as though someone were going away—probably the person whom Swann must on no account meet—after being told that Odette was not at home. And then, when he reflected that merely by coming at an hour when he was not in the habit of coming he had managed to disturb so many arrangements of which she did not wish him to know, he was overcome with a feeling of despondency that amounted almost to anguish. But since he was in love with Odette, since he was in the habit of turning all his thoughts towards her, the pity with which he might have been inspired for himself he felt for her instead, and he murmured: "Poor darling!" When finally he left her, she took up several letters which were lying on the table, and asked him to post them for her. He took them away with him, and having reached home realised that they were still in his pocket. He walked back to the post-office, took the letters out of his pocket, and, before dropping each of them into the box, scanned its address. They were all to tradesmen, except one which was to Forcheville. He kept it in his hand. "If I saw what was in this," he argued, "I should know what she calls him, how she talks to him, whether there really is anything between them. Perhaps indeed by not looking inside I'm behaving shoddily towards Odette, since it's the only way I can rid myself of a suspicion which is perhaps slanderous to her, which must in any case cause her suffering, and which can never possibly be set at rest once the letter is posted."

He left the post-office and went home, but he had kept this last letter with him. He lit a candle and held up close to its flame the envelope which he had not dared open. At first he could distinguish nothing, but the envelope was thin, and by pressing it down on to

131

the stiff card which it enclosed he was able, through the transparent paper, to read the concluding words. They consisted of a stiffly formal ending. If, instead of its being he who was looking at a letter addressed to Forcheville, it had been Forcheville who had read a letter addressed to Swann, he would have found words in it of an altogether more affectionate kind! He took a firm hold of the card which was sliding to and fro, the envelope being too large for it, and then, by moving it with his finger and thumb, brought one line after another beneath the part of the envelope where the paper was not doubled, through which alone it was possible to read.

In spite of these manoeuvres he could not make it out clearly. Not that it mattered, for he had seen enough to assure himself that the letter was about some trifling incident which had no connection with amorous relations; it was something to do with an uncle of Odette's. Swann had read quite plainly at the beginning of the line: "I was right," but did not understand what Odette had been right in doing, until suddenly a word which he had not been able at first to decipher came to light and made the whole sentence intelligible: "I was right to open the door; it was my uncle." To open the door! So Forcheville had been there when Swann rang the bell, and she had sent him away, hence the sound that he had heard.

After that he read the whole letter. At the end she apologised for having treated Forcheville with so little ceremony, and reminded him that he had left his cigarette-case at her house, precisely what she had written to Swann after one of his first visits. But to Swann she had added: "If only you had forgotten your heart! I should never have let you have that back." To Forcheville nothing of that sort: no allusion that might suggest any intrigue between them. And, really, he was obliged to admit that in all this Forcheville had been worse treated than himself, since Odette was writing to him to assure him that the visitor had been her uncle. From which it followed that he, Swann, was the man to whom she attached importance and for whose sake she had sent the other away. And yet, if there was nothing between Odette and Forcheville, why not have opened the door at once, why have said, "I was right to open the door; it was my uncle." If she was doing nothing wrong at that moment, how could Forcheville possibly have accounted for her not opening the door? For some time Swann stood there, disconsolate, bewildered and yet happy, gazing at this envelope which Odette had handed to him without a qualm, so absolute was her trust in his honour, but through the transparent screen of which had been disclosed to him, together with the secret history of an incident which he had despaired of ever being able to learn, a fragment of Odette's life, like a luminous section cut out of the unknown. Then his jealousy rejoiced at the discovery, as though that jealousy had an independent existence, fiercely ego-tistical, gluttonous of everything that would feed its vitality, even at the expense of Swann himself. Now it had something to feed on, and Swann could begin to worry every day about the visits Odette received about five o'clock, could seek to discover where Forcheville had been at that hour. For Swann's affection for Odette still preserved the form which had been imposed on it from the beginning by his ignorance of how she spent her days and by the mental lethargy which prevented him from supplementing that ignorance by imagina-tion. He was not jealous, at first, of the whole of Odette's life, but of those moments only in which an incident, which he had perhaps misinterpreted, had led him to suppose that Odette might have played him false. His jealousy, like an octopus which throws out a first, then a second, and finally a third tentacle, fastened itself firmly to that particular moment, five o'clock in the afternoon, then to another, then to another again. But Swann was incapable of inventing his sufferings. They were only the memory, the perpetuation of a suffering that had come to him from without.

From without, however, everything brought him fresh suffering. He decided to separate Odette from Forcheville by taking her away for a few days to the south. But he imagined that she was coveted by every male person in the hotel, and that she coveted them in return. And so he who in former days, on journeys, used always to seek out new people and crowded places, might now be seen morosely shunning human society as if it had cruelly injured him. And how could he not have turned misanthrope, when in every man he saw a potential lover for Odette? And thus his jealousy did even more than the happy, sensual feeling he had originally experienced for Odette had done to alter Swann's character, completely changing, in the eyes of the world, even the outward signs by which that character had been intelligible.

A month after the evening on which he had intercepted and read Odette's letter to Forcheville, Swann went to a dinner which the Verdurins were giving in the Bois. As the party was breaking up he noticed a series of confabulations between Mme Verdurin and several of her guests, and thought he heard the pianist being reminded to come next day to a party at Chatou, to which he, Swann, had not been invited.

The Verdurins had spoken only in whispers, and in vague terms, but the painter, perhaps without thinking, exclaimed aloud: "There must be no lights of any sort, and he must play the Moonlight Sonata in the dark."

Mme Verdurin, seeing that Swann was within earshot, assumed an expression in which the two-fold desire to silence the speaker and to preserve an air of innocence in the eyes of the listener is neutralised into an intense vacuity wherein the motionless sign of intelligent complicity is concealed beneath an ingenuous smile, an expression which, common to everyone who has noticed a gaffe, instantaneously reveals it, if not to its perpetrator, at any rate to its victim. Odette seemed suddenly to be in despair, as though she had given up the struggle against the crushing difficulties of life, and Swann anxiously counted the minutes that still separated him from the point at which, after leaving the restaurant, while he drove her home, he would be able to ask her for an explanation, make her promise either that she would not go to Chatou next day or that she would procure an invitation for him also, and to lull to rest in her arms the anguish that tormented him. At last the carriages were ordered. Mme Verdurin said to Swann: "Good-bye, then. We shall see you soon, I hope," trying, by the friendliness of her manner and the constraint of her smile, to prevent him from noticing that she was not saying, as she would always have said hitherto: "To-morrow, then, at Chatou, and at my house the day after."

M. and Mme Verdurin invited Forcheville into their carriage. Swann's was drawn up behind it, and he waited for theirs to start before helping Odette into his.

"Odette, we'll take you," said Mme Verdurin, "we've kept a little corner for you, beside M. de Forcheville."

"Yes, Mme Verdurin," said Odette meekly.

"What! I thought I was to take you home," cried Swann, flinging discretion to the wind, for the carriage-door hung open, the seconds were running out, and he could not, in his present state, go home without her.

"But Mme Verdurin has asked me . . ."

"Come, you can quite well go home alone; we've left her with you quite often enough," said Mme Verdurin.

"But I had something important to say to Mme de Crécy."

"Very well, you can write it to her instead."

"Good-bye," said Odette, holding out her hand.

He tried hard to smile, but looked utterly dejected.

"Did you see the airs Swann is pleased to put on with us?" Mme Verdurin asked her husband when they had reached home. "I was afraid he was going to eat me, simply because we offered to take Odette back. It's positively indecent! Why doesn't he say straight out that we keep a bawdy-house? I can't conceive how Odette can stand such manners. He literally seems to be saying, 'You belong to me!' I shall tell Odette exactly what I think about it all, and I hope she'll have the sense to understand me."

A moment later she added, inarticulate with rage: "No, but, don't you agree, the filthy creature . . ." unwittingly using, perhaps in obedience to the same obscure need to justify herself—like Françoise at Combray, when the chicken refused to die—the very words which the last convulsions of an inoffensive animal in its death throes wring from the peasant who is engaged in taking its life.

And when Mme Verdurin's carriage had moved on and Swann's took its place, his coachman, catching sight of his face, asked whether he was unwell, or had heard some bad news.

Swann dismissed him; he wanted to walk, and returned home on foot through the Bois, talking to himself, aloud, in the same slightly artificial tone he used to adopt when enumerating the charms of the "little nucleus" and extolling the magnanimity of the Verdurins. But just as the conversation, the smiles, the kisses of Odette became as odious to him as he had once found them pleasing, if they were addressed to others, so the Verdurin's salon, which, not an hour before, had still seemed to him amusing, inspired with a genuine feeling for art and even with a sort of moral nobility, exhibited to him all its absurdities, its foolishness, its ignominy, now that it was another than himself whom Odette was going to meet there, to love there without restraint.

He pictured to himself with disgust the party next evening at Chatou. "Imagine going to Chatou, of all places! Like a lot of drapers after shutting up shop! Upon my word, these people are really sublime in their bourgeois mediocrity, they can't be real, they must all have come out of a Labiche comedy!"

The Cottards would be there; possibly Brichot. "Could anything be more grotesque than the lives of these nonentities, hanging on to one another like that. They'd imagine they were utterly lost, upon my soul they would, if they didn't all meet again to-morrow at *Chatou*!" Alas! there would also be the painter, the painter who enjoyed match-making, who would invite Forcheville to come with Odette to his studio. He could see Odette in a dress far too smart for a country outing, "because she's so vulgar, and, poor little thing, such an absolute fool!"

He could hear the jokes that Mme Verdurin would make after dinner, jokes which, whoever the "bore" might be at whom they were aimed, had always amused him because he could watch Odette laughing at them, laughing with him, her laughter almost a part of his. Now he felt that it was possibly at him that they would make Odette laugh. "What fetid humour!" he exclaimed, twisting his mouth into an expression of disgust so violent that he could feel the muscles of his throat stiffen against his collar. "How in God's name can a creature made in his image find anything to laugh at in those nauseating witticisms? The least sensitive nose must turn away in horror from such stale exhalations. It's really impossible to believe that a human being can fail to understand that, in allowing herself to smile at the expense of a fellow-creature who has loyally held out his hand to her, she is sinking into a mire from which it will be impossible, with the best will in the world, ever to rescue her. I inhabit a plane so infinitely far above the sewers in which these filthy vermin sprawl and crawl and bawl their cheap obscenities, that I cannot possibly be spattered by the witticisms of a Verdurin!" he shouted, tossing up his head and proudly throwing back his shoulders. "God knows I've honestly tried to pull Odette out of that quagmire, and to teach her to breathe a nobler and a purer air. But human patience has its limits, and mine is at an end," he concluded, as though this sacred mission to tear Odette away from an atmosphere of sarcasms dated from longer than a few minutes ago, as though he had not undertaken it only since it had occurred to him that those sarcasms might perhaps be directed at himself, and might have the effect of detaching Odette from him.

He could see the pianist sitting down to play the Moonlight Sonata, and the grimaces of Mme Verdurin in terrified anticipation of the wrecking of her nerves by Beethoven's music. "Idiot, liar!" he shouted, "and a creature like that imagines that she loves *Art*!" She would say to Odette, after deftly insinuating a few words of praise for Forcheville, as she had so often done for him: "You can make room for M. de Forcheville, there, can't you, Odette?"..."'In the dark!' (he remembered the painter's words), filthy old procuress!" "Procuress" was the name he applied also to the music which would invite them to sit in silence, to dream together, to gaze into each other's eyes, to feel for each other's hands. He felt that there was much to be said, after all, for a sternly censorious attitude towards the arts, such as Plato adopted, and Bossuet, and the old school of education in France.

In a word, the life they led at the Verdurins', which he had so often described as "the true life", seemed to him now the worst of all, and their "little nucleus" the lowest of the low. "It really is," he said, "beneath the lowest rung of the social ladder, the nethermost circle of Dante. No doubt about it, the august words of the Florentine refer to the Verdurins! When you come to think of it, surely people 'in society' (with whom one may find fault now and then but who are after all a very different matter from that riffraff) show a profound sagacity in refusing to know them, or even to soil the tips of their fingers with them. What a sound intuition there is in that 'Noli me tangere' of the Faubourg Saint-Germain."

He had long since emerged from the paths and avenues of the Bois, had almost reached his own house, and still, having not yet shaken off the intoxication of his misery and pain and the inspired insincerity which the counterfeit tones and artificial sonority of his own voice raised to ever more exhilarating heights, he continued to perorate aloud in the silence of the night: "Society people have their failings, as no one knows better than I; but there are certain things they simply wouldn't stoop to. So-and-so" (a fashionable woman whom he had known) "was far from being perfect, but she did after all have a fundamental decency, a sense of honour in her dealings which would have made her incapable, whatever happened, of any sort of treachery and which puts a vast gulf between her and an old hag like Verdurin. Verdurin! What a name! Oh, it must be said that they're perfect specimens of their disgusting kind! Thank God, it was high time that I stopped condescending to promiscuous intercourse with such infamy, such dung."

But, just as the virtues which he had still attributed to the Verdurins an hour or so earlier would not have sufficed, even if the Verdurins had actually possessed them, if they had not also encouraged and protected his love, to excite Swann to that state of intoxication in which he waxed tender over their magnanimity—an intoxication which, even when disseminated through the medium of other persons, could have come to him from Odette alone—so the immorality (had it really existed) which he now found in the Verdurins would have been powerless, if they had not invited Odette with Forcheville and without him, to unstop the vials of his wrath and to make him scarify their "infamy." And doubtless Swann's voice was more perspicacious than Swann himself when it refused to utter those words full of disgust with the Verdurins and their circle, and of joy at having shaken himself free of it, save in an artificial and rhetorical tone and as though they had been chosen rather to appease his anger than to express his thoughts. The latter, in fact, while he abandoned himself to his invective, were probably, though he did not realise it, occupied with a wholly different matter, for having reached home, no sooner had he closed the front-door behind him than he suddenly struck his forehead, and reopening it, dashed out again exclaiming, in a voice which, this time, was quite natural: "I think

I've found a way of getting invited to the dinner at Chatou to-morrow!" But it must have been a bad way, for Swann was not invited. Dr Cottard, who, having been summoned to attend a serious case in the country, had not seen the Verdurins for some days and had been prevented from appearing at Chatou, said on the evening after this dinner, as he sat down to table at their house: "But aren't we going to see M. Swann this evening? He's quite what you might call a personal friend of . . ."

"I sincerely trust we shan't!" cried Mme Verdurin. "Heaven preserve us from him; he's too deadly for words, a stupid, ill-bred boor."

On hearing these words Cottard exhibited an intense astonishment blended with entire submission, as though in the face of a scientific truth which contradicted everything that he had previously believed but was supported by an irresistible weight of evidence; and bowing his head over his plate with timorous emotion, he simply replied: "Oh—oh—oh—oh—oh!" traversing, in an orderly withdrawal of his forces into the depths of his being, along a descending scale, the whole compass of his voice. After which there was no more talk of Swann at the Verdurins'.

And so that drawing-room which had brought Swann and Odette together became an obstacle in the way of their meeting. She no longer said to him, as in the early days of their love: "We shall meet, anyhow, to-morrow evening; there's a supper-party at the Verdurins," but "We shan't be able to meet to-morrow evening; there's a supper-party at the Verdurins." Or else the Verdurins were taking her to the Opéra-Comique, to see *Une Nuit de Cléopâtre*, and Swann could read in her eyes that terror lest he should ask her not to go, which not long since he could not have refrained from greeting with a kiss as it flitted across the face of his mistress, but which now exasperated him. "Yet it's not really anger," he assured himself, "that I feel when I see how she longs to run away and scratch around in that dunghill of cacophony. It's disappointment, not of course for myself but for her; I'm disappointed to find that, after living for more than six months in daily contact with me, she hasn't changed enough to be able spontaneously to reject Victor Massé—above all, that she hasn't yet reached the stage of understanding that there are evenings when anyone with the least delicacy of feeling should be willing to forgo a pleasure when asked to do so. She ought to have the sense to say 'I won't go,' if only from policy, since it is by her answer that the quality of her heart will be judged once and for all." And having persuaded himself that it was solely, after all, in order that he might arrive at a favourable estimate of Odette's spiritual worth that he wished her to stay at home with him that evening instead of going to the Opéra-Comique, he adopted the same line of reasoning with her, with the same degree of insincerity as he had used with himself, or even a degree more, for in her case he was yielding also to the desire to capture her through her own self-esteem.

"I swear to you," he told her, shortly before she was to leave for the theater, "that, in asking you not to go, I should hope, were I a selfish man, for nothing so much as that you should refuse, for I have a thousand other things to do this evening and I shall feel trapped myself, and rather annoyed, if, after all, you tell me you're not going. But my occupations, my pleasures are not everything; I must think of you too. A day may come when, seeing me irrevocably sundered from you, you will be entitled to reproach me for not having warned you at the decisive hour in which I felt that I was about to pass judgment on you, one of those stern judgments which love cannot long resist. You see, your *Nuit de Cléopâtre* (what a title!) has no bearing on the point. What I must know is whether you are indeed one of those creatures in the lowest grade of mentality and even of charm, one of those contemptible creatures who are incapable of forgoing a pleasure. And if you are such, how could anyone love you, for you are not even a person, a clearly defined entity, imperfect but at least perfectible. You are a formless water that will trickle down any slope that offers itself, a fish devoid of memory, incapable of thought, which all its life long in its aquarium will continue to dash itself a hundred times a day against the glass wall, always mistaking it for water. Do you realise that your answer will have the effect—I won't say of making me cease loving you immediately, of course, but of making you less attractive in my eyes when I realise that you are not a person, that you are beneath everything in the world and incapable of raising yourself one inch higher. Obviously, I should have preferred to ask you as a matter of little or no importance to give up your *Nuit de Cléopâtre* (since you compel me to sully my lips with so abject a name) in the hope that you would go to it none the less. But, having decided to make such an issue of it, to draw such drastic consequences from your reply, I considered it more honourable to give you due warning."

Meanwhile, Odette had shown signs of increasing emotion and uncertainty. Although the meaning of this speech was beyond her, she grasped that it was to be included in the category of "harangues" and scenes of reproach or supplication, which her familiarity with the ways of men enabled her, without paying any heed to the words that were uttered, to conclude that they would not make unless they were in love, and that since they were in love, it was unnecessary to obey them, as they would only be more in love later on. And so she would have heard Swann out with the utmost tranquillity had she not noticed that it was growing late, and that if he went on talking much longer she would "never", as she told him with a fond smile, obstinate if slightly abashed, "get there in time for the Overture."

On other occasions he told her that the one thing that would make him cease to love her more than anything else would be her refusal to abandon the habit of lying. "Even from the point of view of coquetry, pure and simple," he said to her, "can't you see how much of your attraction you throw away when you stoop to lying? Think how many faults you might redeem by a frank admission! You really are far less intelligent than I supposed!" In vain, however, did Swann expound to her thus all the reasons that she had for not lying; they might have succeeded in overthrowing a general system of mendacity, but Odette had no such system; she was simply content, whenever she wished Swann to remain in ignorance of anything she had done, not to tell him of it. So that lying was for her an expedient of a specific order, and the only thing that could make her decide whether she should avail herself of it or confess the truth was a reason that was also of a specific or contingent order, namely the chance of Swann's discovering that she had not told him the truth.

Physically, she was going through a bad phase; she was putting on weight, and the expressive, sorrowful charm, the surprised, wistful expression of old seemed to have vanished with her first youth. So that she had become most precious to Swann as it were just at the moment when he found her distinctly less good-looking. He would gaze at her searchingly, trying to recapture the charm which he had once seen in her, and no longer finding it. And yet the knowledge that within this new chrysalis it was still Odette who lurked, still the same fleeting, sly, elusive will, was enough to keep Swann seeking as passionately as ever to capture her. Then he would look at photographs of her taken two years before, and would remember how exquisite she had been. And that would console him a little for all the agony he suffered on her account.

When the Verdurins took her off to SaintGermain, or to Chatou, or to Meulan, as often as not, if the weather was fine, they would decide to stay the night and return next day. Mme Verdurin would endeavour to set at rest the scruples of the pianist, whose aunt had remained in Paris: "She'll be only too glad to be rid of you for a day. Why on earth should she be anxious, when she knows you're with us? Anyhow, I'll take full responsibility."

If this attempt failed, M. Verdurin would set off across country to find a telegraph office or a messenger, after first finding out which of the "faithful" had someone they must notify. But Odette would thank him and assure him that she had no message for anyone, for she had told Swann once and for all that she could not possibly send messages to him, in front of all those people, without compromising herself. Sometimes she would be absent for several days on end, when the Verdurins took her to see the tombs at Dreux, or to Compiègne, on the painter's advice, to watch the sunsets in the forest—after which they went on to the Château of Pierrefonds.

"To think that she could visit really historic buildings with me, who have spent ten years in the study of architecture, who am constantly bombarded by people who really count to take them to Beauvais or Saint-

Loup-de-Naud, and refuse to take anyone but her; and instead of that she trundles off with the most abject brutes to go into ecstasies over the petrified excretions of Louis-Philippe and Viollet-le-Duc! One hardly needs much knowledge of art, I should say, to do that; surely, even without a particularly refined sense of smell, one doesn't deliberately choose to spend a holiday in the latrines so as to be within range of their fragrant exhalations."

But when she had set off for Dreux or Pierrefonds—alas, without allowing him to turn up there, as though by chance, for that, she said, "would create a deplorable impression"—he would plunge into the most intoxicating romance in the lover's library, the railway timetable, from which he learned the ways of joining her there in the afternoon, in the evening, even that very morning. The ways? More than that, the authority, the right to join her. For after all, the time-table, and the trains themselves, were not meant for dogs. If the public was informed, by means of the printed word, that at eight o'clock in the morning a train left for Pierrefonds which arrived there at ten, that could only be because going to Pierrefonds was a lawful act, for which permission from Odette would be superfluous; an act, moreover, which might be performed from a motive altogether different from the desire to see Odette, since persons who had never even heard of her performed it daily, and in such numbers as justified the labour and expense of stoking the engines.

All things considered, she could not really prevent him from going to Pierrefonds if he felt inclined to do so. And as it happened, he did feel so inclined, and had he not known Odette, would certainly have gone. For a long time past he had wanted to form a more definite impression of Viollet-le-Duc's work as a restorer. And the weather being what it was, he felt an overwhelming desire to go for a walk in the forest of Compiègne.

It really was bad luck that she had forbidden him access to the one spot that tempted him to-day. To-day! Why, if he went there in defiance of her prohibition, he would be able to see her that very day! But whereas, if she had met at Pierrefonds someone who did not matter to her, she would have hailed him with obvious pleasure: "What, you here?" and would have invited him to come and see her at the hotel where she was staying with the Verdurins, if on the other hand it was himself, Swann, that she ran into, she would be offended, would complain that she was being followed, would love him less in consequence, might even turn away in anger when she caught sight of him. "So, I'm not allowed to travel any more!" she would say to him on her return, whereas in fact it was he who was not allowed to travel!

At one moment he had had the idea, in order to be able to visit Compiègne and Pierrefonds without letting it be supposed that his object was to meet Odette, of securing an invitation from one of his friends, the Marquis de Forestelle, who had a country house in that neighbourhood. The latter, whom he apprised of his plan without disclosing its ulterior purpose, was beside himself with joy and astonishment at Swann's consenting at last, after fifteen years, to come down and visit his property, and since he did not (he had told him) wish to stay there, promising at least to spend some days going for walks and excursions with him. Swann imagined himself already down there with M. de Forestelle. Even before he saw Odette, even if he did not succeed in seeing her there, what a joy it would be to set foot on that soil, where not knowing the exact spot in which, at any moment, she was to be found, he would feel all around him the thrilling possibility of her sudden apparition: in the courtyard of the Château, now beautiful in his eyes since it was on her account that he had gone to visit it; in all the streets of the town, which struck him as romantic; down every ride of the forest, roseate with the deep and tender glow of sunset;—innumerable and alternative sanctuaries, in which, in the uncertain ubiquity of his hopes, his happy, vagabond and divided heart would simultaneously take refuge. "We mustn't on any account," he would warn M. de Forestelle, "run across Odette and the Verdurins. I've just heard that they're at Pierrefonds, of all places, to-day. One has plenty of time to see them in Paris; it would hardly be worth while coming down here if one couldn't go a yard without meeting them." And his host would fail to understand why, once they were there, Swann would change his plans twenty times in an hour, inspect the dining-rooms of all the hotels in Compiègne without being able to make up his mind to settle down in any of them, although they had seen no trace anywhere of the Verdurins, seeming to be in search of what he claimed to be most anxious to avoid, and would in fact avoid the moment he found it, for if he had come upon the little "group" he would have hastened away at once with studied indifference, satisfied that he had seen Odette and she him, especially that she had seen him not bothering his head about her. But no; she would guess at once that it was for her sake that he was there. And when M. de Forestelle came to fetch him, and it was time to start, he excused himself: "No, I'm afraid I can't go to Pierrefonds to-day. You see, Odette is there." And Swann was happy in spite of everything to feel that if he, alone among mortals, had not the right to go to Pierrefonds that day, it was because he was in fact, for Odette, someone different from all other mortals, her lover, and because that restriction imposed for him alone on the universal right to freedom of movement was but one of the many forms of the slavery, the love that was so dear to him. Decidedly, it was better not to risk a quarrel with her, to be patient, to wait for her return. He spent his days poring over a map of the forest of Compiègne as though it had been that of the "Pays du Tendre,"[6] and surrounded himself with photographs of the Château of Pierrefonds. When the day dawned on which it was possible that she might return, he opened the timetable again, calculated what train she must have taken, and, should she have postponed her departure, what trains were still left for her to take. He did not leave the house for fear of missing a telegram, did not go to bed in case, having come by the last train, she decided to surprise him with a midnight visit. Yes! The frontdoor bell rang. There seemed some delay in opening the door, he wanted to awaken the porter, he leaned out of the window to shout to Odette if it was she, for in spite of the orders which he had gone downstairs a dozen times to deliver in person, they were quite capable of telling her that he was not at home. It was only a servant coming in. He noticed the incessant rumble of passing carriages, to which he had never paid any attention before. He could hear them, one after another, a long way off, coming nearer, passing his door without stopping, and bearing away into the distance a message which was not for him. He waited all night, to no purpose, for the Verdurins had decided to return early, and Odette had been in Paris since midday. It had not occurred to her to tell him, and not knowing what to do with herself she had spent the evening alone at a theatre, had long since gone home to bed, and was peacefully asleep.

As a matter of fact, she had not even given him a thought. And such moments as these, in which she forgot Swann's very existence, were more useful to Odette, did more to bind him to her, than all her coquetry. For in this way Swann was kept in that state of painful agitation which had already been powerful enough to cause his love to blossom, on the night when he had failed to find Odette at the Verdurins' and had hunted for her all evening. And he did not have (as I had at Combray in my childhood) happy days in which to forget the sufferings that would return with the night. For his days were spent without Odette; and there were times when he told himself that to allow so pretty a woman to go out by herself in Paris was just as rash as to leave a case filled with jewels in the middle of the street. Then he would rail against all the passersby, as though they were so many pickpockets. But their faces—a collective and formless mass—escaped the grasp of his imagination, and failed to feed the flame of his jealousy. The effort exhausted Swann's brain, until, putting his hand over his eyes, he cried out: "Heaven help me!" as people, after lashing themselves into an intellectual frenzy in their endeavours to master the problem of the reality of the external world or the immortality of the soul, afford relief to their weary brains by an unreasoning act of faith. But the thought of his absent mistress was incessantly, indissolubly blended with all the simplest actions of Swann's daily life—when he took his meals, opened his letters, went for a walk or to bed—by the very sadness he felt at having to perform those actions without her; like those initials of Philibert the Fair which, in the church of

Brou, because of her grief and longing for him, Margaret of Austria intertwined everywhere with her own. On some days, instead of staying at home, he would go for luncheon to a restaurant not far off to which he had once been attracted by the excellence of its cookery, but to which he now went only for one of those reasons, at once mystical and absurd, which people call "romantic"; because this restaurant (which, by the way, still exists) bore the same name as the street in which Odette lived: La Pérouse.

Sometimes, when she had been away on a short visit somewhere, several days would elapse before she thought of letting him know that she had returned to Paris. And then she would say quite simply, without taking (as she would once have taken) the precaution of covering herself, just in case, with a little fragment borrowed from the truth, that she had at that very moment arrived by the morning train. These words were mendacious; at least for Odette they were mendacious, insubstantial, lacking (what they would have had if true) a basis of support in her memory of her actual arrival at the station; she was even prevented from forming a mental picture of them as she uttered them, by the contradictory picture of whatever quite different thing she had been doing at the moment when she pretended to have been alighting from the train. In Swann's mind, however, these words, meeting no opposition, settled and hardened until they assumed the indestructibility of a truth so indubitable that, if some friend happened to tell him that he had come by the same train and had not seen Odette, Swann was convinced that it was the friend who had mistaken the day or the hour, since his version did not agree with the words uttered by Odette. These words would have appeared to him false only if he had suspected beforehand that they were going to be. For him to believe that she was lying, an anticipatory suspicion was indispensable. It was also, however, sufficient. Given that, everything Odette said appeared to him suspect. If she mentioned a name, it was obviously that of one of her lovers, and once this supposition had taken shape, he would spend weeks tormenting himself. On one occasion he even approached a firm of "inquiry agents" to find out the address and the occupation of the unknown rival who would give him no peace until he could be proved to have gone abroad, and who (he ultimately learned) was an uncle of Odette who had been dead for twenty years.

Although she would not allow him as a rule to meet her in public, saying that people would talk, it happened occasionally that, at an evening party to which he and she had both been invited—at Forcheville's, at the painter's, or at a charity ball given in one of the Ministries—he found himself in the same room with her. He could see her, but dared not stay for fear of annoying her by seeming to be spying upon the pleasures she enjoyed in other company, pleasures which— as he drove home in utter loneliness, and went to bed as miserable as I was to be some years later on the evenings when he came to dine with us at Combray— seemed to him limitless since he had not seen the end of them. And once or twice he experienced on such evenings the sort of happiness which one would be inclined (did it not originate in so violent a reaction from an anxiety abruptly terminated) to call peaceful, since it consists in a pacifying of the mind. On one occasion he had looked in for a moment at a party in the painter's studio, and was preparing to go home, leaving behind him Odette transformed into a brilliant stranger, surrounded by men to whom her glances and her gaiety, which were not for him, seemed to hint at

some voluptuous pleasures to be enjoyed there or elsewhere (possibly at the Bal des Incohérents, to which he
trembled to think that she might be going on afterwards) which caused Swann more jealousy than the
carnal act itself, since he found it more difficult to
imagine; he was already at the door when he heard
himself called back in these words (which, by cutting
off from the party that possible ending which had so
appalled him, made it seem innocent in retrospect,
made Odette's return home a thing no longer incon-
ceivable and terrible, but tender and familiar, a thing
that would stay beside him, like a part of his daily life,
in his carriage, and stripped Odette herself of the excess
of brilliance and gaiety in her appearance, showed that
it was only a disguise which she had assumed for a
moment, for its own sake and not with a view to any
mysterious pleasures, and of which she had already
wearied)——in these words which Odette tossed at him
as he was crossing the threshold: "Can't you wait a
minute for me? I'm just going; we'll drive back together
and you can take me home."

It was true that on one occasion Forcheville had asked
to be driven home at the same time, but when, on
reaching Odette's door, he had begged to be allowed
to come in too, she had replied, pointing to Swann:
"Ah! That depends on this gentleman. You must ask
him. Very well, you may come in just for a minute, if
you insist, but you mustn't stay long, because I warn
you, he likes to sit and talk quietly with me, and he's
not at all pleased if I have visitors when he's here. Oh,
if you only knew the creature as I know him! Isn't that
so, my love, no one really knows you well except me?"

And Swann was perhaps even more touched by the
spectacle of her addressing to him thus, in front of
Forcheville, not only these tender words of predilection,

but also certain criticisms, such as: "I feel sure you haven't written yet to your friends about dining with them on Sunday. You needn't go if you don't want to, but you might at least be polite," or, "Now, have you left your essay on Vermeer here so that you can do a little more of it to-morrow? What a lazy-bones! I'm going to make you work, I can tell you," which proved that Odette kept herself in touch with his social engagements and his literary work, that they had indeed a life in common. And as she spoke she gave him a smile that told him she was entirely his.

At such moments as these, while she was making them some orangeade, suddenly, just as when an ill-adjusted reflector begins by casting huge, fantastic shadows on an object on the wall which then contract and merge into it, all the terrible and shifting ideas which he had formed about Odette melted away and vanished into the charming creature who stood there before his eyes. He had the sudden suspicion that this hour spent in Odette's house, in the lamp-light, was perhaps, after all, not an artificial hour, invented for his special use (with the object of concealing that frightening and delicious thing which was incessantly in his thoughts without his ever being able to form a satisfactory impression of it, an hour of Odette's real life, of her life when he was not there), with theatrical properties and pasteboard fruits, but was perhaps a genuine hour of Odette's life; that if he himself had not been there she would have pulled forward the same armchair for Forcheville, would have poured out for him, not some unknown brew, but precisely this same orangeade; that the world inhabited by Odette was not that other fearful and supernatural world in which he spent his time placing her—and which existed, perhaps, only in his imagination—but the real world, exhaling no special atmosphere of gloom, comprising that table at which he might sit down presently and write, this drink which he was now being permitted to taste, all these objects which he contemplated with as much curiosity and admiration as gratitude—for if, in absorbing his dreams, they had delivered him from them, they themselves in return had been enriched by them, they showed him the palpable realisation of his fancies, and they impressed themselves upon his mind, took shape and grew solid before his eyes, at the same time as they soothed his troubled heart. Ah, if fate had allowed him to share a single dwelling with Odette, so that in her house he should be in his own, if, when asking the servant what there was for lunch, it had been Odette's menu that he had been given in reply, if, when Odette wished to go for a morning walk in the Avenue du Bois de Boulogne, his duty as a good husband had obliged him, though he had no desire to go out, to accompany her, carrying her overcoat when she was too warm, and in the evening, after dinner, if she wished to stay at home in deshabille, if he had been forced to stay beside her, to do what she asked; then how completely would all the trivial details of Swann's life which seemed to him now so melancholy have taken on, for the very reason that they would at the same time have formed part of Odette's life—like this lamp, this orangeade, this armchair, which had absorbed so much of his dreams, which materialised so much of his longing—a sort of superabundant sweetness and a mysterious density!

And yet he was inclined to suspect that the state for which he so longed was a calm, a peace, which would not have been a propitious atmosphere for his love. When Odette ceased to be for him a creature always absent, regretted, imagined, when the feeling that he had for her was no longer the same mysterious turmoil that was wrought in him by the phrase from the sonata, but affection and gratitude, when normal relations that would put an end to his melancholy madness were established between them—then, no doubt, the actions of Odette's daily life would appear to him as being of little intrinsic interest—as he had several times already felt that they might be, on the day, for instance, when he had read through its envelope her letter to Forcheville. Examining his complaint with as much scientific detachment as if he had inoculated himself with it in order to study its effects, he told himself that, when he was cured of it, what Odette might or might not do would be a matter of indifference to him. But the truth was that in the depths of his morbid condition he feared death itself no more than such a recovery, which would in fact amount to the death of all that he now was.

After these quiet evenings, Swann's suspicions would be temporarily lulled; he would bless the name of Odette, and next day, in the morning would order the finest jewels to be sent to her, because her kindnesses to him overnight had excited either his gratitude, or the desire to see them repeated, or a paroxysm of love for her which had need of some such outlet.

But at other times, his anguish would again take hold of him; he would imagine that Odette was Forcheville's mistress, and that when they had both sat watching him from the depths of the Verdurins' landau in the Bois on the evening before the party at Chatou to which he had not been invited, while he implored her in vain, with that look of despair on his face which even his coachman had noticed, to come home with him, and then turned away, solitary and crushed, she must have glanced at Forcheville, as she drew his attention to him, saying "Look how furious he is!" with the same expression, sparkling, malicious, sidelong and sly, as on the evening when Forcheville had driven Saniette from the Verdurins'.

At such times Swann detested her. "But I've been a fool, too," he would argue. "I'm paying for other men's pleasures with my money. All the same, she'd better take care, and not push her luck, because I might very well stop giving her anything at all. At any rate, we'd better knock off supplementary favours for the time being. To think that only yesterday, when she said she would like to go to Bayreuth for the season, I was such an ass as to offer to take one of those nice little castles the King of Bavaria has in the neighbourhood for the two of us. However she didn't seem particularly keen; she hasn't said yes or no yet. Let's hope she'll refuse. Good God! Think of listening to Wagner for a whole fortnight with a woman who takes about as much interest in music as a tone-deaf newt—that would be fun!" And his hatred, like his love, needing to manifest itself in action, he took pleasure in urging his evil imaginings further and further, because, thanks to the perfidies of which he accused Odette, he detested her still more, and would be able, if it turned out—as he tried to convince himself—that she was indeed guilty of them, to take the opportunity of punishing her, emptying upon her the overflowing vials of his wrath. Thus he went so far as to suppose that he was about to receive a letter from her in which she would ask him for money to take the castle near Bayreuth, but with the warning that he was not to come there himself, as she had promised to invite Forcheville and the Verdurins. How he would have loved it if she had had the audacity to do this! How he would have enjoyed refusing, drawing up the vindictive reply, the terms of which he amused himself by selecting and declaiming aloud, as though he had actually received such a letter!

The very next day, he did. She wrote that the Verdurins and their friends had expressed a desire to attend these performances of Wagner, and that, if he would be so good as to send her the money, she would at last have the pleasure, after going so often to their house, of entertaining the Verdurins in hers. Of him she said not a word; it was to be taken for granted that their presence would be a bar to his.

Then he had the pleasure of sending round to her that annihilating answer, every word of which he had carefully rehearsed overnight without venturing to hope that it could ever be used. Alas! he felt only too certain that with the money she had, or could easily procure, she would be able all the same to take a house at Bayreuth, since she wished to do so, she who was incapable of distinguishing between Bach and Clapisson. Let her take it, then: at least she would have to live in it more frugally. No chance (as there would have been if he had replied by sending her several thousand-franc notes) of organising each evening in some castle those exquisite little suppers after which she might perhaps indulge the whim (which, it was possible, had never yet seized her) of falling into the arms of Forcheville. At any rate it would not be he, Swann, who paid for this loathsome expedition! Ah! if he could only manage to prevent it, if she could sprain her ankle before setting out, if the driver of the carriage which was to take her to the station would consent (at no matter what price) to smuggle her to some place where she could be kept for a time in seclusion—that perfidious woman, her eyes glittering with a smile of complicity for Forcheville, that Odette had become for Swann in the last forty-eight hours!

But she was never that for very long. After a few

days the shining, crafty eyes lost their brightness and their duplicity, the picture of a hateful Odette saying to Forcheville "Look how furious he is!" began to fade and dissolve. Then gradually the face of the other Odette would reappear and rise before him, softly radiant—that Odette who also turned with a smile to Forcheville, but with a smile in which there was nothing but tenderness for Swann, when she said: "You mustn't stay long, because this gentleman doesn't much like my having visitors when he's here. Oh! if you only knew the creature as I know him!"—that same smile with which she used to thank Swann for some instance of his courtesy which she prized so highly, for some advice for which she had asked him in one of those moments of crisis when she would turn to him alone.

And thinking of this other Odette, he would ask himself what could have induced him to write that outrageous letter, of which, probably, until then she would never have supposed him capable, a letter which must have brought him down from the high, from the supreme place which by his generosity, by his loyalty, he had won for himself in her esteem. He would become less dear to her, since it was for those qualities, which she found neither in Forcheville nor in any other, that she loved him. It was for them that Odette so often showed him a reciprocal warmth which counted for less than nothing in his moments of jealousy, because it was not a sign of reciprocal desire, was indeed a proof rather of affection than of love, but the importance of which he began once more to feel in proportion as the spontaneous relaxation of his suspicions, often accelerated by the distraction brought to him by reading about art or by the conversation of a friend, rendered his passion less exacting of reciprocities.

Now that, after this swing of the pendulum, Odette

had naturally returned to the place from which Swann's jealousy had momentarily driven her, to the angle from which he found her charming, he pictured her to himself as full of tenderness, with a look of consent in her eyes, and so beautiful that he could not refrain from proffering her his lips as though she had actually been in the room for him to kiss; and he felt as strong a sense of gratitude towards her for that bewitching, kindly glance as if it had been real, as if it had not been merely his imagination that had portrayed it in order to satisfy his desire.

What distress he must have caused her! Certainly he could find valid reasons for his resentment, but they would not have been sufficient to make him feel that resentment if he had not loved her so passionately. Had he not nourished equally serious grievances against other women, to whom he would none the less willingly render a service to-day, feeling no anger towards them because he no longer loved them? If the day ever came when he found himself in the same state of indifference with regard to Odette, he would then understand that it was his jealousy alone which had led him to find something heinous, unpardonable, in this desire of hers (which was after all so natural, springing from a child-like ingenuousness and also from a certain delicacy in her nature) to be able in her turn, since the opportunity had arisen, to repay the Verdurins for their hospitality, and to play the hostess in a house of her own.

He returned to this other point of view, which was the opposite of the one based on his love and jealousy and to which he resorted at times by a sort of intellectual equity and in order to make allowance for the various probabilities, and tried to judge Odette as though he had not been in love with her, as though she were like any other woman, as though her life (as soon as he was no longer present) had not been different, woven secretly behind his back, hatched against him.

Why should he think that she would enjoy out there with Forcheville or with other men intoxicating pleasures which she had never experienced with him, and which his jealousy alone had fabricated out of nothing? At Bayreuth, as in Paris, if it should happen that Forcheville thought of him at all, it would only be as of someone who counted for a great deal in Odette's life, someone for whom he was obligated to make way when they met at her house. If Forcheville and she gloated at the idea of being there together in spite of him, it was he who would have engineered it by striving in vain to prevent her from going, whereas if he had approved of her plan, which for that matter was quite defensible, she would have had the appearance of being there on his advice, she would have felt that she had been sent there, housed there by him, would have been beholden to him for the pleasure which she derived from entertaining those people who had so often entertained her.

And if—instead of letting her go off on bad terms with him, without having seen him again—he were to send her this money, if he were to encourage her to undertake this journey and go out of his way to make it agreeable for her, she would come running to him, happy and grateful, and he would have the joy of seeing her which he had not known for nearly a week and which nothing else could replace. For once Swann could picture her to himself without revulsion, could see once again the friendliness in her smile, once the desire to tear her away from every rival was no longer imposed by his jealousy upon his love, that love became once again, more than anything, a taste for the sensations which Odette's person gave him, for the pleasure he took in admiring as a spectacle, or in examining as a phenomenon, the dawn of one of her glances, the formation of one of her smiles, the emission of a particular vocal cadence. And this pleasure, different from every other, had in the end created in him a need of her, which she alone by her presence or by her letters could assuage, almost as disinterested, almost as artistic, as perverse, as another need which characterised this new period in Swann's life, when the sereness, the depression of the preceding years had been followed by a sort of spiritual overflowing, without his knowing to what he owed this unlooked-for enrichment of his inner life, any more than a person in delicate health who from a certain moment grows stronger, puts on flesh, and seems for a time to be on the road to a complete recovery. This other need, which developed independently of the visible, material world, was the need to listen to music and improve his knowledge of it.

And so, through the chemical action of his malady, after he had created jealousy out of his love, he began again to manufacture tenderness and pity for Odette. She had become once more the old Odette, charming and kind. He was full of remorse for having treated her harshly. He wished her to come to him, and, before she came, he wished to have already procured for her some pleasure, so as to watch her gratitude taking shape in her face and moulding her smile.

And consequently Odette, certain of seeing him come to her after a few days, as tender and submissive as before, to plead with her for a reconciliation, became inured, was no longer afraid of displeasing him or even of making him angry, and refused him, whenever it suited her, the favours by which he set most store.

Perhaps she did not realize how sincere he had been with her during their quarrel, when he had told her that he would not send her any money and would do everything he could to hurt her. Perhaps she did not realise, either, how sincere he was, if not with her, at any rate with himself, on other occasions when, for the sake of the future of their relationship, to show Odette that he was capable of doing without her, that a rupture was still possible between them, he decided to wait some time before going to see her again.

Sometimes it would be after several days during which she had caused him no fresh anxiety; and since he knew that he was likely to derive no very great pleasure from his impending visits, but more probably some annoyance which would put an end to his present state of calm, he would write to her saying that he was very busy, and would not be able to see her on any of the days that he had suggested. Meanwhile, a letter from her, crossing his, asked him to postpone one of those very meetings. He wondered why; his suspicions, his anguish, again took hold of him. He could no longer abide, in the new state of agitation into which he found himself plunged, by the arrangements which he had made in his preceding state of comparative calm; he would hurry round to her, and would insist upon seeing her on each of the following days. And even if she had not written first, if she merely acknowledged his letter, agreeing to his request for a brief separation, it was enough to make him unable to rest without seeing her. For, contrary to his calculations, Odette's acquiescence had entirely changed his attitude. Like everyone who possesses something precious, in order to know what would happen if he ceased for a moment to possess it, he had detached the precious object from his mind, leaving, as he thought, everything else in the same state as when it was there. But the absence of one part from a whole is not only that, it is not simply a partial lack, it is a derangement of all the other parts, a new state which it was impossible to foresee in the old.

But at other times—when Odette was on the point of going away for a holiday—it was after some trifling quarrel for which he had chosen the pretext that he resolved not to write to her and not to see her until her return, thus giving the appearance (and expecting the reward) of a serious rupture, which she would perhaps regard as final, to a separation the greater part of which was the inevitable consequence of her proposed journey, which he was merely allowing to start a little sooner than it must. At once he could imagine Odette puzzled, anxious, distressed at having received neither visit nor letter from him, and this picture of her, by calming his jealousy, made it easy for him to break himself of the habit of seeing her. At moments, no doubt, in the furthest recesses of his mind where his determination had thrust it away thanks to the long interval of the three weeks' separation which he had accepted, it was with pleasure that he considered the idea that he would see Odette again on her return; but it was also with so little impatience that he began to wonder whether he would not readily consent to the doubling of the period of so easy an abstinence. It had lasted, so far, but three days, a much shorter time than he had often spent without seeing Odette, and without having, as on this occasion, premeditated it. And yet, suddenly, some minor vexation or physical ailment—by inciting him to regard the present moment as an exceptional one, outside the rules, one in which common wisdom would allow him to take advantage of the soothing effects of a pleasure and, until there was some purpose in a re-sumption of effort, to give his will a rest—suspended the operation of the latter, which ceased to exert its inhibitive control; or, without that even, the thought of something he had forgotten to ask Odette, such as whether she had decided in what colour she would have her carriage repainted, or, with regard to some investment, whether they were "ordinary" or "preference" shares that she wished him to buy (for it was all very well to show her that he could live without seeing her, but if, after that, the carriage had to be painted over again, or if the shares produced no dividend, a lot of good it would have done him),—and suddenly, like a stretched piece of elastic which is let go, or the air in a pneumatic machine which is ripped open, the idea of seeing her again sprang back from the distant depths in which it lay dormant into the field of the present and of immediate possibilities.

It sprang back thus without meeting any further resistance, so irresistible, in fact, that Swann had found it far less painful to watch the fortnight he was to spend separated from Odette creeping by day after day than to wait the ten minutes it took his coachman to bring round the carriage which was to take him to her, minutes which he spent in transports of impatience and joy, in which he recaptured a thousand times over, to lavish on it all the wealth of his affection, that idea of meeting her again which, by so abrupt a reversal, at a moment when he supposed it so remote, was once more present and on the very surface of his consciousness. The fact was that his idea no longer found as an obstacle in its course the desire to resist it without further delay, a desire which had ceased to have any place in Swann's mind since, having proved to himself—or so at least he believed—that he was so easily capable of resisting it, he no longer saw any danger in postponing a plan of separation which he was now certain of being able to put into operation whenever he wished. Furthermore, this idea of seeing her again came back to him adorned with a novelty, a seductiveness, armed with a virulence, which long habit had dulled but which had been re-tempered during this privation, not of three days but of a fortnight (for a period of abstinence may be cal-culated, by anticipation, as having lasted already until the final date assigned to it), and had converted what had been until then a pleasure in store which could easily be sacrificed into an unlooked-for happiness which he was powerless to resist. Finally, the idea returned to him embellished by his ignorance of what Odette might have thought, might perhaps have done, on find-ing that he had given no sign of life, with the result that what he was going now to find was the entrancing revelation of an almost unknown Odette.

But she, just as she had supposed that his refusal to send her money was only a sham, saw nothing but a pretext in the questions he was now coming to ask her, about the repainting of her carriage or the purchase of shares. For she could not reconstruct the several phases of these crises through which he was passing, and the notion she had formed of them omitted any attempt to understand their mechanism, but looked only to what she knew beforehand, their necessary, never-failing and always identical termination. An incomplete notion (though possibly all the more profound in consequence), if one were to judge it from the point of view of Swann, who would doubtless have considered himself misun-derstood by Odette, just as a drug-addict or a con-sumptive, each persuaded that he has been held back, one by some outside event at the moment when he was about to shake himself free of his inveterate habit, the other by an accidental indisposition at the moment when he was about to be finally cured, feels himself to be misunderstood by the doctor who does not attach the same importance to these alleged contingencies, mere disguises, according to him, assumed, so as to make themselves felt once more, by the vice of the one and the morbid state of the other, which in reality have never ceased to weigh heavily and incurably upon the patients while they were nursing their dreams of reformation or health. And, as a matter of fact, Swann's love had reached the stage at which the boldest of physicians or (in the case of certain affections) of surgeons ask themselves whether to deprive a patient of his vice or to rid him of his malady is still reasonable or indeed possible.

Certainly, of the extent of this love Swann had no direct awareness. When he sought to measure it, it happened sometimes that he found it diminished, shrunk almost to nothing; for instance, the lack of enthusiasm, amounting almost to distaste, which, in the days before he was in love with Odette, he had felt for her expressive features, her faded complexion, returned on certain days. "Really, I'm making distinct headway," he would tell himself next day. "Looking at things quite honestly, I can't say I got much pleasure last night from being in bed with her. It's an odd thing, but I actually thought her ugly." And certainly he was sincere, but his love extended a long way beyond the province of physical desire. Odette's person, indeed, no longer held any great place in it. When his eyes fell upon the photograph of Odette on his table, or when she came to see him, he had difficulty in identifying her face, either in the flesh or on the pasteboard, with the painful and continuous anxiety which dwelt in his mind. He would say to himself, almost with astonishment, "It's she!" as though suddenly we were to be shown in a detached, externalised form one of our own maladies, and we found it bore no resemblance to what we were suffering. "She"——he tried to ask himself what that meant; for it is a point of resemblance between love and death, far more striking than those which are usually pointed out, that they make us probe deeper, in the fear that its reality may elude us, into the mystery of personality. And this malady which Swann's love had become had so proliferated, was so closely interwoven with all his habits, with all his actions, with his thoughts, his health, his sleep, his life, even with what he hoped for after his death, was so utterly inseparable from him, that it would have been impossible to eradicate it without almost entirely destroying him; as surgeons say, his love was no longer operable.

By this love Swann had been so far detached from all other interests that when by chance he reappeared in society, reminding himself that his social relations, like a beautifully wrought setting (although she would not have been able to form any very exact estimate of its worth), might restore something of his own prestige in Odette's eyes (as indeed they might have done had they not been cheapened by his love itself, which for Odette depreciated everything that it touched by seeming to proclaim such things less precious), he would feel there, side by side with his distress at being in places and among people she did not know, the same detached pleasure as he would have derived from a novel or a painting in which were depicted the amusements of a leisured class; just as, at home, he used to enjoy the thought of the smooth efficiency of his household, the elegance of his wardrobe and of his servants' liveries, the soundness of his investments, with the same relish as when he read in Saint-Simon, who was one of his favourite authors, of the mechanics of daily life at Versailles, what Mme de Maintenon ate and drank, or the shrewd avarice and great pomp of Lulli. And to the small extent to which this detachment was not absolute, the reason for this new pleasure which Swann was tasting was that he could take refuge for a moment in those few and distant parts of himself which had remained more or less extraneous to his love and to his pain. In this respect the personality which my great-aunt attributed to him as "young Swann," as distinct from the more individual personality of Charles Swann, was the one in which he was now happiest. Once, wishing to send the Princesse de Parme some fruit for her birthday (and because she could often be of use indirectly to Odette, by letting her have seats for galas and jubilees and the like) and not being quite sure how to order it, he had entrusted the task to a cousin of his mother who, delighted to do an errand for him, had written to him, when sending him the account, to say that she had not ordered all the fruit from the same place, but the grapes from Crapote, whose speciality they were, the strawberries from Jauret, the pears from Chevet, who always had the best, and so on, "every fruit inspected and examined, one by one, by myself." And in the sequel, by the cordiality with which the Princess thanked him, he had been able to judge of the flavour of the strawberries and of the ripeness of the pears. But, most of all, that "every fruit inspected and examined, one by one, by myself" had brought balm to his sufferings by carrying his mind off to a region which he rarely visited, although it was his by right as the heir to a rich, upper-middle-class family in which had been handed down from generation to generation the knowledge of the "right places" and the art of placing an order.

Indeed, he had too long forgotten that he was "young Swann" not to feel, when he assumed the role again for a moment, a keener pleasure than those he might have felt at other times but which had palled; and if the friendliness of the bourgeoisie, for whom he had never been anything else than "young Swann," was less animated than that of the aristocracy (though more flattering, for all that, since with them it is always inseparable from respect), no letter from a royal personage, whatever princely entertainment is offered, could ever be so agreeable to Swann as a letter inviting him to be a witness, or merely to be present, at a wedding in the family of some old friends of his parents, some of whom had "kept up" with him—like my grandfather, who, the year before these events, had invited him to my mother's wedding—while others barely knew him by sight, but considered themselves in duty bound to show civility to the son, to the worthy successor, of the late M. Swann.

But, by virtue of his intimacy, already time-honoured, with so many of its members, the nobility was in a certain sense also a part of his house, his domestic establishment, and his family. He felt, when his mind dwelt upon his brilliant connections, the same external support, the same solid comfort as when he looked at the fine estates, the fine silver, the fine table-linen which had come to him from his own family. And the thought that, if he were struck down by a sudden illness and confined to the house, the people whom his valet would instinctively run to fetch would be the Duc de Chartres, the Prince de Reuss, the Duc de Luxembourg and the Baron de Charlus, brought him the same consolation as our old Françoise derived from the knowledge that she would one day be buried in her own fine sheets, marked with her name, not darned at all (or so exquisitely darned that it merely enhanced one's idea of the skill and patience of the seamstress), a shroud from the constant image of which in her mind's eye she drew a certain satisfactory sense, if not actually of wealth and prosperity, at any rate of self-esteem. But most of all,—since in every one of his actions and thoughts which had reference to Odette, Swann was constantly obsessed and influenced by the unavowed feeling that he was, perhaps not less dear, but less welcome to her than anyone, even the most tedious of the Verdurin "faithful,"—when he betook himself to a world in which he was the paragon of taste, a man whom no pains were spared to attract, whom people were genuinely sorry not to see, he began once again to believe in the existence of a happier life, almost to feel an appetite for it, as an invalid may feel who has been bedridden for months, on a strict diet, when he picks up a newspaper and reads the account of an official banquet or an advertisement for a cruise round Sicily.

If he was obliged to make excuses to his society friends for not visiting them, it was precisely for visiting her that he sought to excuse himself to Odette. Even so, he paid for his visits (asking himself at the end of the month, should he have overtaxed her patience and gone rather often to see her, whether it would be enough if he sent her four thousand francs), and for each one found a pretext, a present that he had to bring her, a piece of information which she required, M. de Charlus whom he had met actually going to her house and who had insisted on Swann's accompanying him. And, failing an excuse, he would ask M. de Charlus to go round to her house and say to her, as though spontaneously, in the course of conversation, that he had just remembered something he had to say to Swann, and would she please send a message to Swann asking him to come to her then and there; but as a rule Swann waited at home in vain, and M. de Charlus informed him later in the evening that his ruse had not proved successful. With the result that, if she was not frequently away from Paris, even when she was there he scarcely saw her, and she who, when she was in love with him, used to say "I'm always free" and "What do I care what other people think?" now, whenever he wanted to see her, appealed to the proprieties or pleaded some engagement. When he spoke of going to a charity entertainment, or a private view, or a first-night at which she was to be present, she would complain that he wished to advertise their liaison, that he was treating her like a whore. Things came to such a pitch that, in an effort to avoid being debarred from meeting her anywhere, Swann, remembering that she knew and was deeply attached to my great-uncle Adolphe, whose friend he himself had also been, went to see him in his little flat in the Rue de Bellechasse, to ask him to use his influence with Odette. Since she invariably adopted a poetical tone when she spoke to Swann about my uncle, saying: "Ah, yes, he's not in the least like you; it's such an exquisite thing, a great, a beautiful thing, his friendship for me. He's not the sort of man who would have so little consideration for me as to let himself be seen with me everywhere in public," this was embarrassing for Swann, who did not know quite to what rhetorical pitch he should screw himself up in speaking of Odette to my uncle. He began by alluding to her *a priori* excellence, her axiomatic and seraphic super-humanity, the inspiration of her transcendental, inexpressible virtues. "I should like to speak to you about her," he went on. "You know what an incomparably superior woman, what an adorable creature, what an angel Odette is. But you know, also, what life is in Paris. Not everyone knows Odette in the light in which you and I have been privileged to know her. And so there are people who think I'm behaving rather foolishly; she won't even allow me to meet her out of doors, at the theatre. Now you, in whom she has such enormous confidence, couldn't you say a few words for me to her, just to assure her that she exaggerates the harm which my greeting her in public might do her?"

My uncle advised Swann not to see Odette for some days, after which she would love him all the more, and advised Odette to let Swann meet her whenever and as often as he pleased. A few days later Odette told Swann that she had just had a rude awakening, on discovering that my uncle was the same as other men: he had tried to take her by force. She calmed Swann down when he wanted to rush out to challenge my uncle to a duel, but he refused to shake hands with him when they met again. He regretted this rupture all the more because he had hoped, if he had met my uncle Adolphe again a few times and had contrived to talk things over with him in strict confidence, to be able to get him to throw light on certain rumours with regard to the life that Odette had formerly led in Nice. For my uncle Adolphe used to spend the winter there, and Swann thought that it might indeed have been there that he had first known Odette. The few words which someone had let fall in his hearing about a man who, it appeared, had been Odette's lover, had left Swann dumbfounded. But the very things which, before knowing them, he would have regarded as the most terrible to learn and the most impossible to believe, were, once he knew them, absorbed forever into the general mass of his gloom; he accepted them, he could no longer have understood their not existing. Only, each one of them added a new and indelible touch to the picture he had formed of his mistress. At one point indeed he was given to understand that this moral laxity of which he would never have suspected Odette was fairly well known, and that at Baden or Nice, when she used to go to spend several months in one or the other place, she had enjoyed a sort of amorous notoriety. He thought of getting in touch with one or two pleasureseekers and interrogating them; but they were aware that he knew Odette, and besides, he was afraid of putting the thought of her into their heads, of setting them once more upon her track. But he, to whom nothing could have seemed more tedious hitherto than all that pertained to the cosmopolitan life of Baden or of Nice, having learned that Odette had perhaps once led a gay life in those pleasure-cities, although he could never find out whether it had been solely to satisfy a need for money which, thanks to him, she no longer felt, or from some capricious instinct which might at any moment revive in her, now leaned in impotent, blind, dizzy anguish over the bottomless abyss in which those early years of MacMahon's Presidency had been engulfed, years during which one spent the winter on the Promenade des Anglais, the summer beneath the limes of Baden, and he would find in them a painful but magnificent profundity, such as a poet might have lent them; indeed he would have devoted to the reconstruction of the petty details of social life on the Côte d'Azur in those days, if it could have helped him to understand something of Odette's smile and the look in her eyes—candid and simple though they were—as much passion as the aesthete who ransacks the extant documents of fifteenth-century Florence in order to penetrate further into the soul of the Primavera, the fair Vanna or the Venus of Botticelli.

Often he would sit, without saying a word, gazing at her dreamily, and she would say: "You do look sad!" It was not very long since he had switched from the idea that she was a really good person, comparable to the nicest he had known, to that of her being a kept woman; conversely, it had happened to him since to revert from the Odette de Crécy who was perhaps too well known to the roisterers, the ladies' men of Nice and Baden, to this face whose expression was often so gentle and sweet, to this nature so eminently human. He would ask himself: "What does it mean, after all, if everyone at Nice knows who Odette de Crécy is? Reputations of that sort, even when they're true, are always based upon other people's ideas"; he would reflect that this legend—even if it was authentic—was something extraneous to Odette, was not an innate, pernicious and ineradicable part of her personality; that the creature who might have been led astray was a woman with frank eyes, a heart full of pity for the sufferings of others, a docile body which he had clasped in his arms and explored with his hands, a woman whom he might one day come to possess absolutely, if he succeeded in making himself indispensable to her.

She would sit there, often tired, her face momentarily drained of that eager, febrile preoccupation with the unknown things that made Swann suffer; she would push back her hair with both hands, and her forehead, her whole face, would seem to grow larger; then, suddenly, some ordinary human thought, some kindly sentiment such as are to be found in all individuals when, in a moment of rest or reclusion, they are free to express their true selves, would flash from her eyes like a ray of gold. And immediately the whole of her face would light up like a grey landscape swathed in clouds which are suddenly swept aside, leaving it transfigured by the setting sun. The life which occupied Odette at such times, even the future which she seemed to be dreamily contemplating, Swann could have shared with her; no evil disturbance seemed to have left its residue there. Rare though they became, those moments did not occur in vain. By the process of memory, Swann joined the fragments together, abolished the intervals between them, cast, as in molten gold, the image of an Odette compact of kindness and tranquillity, for whom (as we shall see in the second part of this story) he was later to make sacrifices which the other Odette would never have won from him. But how rare those moments were, and how seldom he now saw her! Even in the case of their evening meetings, she would never tell him until the last minute whether she would be able to see him, for, counting on his being always free, she wished first to be certain that no-one else would propose coming round. She would plead that she was obliged to wait for an answer that was of the very greatest importance to her, and if, even after she had allowed Swann to come, any of her friends asked her, half-way through the evening, to join them at some theatre or at supper afterwards, she would jump for joy and dress with all speed. As her toilet progressed, every movement she made brought Swann nearer to the moment when he would have to part from her, when she would fly off with irresistible zest; and when at length she was ready, and, peering into her mirror for the last time with eyes tense and bright with anxiety to look well, added a touch of lipstick, fixed a stray lock of hair over her brow, and called for her cloak of sky-blue silk with golden tassels, Swann looked so wretched that she would be unable to restrain a gesture of impatience as she flung at him: "So that's how you thank me for keeping you here till the last minute! And I thought I was being so nice to you. Well, I shall know better another time!" Sometimes, at the risk of annoying her, he made up his mind that he would find out where she had gone, and even dreamed of an alliance with Forcheville, who might perhaps have been able to enlighten him. In any case, when he knew with whom she was spending the evening, he was usually able to discover, among all his innumerable acquaintance, someone who knew—if only indirectly—the man in question, and could easily obtain this or that piece of information about him. And while he was writing to one of his friends, asking him to try to clear up some point or other, he would feel a sense of relief on ceasing to vex himself with questions to which there was no answer and transferring to someone else the strain of interrogation. It is true that Swann was no better off for such information as he did receive. To know a thing does not always enable us to prevent it, but at least the things we know we do hold, if not in our hands, at any rate in our minds, where we can dispose of them as we choose, and this gives us the illusion of a sort of power over them. He was quite happy whenever M. de Charlus was with Odette. He knew that between M. de Charlus and her nothing untoward could ever happen, that when M. de Charlus went out with her, it was out of friendship for him, and that he would make no difficulty about telling him everything she had done. Sometimes she had declared so emphatically to Swann that it was impossible for her to see him on a particular evening, she seemed to be looking forward so keenly to some outing, that Swann felt it really important that M. de Charlus should be free to accompany her. Next day, without daring to put too many questions to M. de Charlus, he would force him, by appearing not quite to understand his first answers, to give him more, after each of which he would feel increasingly relieved, for he very soon learned that Odette had spent her evening in the most innocent of dissipations.

"But what do you mean, my dear Mémé, I don't quite understand. . . . You didn't go straight from her house to the Musée Grévin? Surely you went somewhere else first? No? How very funny! You've no idea how much you amuse me, my dear Mémé. But what an odd idea of hers to go on to the Chat Noir afterwards. it was her idea, I suppose? No? Yours? How strange. But after all, it wasn't such a bad idea; she must have known dozens of people there? No? She never spoke to a soul? How extraordinary! Then you sat there like that, just you and she, all by yourselves? I can just picture you. What a nice fellow you are, my dear Mémé. I'm exceedingly fond of you."

Swann was relieved. So often had it happened to him, when chatting with chance acquaintances to whom he was hardly listening, to hear certain detached sentences (as, for instance, "I saw Mme de Crécy yesterday with a man I didn't know"), sentences which dropped into his heart and turned at once into a solid state, grew hard as stalagmites, and seared and tore him as they lay there, irremovable, that the words "She didn't know a soul, she never spoke to a soul" were, by way of contrast, like a soothing balm. How freely they coursed through him, how fluid they were, how vaporous, how easy to breathe! And yet, a moment later, he was telling himself that Odette must find him very dull if those were the pleasures she preferred to his company. And their very insignificance, though it reassured him, pained him as if her enjoyment of them had been an act of treachery.

Even when he could not discover where she had gone, it would have sufficed him, to alleviate the anguish which he then felt, and against which Odette's presence, the joy of being with her, was the sole specific (a specific which in the long run served to aggravate the disease, but at least brought temporary relief to his sufferings), it would have sufficed him, if only Odette had allowed it, to remain in her house while she was out, to wait for her there until the hour of her return, into whose stillness and peace would have flowed and dissolved those intervening hours which some sorcery, some evil spell had made him imagine as somehow different from the rest. But she would not; he had to return home; he forced himself, on the way, to form various plans, ceased to think of Odette; he even succeeded, while he undressed, in turning over some quite happy ideas in his mind; and it was with a light heart, buoyed with the anticipation of going to see some favourite work of art the next day, that he got into bed and turned out the light; but no sooner, in preparing himself for sleep, did he relax the self-control of which he was not even conscious so habitual had it become, than an icy shudder convulsed him and he began to sob. He did not even wish to know why, but wiped his eyes and said to himself with a smile: "This is delightful; I'm getting neurotic." After which he felt a profound lassitude at the thought that, next day, he must begin afresh his attempts to find out what Odette had been doing, must use all his influence to contrive to see her. This compulsion to an activity without respite, without variety, without results, was so cruel a scourge that one day, noticing a swelling on his stomach, he felt genuinely happy at the thought that he had, perhaps, a tumour which would prove fatal, that he need no longer concern himself with anything, that illness was going to govern his life, to make a plaything of him, until the not-distant end. And indeed if, at this period, it often happened that, without admitting it to himself, he longed for death, it was in order to escape not so much from the acuity of his sufferings as from the monotony of his struggle.

And yet he would have liked to live until the time

came when he no longer loved her, when she would have no reason for lying to him, when at length he might learn from her whether, on the day when he had gone to see her in the afternoon, she had or had not been in bed with Forcheville. Often for several days on end the suspicion that she was in love with someone else would distract his mind from the question of Forcheville, making it almost immaterial to him, like those new developments in a continuous state of ill-health which seem momentarily to have delivered us from their predecessors. There were even days when he was not tormented by any suspicion. He fancied that he was cured. But next morning, when he awoke, he felt in the same place the same pain, the sensation of which, the day before, he had as it were diluted in the stream of different daytime impressions. But it had not stirred from its place. Indeed, it was the sharpness of this pain that had awakened him.

Since Odette never gave him any information as to those vastly important matters which took up so much of her time every day (although he had lived long enough to know that such matters are never anything else than pleasures), he could not sustain for any length of time the effort of imagining them; his brain would become a void; then he would draw a finger over his tired eyelids as he might have wiped his eye-glass, and would cease altogether to think. There emerged, however, from this terra incognita, certain landmarks which reappeared from time to time, vaguely connected by Odette with some obligation towards distant relatives or old friends who, inasmuch as they were the only people whom she was in the habit of mentioning as preventing her from seeing him, seemed to Swann to compose the necessary, unalterable setting of her life. Because of the tone in which she referred from time to time to "the day when

I go with my friend to the races," if, having suddenly felt unwell and thought, "Perhaps Odette would be kind enough to come and see me," he remembered that it was one of those very days, he would say to himself: "Oh, no! There's no point in asking her to come. I should have thought of it before, this is the day when she goes with her friend to the races. We must confine ourselves to what's possible; no use wasting time proposing things that are *ipso facto* unacceptable." And the duty incumbent upon Odette of going to the races, to which Swann thus gave way, seemed to him to be not merely ineluctable in itself, but the mark of necessity with which it was stamped seemed to make plausible and legitimate everything that was even remotely connected with it. If, having acknowledged a greeting from a passer-by in the street which had aroused Swann's jealousy, Odette replied to his questions by associating the stranger with one of the two or three paramount duties of which she had often spoken to him—if, for instance, she said: "That's a gentleman who was in my friend's box at the races the other day"—this explanation would set Swann's suspicions at rest; it was, after all, inevitable that this friend should have other guests than Odette in her box at the races, though he had never sought to form or succeeded in forming any coherent impression of them. Ah, how he would have loved to know her, the friend who went to the races! If only she would invite him there with Odette. How readily he would have sacrificed all his grand connections for no matter what person who was in the habit of seeing Odette, even if she were a manicurist or a shop assistant! He would have put himself out for her, taken more trouble than he would have done for a queen. Would they not have supplied him, from their store of knowledge of the life of Odette, with the one effective anodyne for his pain? With what joy would he have hastened to spend his days with one or other of those humble folk with whom Odette kept up friendly relations, either with some ulterior motive or from genuine simplicity of nature! How willingly would he have taken up residence for ever in the attic of some sordid but enviable house where Odette went but never took him and where, if he had lived with the little retired dressmaker, whose lover he would readily have pretended to be, he would have been visited by Odette almost daily! In those almost plebeian districts, what a modest existence, abject even, but happy, nourished by tranquillity and peace of mind, he would have consented to lead indefinitely!

It sometimes happened, again, that when, after meeting Swann, she saw some man approaching whom he did not know, he could distinguish upon Odette's face that look of dismay which she had worn on the day when he had come to her while Forcheville was there. But this was rare; for on the days when, in spite of all that she had to do, and of her dread of what people might think, she did actually manage to see Swann, what predominated in her attitude now was self-assurance; a striking contrast, perhaps an unconscious revenge for, or a natural reaction from, the timorous emotion which, in the early days of their friendship, she had felt in his presence, and even in his absence, when she began a letter to him with the words: "My dear, my hand trembles so that I can scarcely write" (so, at least, she pretended, and a little of that emotion must have been sincere, or she would not have wanted to feign more). She had been attracted to Swann then. We do not tremble except for ourselves, or for those whom we love. When our happiness is no longer in their hands, how calm, how relaxed, how bold we become in their presence! In speaking to him, in writing to him now, she no longer employed those words by which she had sought to give herself the illusion that he belonged to her, creating opportunities for saying "my" and "mine" when she referred to him—"You are my very own; it is the perfume of our friendship, I shall keep it"—for speaking to him of the future, of death itself, as of a single adventure which they would share. In those early days, whatever he might say to her she would answer admiringly: "You know, you'll never be like other people!"—she would gaze at that long face and slightly bald head, of which people who knew of his successes with women used to think: "He's not conventionally good-looking, if you like, but he has style: that toupee, that eyeglass, that smile!"—and, with more curiosity perhaps to know him as he really was than desire to become his mistress, she would sigh: "If only I knew what was in that head of yours!"

But now, whatever he said, she would answer in a tone that was sometimes irritable, sometimes indulgent: "Ah! won't you ever be like other people!" And gazing at that face which was only a little aged by his recent anxieties (though people now thought of it, by the same mental process which enables one to discover the meaning of a piece of symphonic music of which one has read the programme, or the resemblance of a child whose family one knows: "He's not positively ugly, if you like, but he's really rather absurd: that eyeglass, that toupee, that smile!"—adumbrating in their suggestible imaginations the invisible boundary which separates, at a few months' interval, the face of a successful lover from that of a cuckold), she would say: "Oh, I do wish I could change you, put some sense into that head of yours."

Always ready to believe in the truth of what he

hoped, if Odette's way of behaving to him left the slightest room for doubt, he would fling himself greedily upon her words: "You can if you like," he would say to her.

And he tried to explain to her that to comfort him, to guide him, to make him work, would be a noble task, to which numbers of other women asked for nothing better than to be allowed to devote themselves, though it is only fair to add that in those other women's hands the noble task would have seemed to Swann a tactless and intolerable usurpation of his freedom. "If she didn't love me just a little," he told himself, "she wouldn't want to change me. And to change me, she will have to see me more often." Thus he saw her very reproaches as proofs of her interest, perhaps of her love; and indeed she now gave him so few that he was obliged to regard as such the various prohibitions which she imposed on him from time to time. One day she announced that she did not care for his coachman, who, she thought, might be setting Swann against her, and anyhow did not show the promptness and deference to Swann's orders which she would have liked to see. She felt that he wanted to hear her say: "Don't take him again when you come to me," just as he might have wanted her to kiss him. So, being in a good mood, she said it: and he was touched. That evening, talking to M. de Charlus, with whom he had the consolation of being able to speak of her openly (for the most trivial remarks that he uttered now, even to people who had never heard of her, always somehow related to Odette), he said to him: "I believe, all the same, that she loves me. She's so nice to me, and she certainly takes an interest in what I do."

And if, when he was setting off for her house, climbing into his carriage with a friend whom he was to drop somewhere on the way, his friend said: "Hullo! that isn't Loredan on the box?" with what melancholy joy Swann would answer him:

"Oh! Good heavens, no! I can tell you, I daren't take Loredan when I go to the Rue La Pérouse. Odette doesn't like me to take Loredan, she doesn't think he treats me properly. What on earth is one to do? Women, you know, women. My dear fellow, she'd be furious. Oh, lord, yes; if I took Rémi there I should never hear the last of it!"

This new manner, indifferent, offhand, irritable, which Odette now adopted with Swann, undoubtedly made him suffer; but he did not realise how much he suffered; since it was only gradually, day by day, that Odette had cooled towards him, it was only by directly contrasting what she was to-day with what she had been at first that he could have measured the extent of the change that had taken place. But this change was his deep, secret wound, which tormented him day and night, and whenever he felt that his thoughts were straying too near it, he would quickly turn them into another channel for fear of suffering too much. He might say to himself in an abstract way: "There was a time when Odette loved me more," but he never formed any definite picture of that time. Just as he had in his study a chest of drawers which he contrived never to look at, which he made a detour to avoid whenever he went in or out of the room, because in one of its drawers he had locked away the chrysanthemum which she had given him on one of those first evenings when he had taken her home in his carriage, and the letters in which she said: "If only you had forgotten your heart also. I should never have let you have that back," and "At whatever hour of the day or night you may need me, just send me a word, and dispose of me as you please," so there was a place in his heart where he would never allow his thoughts to trespass, forcing them, if need be, into a long divagation so that they should not have to pass within reach of it; the place in which lingered his memory of happier days.

But his meticulous prudence was defeated one evening when he had gone out to a party.

It was at the Marquise de Saint-Euverte's, the last, for that season, of the evenings on which she invited people to listen to the musicians who would serve, later on, for her charity concerts. Swann, who had intended to go to each of the previous evenings in turn but never succeeded in making up his mind, received, while he was dressing for this one, a visit from the Baron de Charlus, who came with an offer to accompany him to the party, if this would help him to feel a little less bored and unhappy when he got there. Swann thanked him and said:

"You can't conceive how glad I should be of your company. But the greatest pleasure you can give me is to go instead to see Odette. You know what an excellent influence you have over her. I don't suppose she'll be going anywhere this evening before she goes to see her old dressmaker, and I'm sure she'd be delighted if you accompanied her there. In any case, you'll find her at home before then. Try to entertain her, and also to give her a little sound advice. If you could arrange something for to-morrow that would please her, something we could all three do together. . . . Try to put out a feeler, too, for the summer; see if there's anything she wants to do, a cruise that the three of us might take, or something. I don't expect to see her to-night myself; still, if she'd like me to come, or if you find a loophole, you've only to send me a word at Mme. de Saint-Euverte's up till midnight, and afterwards here. Thank you for all your kindness—you know how fond I am of you."

The Baron promised to do as Swann wished as soon as he had deposited him at the door of the Saint-Euverte house, where Swann arrived soothed by the thought that M. de Charlus would be spending the evening at the Rue La Pérouse, but in a state of melancholy indifference to everything that did not concern Odette, and in particular to the details of fashionable life, a state which invested them with the charm that is to be found in anything which, being no longer an object of our desire, appears to us in its own guise. On alighting from his carriage, in the foreground of that fictitious summary of their domestic existence which hostesses are pleased to offer to their guests on ceremonial occasions, and in which they show a great regard for accuracy of costume and setting, Swann was delighted to see the heirs and successors of Balzac's "tigers"— now "grooms"—who normally followed their mistress on her daily drive, now hatted and booted and posted outside in the roadway in front of the house, or in front of the stables, like gardeners drawn up for inspection beside their flower-beds. The tendency he had always had to look for analogies between living people and the portraits in galleries reasserted itself here, but in a more positive and more general form; it was society as a whole, now that he was detached from it, which presented itself to him as a series of pictures. In the hall, which in the old days, when he was still a regular attender at such functions, he would have entered swathed in his overcoat to emerge from it in his tails, without noticing what had happened during the few moments he had spent there, his mind having been either still at the party which he had just left or already at the party into which he was about to be ushered, he now noticed for the first time, roused by the unexpected arrival of so belated a guest, the scattered pack of tall, magnificent, idle footmen who were drowsing here and there upon benches and chests and who, pointing their noble greyhound profiles, now rose to their feet and gathered in a circle round about him.

One of them, of a particularly ferocious aspect, and not unlike the headsman in certain Renaissance pictures which represent executions, tortures and the like, advanced upon him with an implacable air to take his "things." But the harshness of his steely glare was compensated by the softness of his cotton gloves, so that, as he approached Swann, he seemed to be exhibiting at once an utter contempt for his person and the most tender regard for his hat. He took it with a care to which the precision of his movements imparted something that was almost over-fastidious, and with a delicacy that was rendered almost touching by the evidence of his splendid strength. Then he passed it to one of his satellites, a timid novice who expressed the panic that overpowered him by casting furious glances in every direction, and displayed all the dumb agitation of a wild animal in the first hours of its captivity.

A few feet away, a strapping great fellow in livery stood musing, motionless, statuesque, useless, like that purely decorative warrior whom one sees in the most tumultuous of Mantegna's paintings, lost in thought, leaning upon his shield, while the people around him are rushing about slaughtering one another; detached from the group of his companions who were thronging about Swann, he seemed as determined to remain aloof from that scene, which he followed vaguely with his cruel, glaucous eyes, as if it had been the Massacre of the Innocents or the Martyrdom of St. James. He seemed precisely to have sprung from that vanished race—if,

indeed, it ever existed, save in the reredos of San Zeno
and the frescoes of the Eremitani, where Swann had
come in contact with it, and where it still dreams—
fruit of the impregnation of a classical statue by one of
the Master's Paduan models or an Albrecht Dürer Saxon.
And the locks of his reddish hair, crinkled by nature
but glued to his head by brilliantine, were treated broadly
as they are in that Greek sculpture which the Mantuan
painter never ceased to study, and which, if in its creator's purpose it represents but man, manages at least
to extract from man's simple outlines such a variety of
richness, borrowed, as it were, from the whole of animate nature, that a head of hair, by the glossy un-
dulation and beak-like points of its curls, or in the
superimpositon of the florid triple diadem of its tresses,
can suggest at once a bunch of seaweed, a brood of
fledgling doves, a bed of hyacinths and a coil of snakes.

Others again, no less colossal, were disposed upon
the steps of a monumental staircase for which their
decorative presence and marmorean immobility might
have earned, like the one in the Palace of the Doges,
the name "Staircase of the Giants," and on which Swann
now set foot, saddened by the thought that Odette had
never climbed it. Ah, with what joy by contrast would
he have raced up the dark, evil-smelling, breakneck
flights to the little dressmaker's, in whose attic he
would so gladly have paid the price of a weekly stage-
box at the Opera for the right to spend the evening
there when Odette came, and other days too, for the
privilege of talking about her, of living among people
whom she was in the habit of seeing when he was not
there, and who on that account seemed to be possessed
of some part of his mistress's life that was more real,
more inaccessible and more mysterious than anything
that he knew. Whereas upon that pestilential but longed-

for staircase to the old dressmaker's, since there was no other, no service stair in the building, one saw in the evening outside every door an empty, unwashed milk-can set out upon the door-mat in readiness for the morning round, on the splendid but despised staircase which Swann was now climbing, on either side of him, at different levels, before each anfractuosity made in its walls by the window of the porter's lodge or the entrance to a set of rooms, representing the departments of in-door service which they controlled and doing homage for them to the guests, a concierge, a major-domo, a steward (worthy men who spent the rest of the week in semi-independence in their own domains, dined there by themselves like small shop-keepers, and might to-morrow lapse to the bourgeois service of some successful doctor or industrial magnate), scrupulous in observing to the letter all the instructions they had been given before being allowed to don the brilliant livery which they wore only at rare intervals and in which they did not feel altogether at their ease, stood each in the arcade of his doorway with a pompous splendour tempered by democratic good-fellowship, like saints in their niches, while a gigantic usher, dressed Swiss Guard fashion like the beadle in a church, struck the floor with his staff as each fresh arrival passed him. Coming to the top of the staircase, up which he had been followed by a ser-vant with a pallid countenance and a small pigtail clubbed at the back of his head, like a Goya sacristan or a tabellion in an old play, Swann passed in front of a desk at which lackeys seated like notaries before their massive register rose solemnly to their feet and inscribed his name. He next crossed a little hall which—like certain rooms that are arranged by their owners to serve as the setting for a single work of art (from which they take their name), and, in their studied bareness, contain nothing else—displayed at its entrance, like some priceless effigy by Benvenuto Cellini of an armed watchman, a young footman, his body slightly bent forward, rearing above his crimson gorget an even more crimson face from which gushed torrents of fire, timidity and zeal, who, as he pierced with his impetuous, vigilant, desperate gaze the Aubusson tapestries screening the door of the room in which the music was being given, appeared, with a soldierly impassiveness or a supernatural faith—an allegory of alarums, incarnation of alertness, commemoration of the call to arms—to be watching, angel or sentinel, from the tower of a castle or cathedral, for the approach of the enemy or for the hour of Judgment. Swann had now only to enter the concert-room, the doors of which were thrown open to him by an usher loaded with chairs, who bowed low before him as though tendering to him the keys of a conquered city. But he thought of the house in which at that very moment he might have been if Odette had only permitted it, and the remembered glimpse of an empty milk-can upon a door-mat wrung his heart.

Swann speedily recovered his sense of the general ugliness of the human male when, on the other side of the tapestry curtain, the spectacle of the servants gave place to that of the guests. But even this ugliness of faces which of course were mostly familiar to him seemed something new now that their features—instead of being to him symbols of practical utility in the identification of this or that person who until then had represented merely so many pleasures to be pursued, boredoms to be avoided, or courtesies to be acknowledged—rested in the autonomy of their lines, measurable by aesthetic co-ordinates alone. And in these men by whom Swann now found himself surrounded there was nothing, down to the monocles which many of them wore (and which previously would at the most have enabled Swann to say that so-and-so wore a monocle) which, no longer restricted to the general connotation of a habit, the same in all of them, did not now strike him with a sense of indiviuality in each. Perhaps because he regarded General de Froberville and the Marquis de Bréauté, who were talking to each other just inside the door, simply as two figures in a picture, whereas they were the old and useful friends who had put him up for the Jockey Club and had supported him in duels, the General's monocle, stuck between his eyelids like a shell-splinter in his vulgar, scarred and overbearing face, in the middle of a forehead which it dominated like the single eye of the Cyclops, appeared to Swann as a monstrous wound which it might have been glorious to receive but which it was indecent to expose, while that which M. de Bréauté sported, as a festive badge, with his pearl-grey gloves, his crush hat and white tie, substituting it for the familiar pair of glasses (as Swann himself did) when he went to society functions, bore, glued to its other side, like a specimen prepared on a slide for the microscope, an infinitesimal gaze that swarmed with affability and never ceased to twinkle at the loftiness of the ceilings, the delightfulness of the entertainment, the interestingness of the programmes and the excellence of the refreshments.

"Hallo, you here! Why, it's ages since we've seen you," the General greeted Swann and, noticing his drawn features and concluding that it was perhaps a serious illness that had kept him away, added: "You're looking well, old man!" while M. de Bréauté exclaimed: "My dear fellow, what on earth are you doing here?" to a society novelist who had just fitted into the angle of eyebrow and cheek a monocle that was his sole instrument of psychological investigation and remorseless analysis, and who now replied with an air of mystery and self-importance, rolling the "r": "I am observing!"

The Marquis de Forestelle's monocle was minute and rimless, and, by enforcing an incessant and painful contraction of the eye in which it was embedded like a superfluous cartilage the presence of which is inexplicable and its substance unimaginable, gave to his face a melancholy refinement, and led women to supose him capable of suffering greatly from the pangs of love. But that of M. de Saint-Candé, encircled, like Saturn, with an enormous ring, was the centre of gravity of a face which adjusted itself constantly in relation to it, a face whose quivering red nose and swollen sarcastic lips endeavoured by their grimaces to keep up with the running fire of wit that sparkled in the polished disk, and saw itself preferred to the most handsome looks in the world by snobbish and depraved young women whom it set dreaming of artificial charms and a refinement of sensual bliss. Meanwhile, behind him, M. de Palancy, who with his huge carp's head and goggling eyes moved slowly through the festive gathering, periodically unclenching his mandibles as though in search of his orientation, had the air of carrying about upon his person only an accidental and perhaps purely symbolical fragment of the glass wall of his aquarium, a part intended to suggest the whole, which recalled to Swann, a fervent admirer of Giotto's Vices and Virtues at Padua, that figure representing Injustice by whose side a leafy bough evokes the idea of the forests that enshroud his secret lair.

Swann had gone forward into the room at Mme de Saint-Euverte's insistence, and in order to listen to an air from *Orfeo* which was being rendered on the flute, had taken up a position in a corner from which, unfortunately, his horizon was bounded by two ladies of

mature years seated side by side, the Marquise de Cambremer and the Vicomtesse de Franquetot, who, because
they were cousins, spent their time at parties wandering
through the room each clutching her bag and followed
by her daughter, hunting for one another like people
at a railway station, and could never be at rest until
they had reserved two adjacent chairs by marking them
with their fans or handkerchiefs—Mme de Cambremer,
since she knew scarcely anyone, being all the more glad
of a companion, while Mme de Franquetot, who, on
the contrary, was extremely well-connected, thought it
elegant and original to show all her fine friends that
she preferred to their company that of an obscure country cousin with whom she had childhood memories in
common. Filled with melancholy irony, Swann watched
them as they listened to the pianoforte intermezzo (Liszt's
"Saint Francis preaching to the birds") which had succeeded the flute and followed the virtuoso in his dizzy
flight, Mme de Franquetot anxiously, her eyes starting
from her head as though the keys over which his fingers
skipped with such agility were a series of trapezes from
any one of which he might come crashing a hundred
feet to the ground, stealing now and then a glance of
astonishment and unbelief at her companion, as who
should say: "It isn't possible, I'd never have believed
that a human being could do that!", Mme de Cambremer, as a woman who had received a sound musical
education, beating time with her head, transformed for
the nonce into the pendulum of a metronome, the sweep
and rapidity of whose oscillations from one shoulder to
the other (performed with that look of wild abandonment in her eye which a sufferer shows when he has
lost control of himself and is no longer able to master
his pain, saying merely "I can't help it") so increased
that at every moment her diamond earrings caught in

the trimming of her bodice, and she was obliged to straighten the bunch of black grapes which she had in her hair, though without any interruption of her constantly accelerated motion. On the other side (and a little way in front) of Mme de Franquetot was the Marquise de Gallardon, absorbed in her favourite subject of meditation, namely her kinship with the Guermantes family, from which she derived both publicly and in private a good deal of glory not unmingled with shame, the most brilliant ornaments of that house remaining somewhat aloof from her, perhaps because she was boring, or because she was disagreeable, or because she came of an inferior branch of the family, or very possibly for no reason at all. When she found herself seated next to someone whom she did not know, as she was at this moment next to Mme de Franquetot, she suffered acutely from the feeling that her own consciousness of her Guermantes connection could not be made externally manifest in visible characters like those which, in the mosaics in Byzantine churches, placed one beneath another, inscribe in a vertical column by the side of some holy personage the words which he is supposed to be uttering. At this moment she was pondering the fact that she had never received an invitation, or even a call, from her young cousin the Princesse des Laumes during the six years that had elapsed since the latter's marriage. The thought filled her with anger, but also with pride; for, by dint of telling everyone who expressed surprise at never seeing her at Mme des Laumes's that it was because of the risk of meeting the Princesse Mathilde there—a degradation which her own ultra-Legitimist family would never have forgiven her— she had come to believe that this actually was the reason for her not visiting her young cousin. She remembered, it is true, that she had several times inquired of Mme des Laumes how they might contrive to meet, but she remembered it only confusedly and, besides, more than neutralised this slightly humiliating reminiscence by murmuring, "After all, it isn't for me to take the first step; I'm at least twenty years older than she is." And fortified by these unspoken words she flung her shoulders proudly back until they seemed to part company with her bust, while her head, which lay almost horizontally upon them, was reminiscent of the "detachable" head of a pheasant which is brought to the table regally adorned with its feathers. Not that she in the least resembled a pheasant, having been endowed by nature with a squat, dumpy and masculine figure; but successive mortifications had given her a backward tilt, such as one may observe in trees which have taken root on the edge of a precipice and are forced to grow backwards to preserve their balance. Since she was obliged, in order to console herself for not being quite the equal of the rest of the Guermantes clan, to repeat to herself incessantly that it was owing to the uncompromising rigidity of her principles and pride that she saw so little of them, the constant iteration had ended up by re-moulding her body and giving her a sort of presence which was accepted by bourgeois ladies as a sign of breeding, and even kindled at times a momentary spark in the jaded eyes of old clubmen. Had anyone subjected Mme de Gallardon's conversation to that form of analysis which by noting the relative frequency of its several terms enables one to discover the key to a coded text, they would at once have remarked that no expression, not even the commonest, occurred in it nearly so often as "at my cousins the Guermantes'," "at my aunt Guermantes's," "Elzéar de Guermantes's health," "my cousin Guermantes's box." If anyone spoke to her of a distinguished personage, she would reply that, although she was not personally acquainted with him, she had seen him hundreds of times at her aunt Guermantes's, but she would utter this reply in so icy a tone, in such a hollow voice, that it was clear that if she did not know the celebrity personally it was by virtue of all the stubborn and ineradicable principles against which her shoulders leaned, as against one of those ladders on which gymnastic instructors make us stretch in order to develop the expansion of our chests.

As it happened, the Princesse des Laumes, whom no one would have expected to appear at Mme de Saint-Euverte's, had just arrived there. To show that she did not wish to flaunt her superior rank in a salon to which she had come only out of condescension, she had sidled in with her arms pressed close to her sides, even when there was no crowd to be squeezed through and no one attempting to get past her, staying purposely at the back, with the air of being in her proper place, like a king who stands in the queue at the doors of a theatre where the management have not been warned of his coming; and, restricting her gaze—so as not to seem to be advertising her presence and claiming the consideration that was her due—to the study of a pattern in the carpet or her own skirt, she stood there on the spot which had struck her as the most modest (and from which, as she very well knew, a rapturous exclamation from Mme de Saint-Euverte would extricate her as soon as her presence there was noticed), next to Mme de Cambremer, whom she did not know. She observed the dumbshow by which her neighbour was expressing her passion for music, but she refrained from imitating it. This was not to say that, having for once consented to spend a few minutes in Mme de Saint-Euverte's house, the Princesse des Laumes would not have wished (so that the courtesy she was doing her hostess might, so

to speak, "count double") to show herself as friendly
and obliging as possible. But she had a natural horror
of what she called "exaggerating," and always made a
point of letting people see that she "had no desire" to
indulge in displays of emotion that were not in keeping
with the tone of the circle in which she moved, although
on the other hand such displays could not help but
make an impression upon her, by virtue of that spirit
of imitation, akin to timidity, which is developed in
the most self-confident persons by contact with an unfamiliar environment, even though it be inferior to their
own. She began to ask herself whether these gesticu-
lations might not, perhaps, be a necessary concomitant
of the piece of music that was being played—a piece
which did not quite come within the scope of the music
she was used to hearing—whether to abstain from them
might not be evidence of incomprehension as regards
the music and of discourtesy towards the lady of the
house; with the result that, in order to express by a
compromise both of her contradictory inclinations in
turn, at one moment she would confine herself to
straightening her shoulder-straps or feeling in her golden
hair for the little balls of coral or of pink enamel, frosted
with tiny diamonds, which formed its simple but
charming ornament, scrutinising her impassioned
neighbour with cold curiosity the while, and at the next
would beat time for a few bars with her fan, but, so as
not to forfeit her independence, against the rhythm.
The pianist having finished the Liszt intermezzo and
begun a prelude by Chopin, Mme de Cambremer turned
to Mme de Franquetot with a fond smile of knowing
satisfaction and allusion to the past. She had learned in
her girlhood to fondle and cherish those long sinuous
phrases of Chopin, so free, so flexible, so tactile, which
begin by reaching out and exploring far outside and

away from the direction in which they started, far beyond the point which one might have expected their notes to reach, and which divert themselves in those fantastic bypaths only to return more deliberately— with a more premeditated reprise, with more precision, as on a crystal bowl that reverberates to the point of exquisite agony—to clutch at one's heart.

Brought up in a provincial household with few connections, hardly ever invited to a ball, she had revelled, in the solitude of her old manor-house, in setting the pace, now slow, now breathlessly whirling, for all those imaginary waltzing couples, in picking them off like flowers, leaving the ball-room for a moment to listen to the wind sighing among the pine-trees on the shore of the lake, and seeing all of a sudden advancing towards her, more different from anything one has ever dreamed of than earthly lovers are, a slender young man with a slightly sing-song voice, strange and out of tune, in white gloves. But nowadays the old-fashioned beauty of this music seemed to have become a trifle stale. Having forfeited, some years back, the esteem of the connoisseurs, it had lost its distinction and its charm, and even those whose taste was frankly bad had ceased to find in it more than a moderate pleasure to which they hardly liked to confess. Mme de Cambremer cast a furtive glance behind her. She knew that her young daughter-in-law (full of respect for her new family, except as regards the things of the mind, upon which, having "got as far" as Harmony and the Greek alphabet, she was specially enlightened) despised Chopin, and felt quite ill when she heard him played. But finding herself free from the scrutiny of this Wagnerian, who was sitting at some distance in a group of her own contemporaries, Mme de Cambremer let herself drift upon a stream of exquisite sensations. The Princesse

des Laumes felt them too. Though without any natural
gift for music, she had had lessons some fifteen years
earlier from a piano-teacher of the Faubourg Saint-Germain, a woman of genius who towards the end of her
life had been reduced to penury and had returned, at
seventy, to instruct the daughters and granddaughters
of her old pupils. This lady was now dead. But her
method, her beautiful tone, came to life now and then
beneath the fingers of her pupils, even of those who
had become in other respects quite mediocre, had given
up music, and hardly ever opened a piano. Thus Mme
des Laumes could wave her head to and fro with complete conviction, with a just appreciation of the manner
in which the pianist was rendering this prelude, since
she knew it by heart. The closing notes of the phrase
that he had begun sounded already on her lips. And
she murmured "How *ch*arming it is!" with a double *ch*
at the beginning of the word which was a mark of
refinement and by which she felt her lips so romantically
crinkled, like the petals of a beautiful, budding flower,
that she instinctively brought her eyes into harmony
with them, illuminating them for a moment with a
vague and sentimental gaze. Meanwhile Mme de Gallardon was saying to herself how annoying it was that
she had so few opportunities of meeting the Princesse
des Laumes, for she meant to teach her a lesson by not
acknowledging her greeting. She did not know that her
cousin was in the room. A movement of Mme Franquetot's head disclosed the Princess. At once Mme de
Gallardon dashed towards her, disturbing everybody;
although determined to preserve a distant and glacial
manner which should remind everyone present that she
had no desire to be on friendly terms with a person in
whose house one might find oneself cheek by jowl with
the Princesse Mathilde, and to whom it was not for her

to make advances since she was not "of her generation," she felt bound to modify this air of dignity and reserve by some non-committal remark which would justify her overture and force the Princess to engage in conversation; and so, when she reached her cousin, Mme de Gallardon, with a stern countenance and one hand thrust out as though she were trying to "force" a card, said to her: "How is your husband?" in the same anxious tone that she would have used if the Prince had been seriously ill. The Princess, breaking into a laugh which was characteristic of her and was intended at once to draw attention to the fact that she was making fun of someone and also to enhance her beauty by concentrating her features around her animated lips and sparkling eyes, answered: "Why, he's never been better in his life!" And she went on laughing.

Whereupon Mme de Gallardon drew herself up and, putting on an even chillier expression, though still apparently concerned about the Prince's health, said to her cousin:

"Oriane" (at once Mme des Laumes looked with amused astonishment towards an invisible third person, whom she seemed to call to witness that she had never authorised Mme de Gallardon to use her Christian name), "I should be so pleased if you would look in for a moment to-morrow evening to hear a clarinet quintet by Mozart. I should like to have your opinion of it."

She seemed not so much to be issuing an invitation as to be asking a favour, and to want the Princess's opinion of the Mozart quintet just as though it had been a dish invented by a new cook, whose talent it was most important that an epicure should come to judge.

"But I know that quintet quite well. I can tell you now—that I adore it."

"You know my husband isn't at all well—his liver... He would so much like to see you," Mme de Gallardon went on, making it now a charitable obligation for the Princess to appear at her party.

The Princess never liked to tell people that she would not go to their houses. Every day she would write to express her regret at having been kept away—by the sudden arrival of her husband's mother, by an invitation from her brother-in-law, by the Opera, by some excursion to the country—from some party to which she would never have dreamed of going. In this way she gave many people the satisfaction of feeling that she was on intimate terms with them, that she would gladly have come to their houses, and that she had been prevented from doing so only by some princely obstacle which they were flattered to find competing with their own humble entertainment. And then, as she belonged to that witty Guermantes set in which there survived something of the mental briskness, stripped of all commonplace phrases and conventional sentiments, which goes back to Mérimée and has found its final expression in the plays of Meilhac and Halévy, she adapted it even for the purposes of her social relations, transposed it into the form of politeness which she favoured and which endeavoured to be positive and precise, to approximate itself to the plain truth. She would never develop at any length to a hostess the expression of her anxiety to be present at her party; she thought it more amiable to put to her a few little facts on which it would depend whether or not it was possible for her to come.

"Listen, and I'll explain," she said to Mme de Gallardon. "To-morrow evening I must go to a friend of mine who has been pestering me to fix a day for ages. If she takes us to the theatre afterwards, with the best

will in the world there'll be no possibility of my coming
to you; but if we just stay in the house, since I know
there won't be anyone else there, I shall be able to slip
away."

"Tell me, have you seen your friend M. Swann?"

"No! my beloved Charles! I never knew he was here.
I must catch his eye."

"It's odd that he should come to old Saint-Euverte's,"
Mme de Gallardon went on. "Oh, I know he's very
clever," meaning by that "very cunning," "but that
makes no difference—the idea of a Jew in the house
of a sister and sister-in-law of Archbishops!"

"I'm ashamed to confess that I'm not in the least
shocked," said the Princesse des Laumes.

"I know he's a convert and all that, and even his
parents and grandparents before him. But they do say
that the converted ones remain more attached to their
religion than the practising ones, that it's all just a
pretense; is that true, d'you think?"

"I can throw no light at all on the matter."

The pianist, who was "down" to play two pieces by
Chopin, after finishing the Prelude had at once attacked
a Polonaise. But once Mme de Gallardon had informed
her cousin that Swann was in the room, Chopin himself
might have risen from the grave and played all his works
in turn without Mme des Laumes paying him the slightest attention. She belonged to that half of the human
race in whom the curiosity the other half feels about
the people it does not know is replaced by an interest
in the people it does. As with many women of the
Faubourg Saint-Germain, the presence in any room in
which she might find herself of another member of her
set, even though she had nothing in particular to say
to him, monopolised her attention to the exclusion of
everything else. From that moment, in the hope that

Swann would catch sight of her, the Princess spent her whole time (like a tame white mouse when a lump of sugar is put down before its nose and then taken away) turning her face, which was filled with countless signs of complicity, none of them with the least relevance to the sentiment underlying Chopin's music, in the direction where Swann as standing and, if he moved, diverting accordingly the course of her magnetic smile.

"Oriane, don't be angry with me," resumed Mme de Gallardon, who could never restrain herself from sacrificing her highest social ambitions, and the hope that she might one day dazzle the world, to the immediate, obscure and private satisfaction of saying something disagreeable, "people do say about your M. Swann that he's the sort of man one can't have in one's house; is that true?"

"Why, you of all people ought to know that it's true," replied the Princesse des Laumes, "since you must have asked him a hundred times, and he's never been to your house once."

And leaving her cousin mortified, she burst out laughing again, scandalising everyone who was trying to listen to the music, but attracting the attention of Mme de Saint-Euverte, who had stayed, out of politeness, near the piano, and now caught sight of the Princess for the first time. Mme de Saint-Euverte was all the more delighted to see Mme des Laumes as she imagined her to be still at Guermantes, looking after her sick father-in-law.

"My dear Princess, you here?"

"Yes, I tucked myself away in a corner, and I've been hearing such lovely things."

"What, you've been here for quite a time?"

"Oh, yes, a very long time which seemed very short, long only because I couldn't see you."

Mme de Saint-Euverte offered her own chair to the Princess, who declined it, saying:

"Oh, please, no! Why should you? I don't mind in the least where I sit." And deliberately picking out, the better to display the simplicity of a really great lady, a low seat without a back: "There now, that pouf, that's all I need. It will make me keep my back straight. Oh! good heavens, I'm making a noise again; they'll be telling you to have me chucked out."

Meanwhile, the pianist having redoubled his speed, the musical excitement was at its height, a servant was handing refreshments round on a salver, and was making the spoons rattle, and, as happened every week, Mme de Saint-Euverte was making unavailing signs to him to go away. A recent bride, who had been told that a young woman ought never to appear bored, was smiling vigorously, trying to catch her hostess's eye so as to flash her a look of gratitude for having "thought of her" in connection with so delightful an entertainment. However, although she remained calmer than Mme de Franquetot, it was not without some uneasiness that she followed the flying fingers, the object of her concern being not the pianist but the piano, on which a lighted candle, jumping at each *fortissimo*, threatened, if not to set its shade on fire, at least to spill wax upon the rosewood. At last she could contain herself no longer, and, running up the two steps of the platform on which the piano stood, flung herself on the candle to adjust its sconce. But scarcely had her hand come within reach of it when, on a final chord, the piece came to an end and the pianist rose to his feet. Nevertheless the bold initiative shown by this young woman and the brief promiscuity between her and the instrumentalist which resulted from it, produced a generally favourable impression.

"Did you see what that girl did just now, Princess?" asked General de Froberville, who had come up to Mme des Laumes as her hostess left her for a moment. "Odd, wasn't it? Is she one of the performers?"

"No, she's a little Mme de Cambremer," replied the Princess without thinking, and then added hurriedly: "I'm only repeating what I've heard—I haven't the faintest notion who she is; someone behind me said that they were neighbours of Mme de Saint-Euverte in the country, but I don't believe anyone knows them, really. They must be 'country cousins'! By the way, I don't know whether you're particularly familiar with the brilliant society which we see before us, because I've no idea who all these astonishing people can be. What do you suppose they do with themselves when they're not at Mme de Saint-Euverte's parties? She must have ordered them along with the musicians and the chairs and the food. 'Universal providers,' you know. You must admit they're rather splendid, General. But can she really have the heart to hire the same 'supers' every week? It isn't possible!"

"Oh, but Cambremer is quite a good name—old, too," protested the General.

"I see no objection to its being old," the Princess answered dryly, "but whatever else it is it's not *euphonious*," she went on, isolating the word euphonious as though between inverted commas, a little affectation to which the Guermante set were addicted.

"You think not, eh! She's a regular little peach, though," said the General, whose eyes never strayed from Mme de Cambremer. "Don't you agree with me, Princess?"

"She thrusts herself forward too much. I think, in so young a woman, that's not very nice—for I don't suppose she's my generation," replied Mme des Laumes (this expression being common, it appeared, to Gallardon and Guermantes). And then, seeing that M. de Froberville was still gazing at Mme de Cambremer, she added, half out of malice towards the latter, half out of amiability towards the General: "Not very nice . . . for her husband! I'm sorry I don't know her, since you've set your heart on her—I might have introduced you to her," said the Princess, who, if she had known the young woman, would probably have done nothing of the sort. "And now I must say good night, because one of my friends is having a birthday party, and I must go and wish her many happy returns," she explained in a tone of modest sincerity, reducing the fashionable gathering to which she was going to the simple proportions of a ceremony which would be boring in the extreme but which it was obligatory and touching to attend. "Besides, I must pick up Basin who while I've been here has gone to see those friends of his—you know them too I believe,—who are called after a bridge—oh, yes, the Iénas."

"It was a victory before it was a bridge, Princess," said the General. "I mean to say, to an old soldier like me," he went on, wiping his monocle and replacing it, as though he were laying a fresh dressing on the raw wound beneath, while the Princess instinctively looked away, "that Empire nobility, well of course it's not the same thing, but, after all, taking it for what it is, it's very fine of its kind—they were people who really did fight like heroes."

"But I have the deepest respect for heroes," the Princess assented with a faint trace of irony. "If I don't go with Basin to see this Princess d'Iéna, it isn't at all because of that, it's simply because I don't know them. Basin knows them, and is deeply attached to them. Oh, no, it's not what you think, it's not a flirtation.

I've no reason to object. Besides, what good has it ever done when I have objected," she added in a melancholy voice, for the whole world knew that, ever since the day when the Prince des Laumes had married his ravishing cousin, he had been consistently unfaithful to her. "Anyhow, it isn't that at all. They're people he has known for a long time, he takes advantage of them, and that suits me down to the ground. In any case, what he's told me about their house is quite enough. Can you imagine it, all their furniture is 'Empire'!"

"But, my dear Princess, that's only natural; it belonged to their grandparents."

"I don't say it didn't, but that doesn't make it any less ugly. I quite understand that people can't always have nice things, but at least they needn't have things that are merely grotesque. I'm sorry, but I can think of nothing more pretentious and bourgeois than that hideous style—cabinets with swans' heads, like baths!"

"But I believe, all the same, that they've got some fine things; why, they must have that famous mosaic table on which the Treaty of . . ."

"Oh, I don't deny they may have things that are interesting enough from the historic point of view. But things like that can't ever be beautiful . . . because they're simply horrible! I've got things like that myself, that came to Basin from the Montesquious. Only, they're up in the attics at Guermantes, where nobody ever sees them. But in any case that's not the point, I would rush round to see them with Basin, I'd even go to see them among all their sphinxes and brasses if I knew them, but—I don't know them! D'you know, I was always taught when I was a little girl that it wasn't polite to call on people one didn't know." She assumed a tone of childish gravity. "And so I'm just doing what I was taught to do. Can't you see those good people, with a totally strange woman bursting into their house? Why, I might get a most hostile reception."

And she coquettishly enhanced the charm of the smile which that supposition had brought to her lips, by giving to her blue eyes, which were fixed on the General, a gentle, dreamy expression.

"My dear Princess, you know that they'd be simply wild with joy."

"No, why?" she inquired with the utmost vivacity, either to give the impression of being unaware that it would be because she was one of the first ladies in France, or in order to have the pleasure of hearing the General tell her so. "Why? How can you tell? Perhaps they might find it extremely disagreeable. I don't know, but if they're anything like me, I find it quite boring enough to see the people I do know, and I'm sure if I had to see people I didn't know as well, even if they had 'fought like heroes,' I should go stark mad. Besides, except when it's an old friend like you, whom one knows quite apart from that, I'm not sure that heroism takes one very far in society. It's often quite boring enough to have to give a dinner-party, but if one had to offer one's arm to Spartacus to go into dinner . . . Really, no, it would never be Vercingetorix I should send for to make a fourteenth. I feel sure I should keep him for really big 'crushes.' And as I never give any . . ."

"Ah! Princess, it's easy to see you're not a Guermantes for nothing. You have your share of it, all right, the 'wit of the Guermantes'!"

"But people always talk about the wit of *the* Guermantes in the plural. I never could make out why. Do you really know any *others* who have it?" she rallied him, with a rippling flow of laughter, her features concentrated, yoked to the service of her animation, her eyes sparkling, blazing with a radiant sunshine of gaiety which could be kindled only by such observations—even if the Princess had to make them herself—as were in praise of her wit or of her beauty. "Look, there's Swann talking to your Cambremer; over there, beside old mother Saint-Euverte, don't you see him? Ask him to introduce you. But hurry up, he seems to be just going!"

"Did you notice how dreadfully ill he's looking?" asked the General.

"My precious Charles? Ah, he's coming at last. I was beginning to think he didn't want to see me!"

Swann was extremely fond of the Princess des Laumes, and the sight of her reminded him of Guermantes, the estate next to Combray, and all the country which he so dearly loved and had ceased to visit in order not to be separated from Odette. Slipping into the manner, half-artistic, half-amorous, with which he could always manage to amuse the Princess—a manner which came to him quite naturally whenever he dipped for a moment into the old social atmosphere—and wishing also to express in words, for his own satisfaction, the longing that he felt for the country:

"Ah!" he began in a declamatory tone, so as to be audible at once to Mme de Saint-Euverte, to whom he was speaking, and to Mme des Laumes, for whom he was speaking, "Behold our charming Princess! Look, she has come up on purpose from Guermantes to hear Saint Francis preach to the birds, and has only just had time, like a dear little titmouse, to go and pick a few little hips and haws and put them in her hair; there are even some drops of dew upon them still, a little of the hoarfrost which must be making the Duchess shiver. It's very pretty indeed, my dear Princess."

"What! The Princess came up on purpose from Guermantes? But that's too wonderful! I never knew; I'm

quite overcome," Mme de Saint-Euverte protested with
quaint simplicity, being but little accustomed to Swann's
form of wit. And then, examining the Princess's head-
dress, "Why, you're quite right; it is copied from . . . what
shall I say, not chestnuts, no,—oh, it's a delightful
idea, but how can the Princess have known what was
going to be on my programme? The musicans didn't
tell me, even."

Swann, who was accustomed, when he was with a
woman whom he had kept up the habit of addressing
in terms of gallantry, to pay her delicate compliments
which most society people were incapable of understanding, did not condescend to explain to Mme de
Saint-Euverte that he had been speaking metaphori-
cally. As for the Princess, she was in fits of laughter,
both because Swann's wit was highly appreciated by
her set, and because she could never hear a compliment
addressed to herself without finding it exquisitely subtle
and irresistibly amusing.

"Well, I'm delighted, Charles, if my little hips and
haws meet with your approval. But tell me, why did
you pay your respects to that Cambremer person, are
you also her neighbour in the country?"

Mme de Saint-Euverte, seeing that the Princess
seemed quite happy talking to Swann, had drifted away.

"But you are yourself, Princess!"

"I! Why, they must have 'countries' everywhere, those
people! Don't I wish I had!"

"No, not the Cambremers; her own people. She was
a Legrandin, and used to come to Combray. I don't
know whether you're aware that you are Comtesse de
Combray, and that the Chapter owes you a due."

"I don't know what the Chapter owes me, but I do
know that I'm touched for a hundred francs every year
by the Curé, which is a due that I could do very well

without. But surely these Cambremers have rather a startling name. It ends just in time, but it ends badly!" she said with a laugh.[7]

"It begins no better." Swann took the point.

"Yes; that double abbreviation!"

"Someone very angry and very proper who didn't dare to finish the first word."

"But since he couldn't stop himself beginning the second, he'd have done better to finish the first and be done with it. I must say our jokes are in really charming taste, my dear Charles . . . but how tiresome it is that I never see you now," she went on in a winning tone, "I do so love talking to you. Just imagine, I couldn't even have made that idiot Froberville see that there was anything funny about the name Cambremer. Do you agree that life is a dreadful business. It's only when I see you that I stop feeling bored."

Which was probably not true. But Swann and the Princess had a similar way of looking at the little things of life, the effect — if not the cause — of which was a close analogy between their modes of expression and even of pronunciation. This similarity was not immediately striking because no two things could have been more unlike than their voices. But if one took the trouble to imagine Swann's utterances divested of the sonority that enwrapped them, of the moustache from under which they emerged, one realised that they were the same phrases, the same inflexions, that they had the "tone" of the Guermantes set. On important matters, Swann and the Princess had not an idea in common. But since Swann had become so melancholy, and was always in that tremulous condition which precedes the onset of tears, he felt the same need to speak about his grief as a murderer to speak about his crime. And when he heard the Princess say that life was a dreadful business, it gave him a feeling of solace as if she had spoken to him of Odette.

"Yes, life is a dreadful business! We must meet more often, my dear Princess. What is so nice about you is that you're not cheerful. We might spend an evening together."

"By all means. Why not come down to Guermantes? My mother-in-law would be wild with joy. It's supposed to be very ugly down there, but I must say I find the neighbourhood not at all unattractive; I have a horror of 'picturesque spots'."

"Yes, I know, it's delightful!" replied Swann. "It's almost too beautiful, too alive for me just at present; it's a country to be happy in. It's perhaps because I've lived there, but things there speak to me so. As soon as a breath of wind gets up, and the cornfields begin to stir, I feel that someone is going to appear suddenly, that I'm going to hear some news; and those little houses by the water's edge . . . I should be quite wretched!"

"Oh! my dear Charles, look out, there's that appalling Rampillon woman; she's seen me; please hide me. Remind me what it was that happened to her; I get so confused; she's just married off her daughter, or her lover (I never can remember)—perhaps both—to each other! Oh, no, I remember now, she's been dropped by her prince . . . Pretend to be talking to me, so that the poor old Berenice shan't come and invite me to dinner. Anyhow, I'm going. Listen, my dearest Charles, now that I've seen you for once, won't you let me carry you off and take you to the Princesse de Parme's? She'd be so pleased to see you, and Basin too, for that matter— he's meeting me there. If one didn't get news of you, sometimes, from Mémé . . . Imagine, I never see you at all now!"

Swann declined. Having told M. de Charlus that on

leaving Mme de Saint-Euverte's he would go straight home, he did not care to run the risk, by going on now to the Princesse de Parme's, of missing a message which he had all the time been hoping to see brought in to him by one of the footmen during the party, and which he might perhaps find with his own porter when he got home.

"Poor Swann," said Mme des Laumes that night to her husband, "he's as charming as ever, but he does look so dreadfully unhappy. You'll see for yourself, as he has promised to dine with us one of these days. I do feel it's absurd that a man of his intelligence should let himself suffer for a woman of that sort, and one who isn't even interesting, for they tell me she's an absolute idiot!" she added with the wisdom invariably shown by people who, not being in love themselves, feel that a clever man should only be unhappy about a person who is worth his while; which is rather like being astonished that anyone should condescend to die of cholera at the bidding of so insignificant a creature as the comma bacillus.

Swann wanted to go home, but just as he was making his escape, General de Froberville caught him and asked for an introduction to Mme de Cambremer, and he was obliged to go back into the room to look for her.

"I say, Swann, I'd rather be married to that little woman than slaughtered by savages, what do you say?"

The words "slaughtered by savages" pierced Swann's aching heart; and at once he felt the need to continue the conversation. "Ah!" he began, "some fine lives have been lost in that way . . . There was, you remember, that navigator whose remains Dumont d'Urville brought back, La Pérouse . . ." (and he was at once happy again, as though he had named Odette). "He was a fine char-

acter, and interests me very much, does La Pérouse,"
he added with a melancholy air.

"Oh, yes, of course, La Pérouse," said the General.
"It's quite a well-known name. There's a street called
that."

"Do you know anyone in the Rue La Pérouse?" asked
Swann excitedly.

"Only Mme de Chanlivault, the sister of that good
fellow Chaussepierre. She gave a most amusing theatre-
party the other evening. That'll be a really elegant salon
one of these days, you'll see!"

"Oh, so she lives in the Rue La Pérouse. It's attractive, a delightful street, so gloomy."

"Not at all. You can't have been in it for a long
time; it isn't gloomy now; they're beginning to build
all round there."

When Swann did finally introduce M. de Froberville
to the young Mme de Cambremer, since it was the first
time she had heard the General's name she offered him
the smile of joy and surprise with which she would
have greeted him if no one had ever uttered any other;
for, not knowing any of the friends of her new family,
whenever someone was presented to her she assumed
that he must be one of them, and thinking that she
was showing evidence of tact by appearing to have heard
"such a lot about him" since her marriage, she would
hold out her hand with a hesitant air that was meant
as a proof at once of the inculcated reserve which she
had to overcome and of the spontaneous friendliness
which successfully overcame it. And so her parents-in-
law, whom she still regarded as the most eminent people in France, declared that she was an angel; all the
more so because they preferred to appear, in marrying
their son to her, to have yielded to the attraction rather

of her natural charm than of her considerable fortune.

"It's easy to see that you're a musician heart and soul, Madame," said the General, alluding to the incident of the candle.

Meanwhile the concert had begun again, and Swann saw that he could not now go before the end of the new number. He suffered greatly from being shut up among all these people whose stupidity and absurdities struck him all the more painfully since, being ignorant of his love and incapable, had they known of it, of taking any interest or of doing more than smile at it as at some childish nonsense or deplore it as an act of folly, they made it appear to him in the aspect of a subjective state which existed for himself alone, whose reality there was nothing external to confirm; he suffered above all, to the point where even the sound of the instruments made him want to cry out, from having to prolong his exile in this place to which Odette would never come, in which no one, nothing was aware of her existence, from which she was entirely absent.

But suddenly it was as though she had entered, and this apparition was so agonisingly painful that his hand clutched at his heart. The violin had risen to a series of high notes on which it rested as though awaiting something, holding on to them in a prolonged expectancy, in the exaltation of already seeing the object of its expectation approaching, and with a desperate effort to last out until its arrival, to welcome it before itself expiring, to keep the way open for a moment longer, with all its remaining strength, so that the stranger might pass, as one holds a door open that would otherwise automatically close. And before Swann had had time to understand what was happening and to say to himself: "It's the little phrase from Vinteuil's sonata—I mustn't listen!", all his memories of the days when Odette had been in love with him, which he had succeeded until that moment in keeping invisible in the depths of his being, deceived by this sudden reflection of a season of love whose sun, they supposed, had dawned again, had awakened from their slumber, had taken wing and risen to sing maddeningly in his ears, without pity for his present desolation, the forgotten strains of happiness.

In place of the abstract expressions "the time when I was happy," "the time when I was loved," which he had often used before then without suffering too much since his intelligence had not embodied in them anything of the past save fictitious extracts which preserved none of the reality, he now recovered everything that had fixed unalterably the specific, volatile essence of that lost happiness; he could see it all: the snowy, curled petals of the chrysanthemum which she had tossed after him into his carriage, which he had kept pressed to his lips—the address "Maison Dorée" embossed on the note-paper on which he had read "My hand trembles so as I write to you"—the contraction of her eyebrows when she said pleadingly: "You won't leave it too long before getting in touch with me?"; he could smell the heated iron of the barber whom he used to have singe his hair while Loredan went to fetch the little seamstress; could feel the showers which fell so often that spring, the ice-cold homeward drive in his victoria, by moonlight; all the network of mental habits, of seasonal impressions, of sensory reactions, which had extended over a series of weeks its uniform meshes in which his body found itself inextricably caught. At that time he had been satisfying a sensual curiosity in discovering the pleasures of those who live for love alone. He had supposed that he could stop there, that he would not be obliged to learn their sorrows also; yet how small a

thing the actual charm of Odette was now in comparison
with the fearsome terror which extended it like a cloudy
halo all around her, the immense anguish of not knowing at every hour of the day and night what she had
been doing, of not possessing her wholly, always and
everywhere! Alas, he recalled the accents in which she
had exclaimed: "But I can see you at any time; I'm
always free!"—she who was never free now; he remembered the interest, the curiosity she had shown in his
life, her passionate desire that he should do her the
favour—which it was he who had dreaded at that time
as a possibly tedious waste of his time and disturbance
of his arrangements—of granting her access to his study;
how she had been obliged to beg him to let her take
him to the Verdurins'; and, when he allowed her to
come to him once a month, how she had had to repeat
to him time and again, before he let himself be swayed,
what a joy it would be to see each other daily, a custom
for which she longed when to him it seemed only a
tiresome distraction, which she had then grown tired
of and finally broken while for him it had become so
irresistible and painful a need. Little had he suspected
how truly he spoke, when at their third meeting, as
she repeated: "But why don't you let me come to you
oftener?" he had told her, laughing, and in a vein of
gallantry, that it was for fear of forming a hopeless
passion. Now, alas, it still happened at times that she
wrote to him from a restaurant or hotel, on paper which
bore a printed address, but printed in letters of fire that
seared his heart. "It's written from the Hôtel Vouil-
lemont. What on earth can she have gone there for?
With whom? What happened there?" He remembered
the gas-jets being extinguished along the Boulevard des
Italiens when he had met her against all expectations
among the errant shades on that night which had seemed

to him almost supernatural and which indeed—a night from a period when he had not even to ask himself whether he would be annoying her by looking for her and finding her, so certain was he that she knew no greater happiness than to see him and to let him take her home—belonged to a mysterious world to which one never may return again once its doors are closed. And Swann could distinguish, standing motionless before that scene of remembered happiness, a wretched figure who filled him with such pity, because he did not at first recognise who it was, that he had to lower his eyes lest anyone should observe that they were filled with tears. It was himself.

When he had realised this, his pity ceased; he was jealous, now, of that other self whom she had loved, he was jealous of those men of whom he had so often said, without suffering too much: "Perhaps she loves them," now that he had exchanged the vague idea of loving, in which there is no love, for the petals of the chrysanthemum and the "letter-heading" of the Maison d'Or, which were full of it. And then, his anguish becoming too intense, he drew his hand across his forehead, let the monocle drop from his eye, and wiped its glass. And doubtless, if he had caught sight of himself at that moment, he would have added, to the collection of those which he had already identified, this monocle which he removed like an importunate, worrying thought and from whose misty surface, with his handkerchief, he sought to obliterate his cares.

There are in the music of the violin—if one does not see the instrument itself, and so cannot relate what one hears to its form, which modifies the tone—accents so closely akin to those of certain contralto voices that one has the illusion that a singer has taken her place amid the orchestra. One raises one's eyes, and sees only the wooden case, delicate as a Chinese box, but, at moments, one is still tricked by the siren's deceiving call; at times, too, one thinks one is listening to a captive genie, struggling in the darkness of the sapient, quivering and enchanted box, like a devil immersed in a stoup of holy water; sometimes, again, it is in the air, at large, like a pure and supernatural being that unfolds its invisible message as it goes by.

As though the musicians were not nearly so much playing the little phrase as performing the rites on which it insisted before it would consent to appear, and proceeding to utter the incantations necessary to procure, and to prolong for a few moments, the miracle of its apparition, Swann, who was no more able to see it than if it had belonged to a world of ultraviolet light, and who experienced something like the refreshing sense of a metamorphosis in the momentary blindness with which he was struck as he approached it, Swann felt its presence like that of a protective goddess, a confidante of his love, who, in order to be able to come to him through the crowd and to draw him aside to speak to him, had disguised herself in this sweeping cloak of sound. And as she passed, light, soothing, murmurous as the perfume of a flower, telling him what she had to say, every word of which he closely scanned, regretful to see them fly away so fast, he made involuntarily with his lips the motion of kissing, as it went by him, the harmonious, fleeting form. He felt that he was no longer in exile and alone since she, who addressed herself to him, was whispering to him of Odette. For he had no longer, as of old, the impression that Odette and he were unknown to the little phrase. Had it not often been the witness of their joys? True that, as often, it had warned him of their frailty. And indeed, whereas in that earlier time he had divined an element of suffering in its smile, in its limpid, disenchanted tones, tonight he found there rather the grace of a resignation that was almost gay. Of those sorrows which the little phrase foreshadowed to him then, which, without being affected by them himself, he had seen it carry past him, smiling, on its sinuous and rapid course, of those sorrows which had now become his own, without his having any hope of being ever delivered from them, it seemed to say to him, as once it had said of his happiness: "What does it all matter? It means nothing." And Swann's thoughts were borne for the first time on a wave of pity and tenderness towards Vinteuil, towards that unknown, exalted brother who must also have suffered so greatly. What could his life have been? From the depths of what well of sorrow could he have drawn that god-like strength, that unlimited power of creation?

When it was the little phrase that spoke to him of the vanity of his sufferings, Swann found a solace in that very wisdom which, but a little while back, had seemed to him intolerable when he fancied he could read it on the faces of indifferent strangers who regarded his love as an insignificant aberration. For the little phrase, unlike them, whatever opinion it might hold on the transience of these states of the soul, saw in them something not, as all these people did, less serious than the events of everyday life, but, on the contrary, so far superior to it as to be alone worth while expressing. It was the charms of an intimate sadness that it sought to imitate, to re-create, and their very essence, for all that it consists in being incommunicable and in appearing trivial to everyone save him who experiences them, had been captured and made visible by the little phrase. So much so that it caused their value to be acknowledged, their divine sweetness savoured, by all those same onlookers, if they were at all musical—who then would fail to recognise them in real life, in every individual love that came into being beneath their eyes. Doubtless the form in which it had codified those charms could not be resolved into rational discourse. But ever since, more than a year before, discovering to him many of the riches of his own soul, the love of music had, for a time at least, been born in him, Swann had regarded musical *motifs* as actual ideas, of another world, of another order, ideas veiled in shadow, unknown, impenetrable to the human mind, but none the less perfectly distinct from one another, unequal among themselves in value and significance. When, after that first evening at the Verdurins', he had had the little phrase played over to him again, and had sought to disentangle from his confused impressions how it was that, like a perfume or a caress, it swept over and enveloped him, he had observed that it was to the closeness of the intervals between the five notes which composed it and to the constant repetition of two of them that was due that impression of a frigid and withdrawn sweetness; but in reality he knew that he was basing this conclusion not upon the phrase itself, but merely upon certain equivalents, substituted (for his mind's convenience) for the mysterious entity of which he had become aware, before ever he knew the Verdurins, at that earlier party when for the first time he had heard the sonata played. He knew that the very memory of the piano falsified still further the perspective in which he saw the elements of music, that the field open to the musician is not a miserable stave of seven notes, but an immeasurable keyboard (still almost entirely unknown) on which, here and there only, separated by the thick darkness of its unexplored tracts, some few among the millions of keys of tenderness, of passion, of courage, of serenity, which compose it, each one differing from all the rest as one universe differs from another, have been discovered by a few great artists who do us the service, when they awaken in us the emotion corresponding to the theme they have discovered, of showing us what richness, what variety lies hidden, unknown to us, in that vast, unfathomed and forbidding night of our soul which we take to be an impenetrable void. Vinteuil had been one of those musicians. In his little phrase, although it might present a clouded surface to the eye of reason, one sensed a content so solid, so consistent, so explicit, to which it gave so new, so original a force, that those who had once heard it preserved the memory of it on an equal footing with the ideas of the intellect. Swann referred back to it as to a conception of love and happiness whose distinctive character he recognised at once as he would that of the *Princesse de Clèves*, or of *René,* should either of those titles occur to him. Even when he was not thinking of the little phrase, it existed latent in his mind on the same footing as certain other notions without material equivalent, such as our notions of light, of sound, of perspective, of physical pleasure, the rich possessions wherewith our inner temple is diversified and adorned. Perhaps we shall lose them, perhaps they will be obliterated, if we return to nothingness. But so long as we are alive, we can no more bring ourselves to a state in which we shall not have known them than we can with regard to any material object, than we can, for example, doubt the luminosity of a lamp that has just been lit, in view of the changed aspect of everything in the room, from which even the memory of the darkness has vanished. In that way Vinteuil's phrase, like some theme, say, in *Tristan,* which represents to us also a certain emotional accretion, had espoused our mortal state, had endued a vesture of humanity that was peculiarly affecting. Its destiny was linked to the future, to the reality of the human soul, of which it was one of the most special and distinctive ornaments. Perhaps it is not-being that is the true state, and all our dream of life is inexistent; but, if so, we feel that these phrases of music, these conceptions which exist in relation to our dream, must be nothing either. We shall perish, but we have as hostages these divine captives who will follow and share our fate. And death in their company is somehow less bitter, less inglorious, perhaps even less probable.

So Swann was not mistaken in believing that the phrase of the sonata really did exist. Human as it was from this point of view, it yet belonged to an order of supernatural beings whom we have never seen, but whom, in spite of that, we recognise and acclaim with rapture when some explorer of the unseen contrives to coax one forth, to bring it down, from that divine world to which he has access, to shine for a brief moment in the firmament of ours. This was what Vinteuil had done with the little phrase. Swann felt that the composer had been content (with the musical instruments at his disposal) to unveil it, to make it visible, following and respecting its outlines with a hand so loving, so prudent, so delicate and so sure that the sound altered at every moment, softening and blurring to indicate a shadow, springing back into life when it must follow the curve of some bolder projection. And one proof that Swann was not mistaken when he believed in the real existence of this phrase, was that anyone with the least discernment would at once have detected the imposture had Vinteuil, endowed with less power to see and to render its forms, sought to dissemble, by adding a

counterfeit touch here and there, the flaws in his vision
or the deficiencies of his hand.

The phrase had disappeared. Swann knew that it
would come again at the end of the last movement,
after a long passage which Mme Verdurin's pianist always "skipped." There were in this passage some admirable ideas which Swann had not distinguished on
first hearing the sonata and which he now perceived,
as if, in the cloak-room of his memory, they had divested themselves of the uniform disguise of their novelty. Swann listened to all the scattered themes which
would enter into the composition of the phrase, as its
premisses enter into the inevitable conclusion of a syl-
logism; he was assisting at the mystery of its birth.
"An audacity," he exclaimed to himself, "as inspired,
perhaps, as that of a Lavoisier or an Ampère—the audacity of a Vinteuil experimenting, discovering the secret laws that govern an unknown force, driving, across
a region unexplored, towards the one possible goal, the
invisible team in which he has placed his trust and
which he may never discern!" How beautiful the dialogue which Swann now heard between piano and violin, at the beginning of the last passage! The suppression
of human speech, so far from letting fancy reign there
uncontrolled (as one might have thought), had eliminated it altogether; never was spoken language so inex-
orably determined, never had it known questions so
pertinent, such irrefutable replies. At first the piano
complained alone, like a bird deserted by its mate; the
violin heard and answered it, as from a neighbouring
tree. It was as at the beginning of the world, as if there
were as yet only the two of them on the earth, or rather
in this world closed to all the rest, so fashioned by the
logic of its creator that in it there should never be any

but themselves: the world of this sonata. Was it a bird, was it the soul, as yet not fully formed, of the little phrase, was it a fairy—that being invisibly lamenting, whose plaint the piano heard and tenderly repeated? Its cries were so sudden that the violinist must snatch up his bow and race to catch them as they came. Marvellous bird! The violinist seemed to wish to charm, to tame, to capture it. Already it had passed into his soul, already the little phrase which it evoked shook like a medium's the body of the violinist, "possessed" indeed. Swann knew that the phrase was going to speak to him once again. And his personality was now so divided that the strain of waiting for the imminent moment when he would find himself face to face with it again shook him with one of those sobs which a beautiful line of poetry or a sad piece of news will wring from us, not when we are alone, but when we impart them to friends in whom we see ourselves reflected like a third person whose probable emotion affects them too. It reappeared, but this time to remain poised in the air, and to sport there for a moment only, as though immobile, and shortly to expire. And so Swann lost nothing of the precious time for which it lingered. It was still there, like an iridescent bubble that floats for a while unbroken. As a rainbow whose brightness is fading seems to subside, then soars again and, before it is extinguished, shines forth with greater splendour than it has ever shown; so to the two colours which the little phrase had hitherto allowed to appear it added others now, chords shot with every hue in the prism, and made them sing. Swann dared not move, and would have liked to compel all the other people in the room to remain still also, as if the slightest movement might imperil the magic presence, supernatural, delicious, frail, that was so soon to vanish. But no one, as it happened, dreamed of speaking. The ineffable utterance of one solitary man, absent, perhaps dead (Swann did not know whether Vinteuil was still alive), breathed out above the rites of those two hierophants, sufficed to arrest the attention of three hundred minds, and made of that platform on which a soul was thus called into being one of the noblest altars on which a supernatural ceremony could be performed. So that when the phrase had unravelled itself at last, and only its fragmentary echoes floated among the subsequent themes which had already taken its place, if Swann at first was irritated to see the Comtesse de Monteriender, famed for her imbecilities, lean over towards him to confide her impressions to him before even the sonata had come to an end, he could not refrain from smiling, and perhaps also found an underlying sense, which she herself was incapable of perceiving, in the words that she used. Dazzled by the virtuosity of the performers, the Comtesse exclaimed to Swann: "It's astonishing! I've never seen anything to beat it..." But a scrupulous regard for accuracy making her correct her first assertion, she added the reservation: "anything to beat it... since the table-turning!"

From that evening onwards, Swann understood that the feeling which Odette had once had for him would never revive, that his hopes of happiness would not be realised now. And on the days on which she happened to be once more kind and affectionate towards him, had shown him some thoughtful attention, he recorded these deceptive signs of a change of feeling on her part with the fond and sceptical solicitude, the desperate joy of people who, nursing a friend in the last days of an incurable illness, relate as facts of infinitely precious significance: "Yesterday he went through his accounts himself, and actually corrected a mistake we had made in adding them up; he ate an egg to-day and seemed quite to enjoy it, and if he digests it properly we shall try him with a cutlet to-morrow,"—although they themselves know that these things are meaningless on the eve of an inevitable death. No doubt Swann was assured that if he had now been living at a distance from Odette he would gradually have lost interest in her, so that he would have been glad to learn that she was leaving Paris for ever; he would have had the heart to remain there; but he hadn't the heart to go.

He had often thought of going. Now that he was once again at work upon his essay on Vermeer, he needed to return, for a few days at least, to The Hague, to Dresden, to Brunswick. He was convinced that a picture of "Diana and her Companions" which had been acquired by the Mauritshuis at the Goldschmidt sale as a Nicholas Maes was in reality a Vermeer. And he would have liked to be able to examine the picture on the spot, in order to buttress his conviction. But to leave Paris while Odette was there, and even when she was not there—for in strange places where our sensations have not been numbed by habit, we revive, we resharpen an old pain—was for him so cruel a project that he felt capable of entertaining it incessantly in his mind only because he knew he was determined never to put it into effect. But it sometimes happened that, while he was asleep, the intention to travel would re-awaken in him (without his remembering that it was out of the question) and would actually take place. One night he dreamed that he was going away for a year; leaning from the window of the train towards a young man on the platform who wept as he bade him farewell, he was trying to persuade this young man to come away also. The train began to move, he awoke in alarm, and remembered that he was not going away, that he would

see Odette that evening, and the next day and almost
every day. And then, being still deeply affected by his
dream, he thanked heaven for those special circumstances which made him independent, thanks to which
he could remain close to Odette, and could even succeed
in getting her to allow him to see her sometimes; and,
recapitulating all his advantages: his social position—
his wealth, from which she stood too often in need of
assistance not to shrink from the prospect of a definite
rupture (having even, so people said, an ulterior plan
of getting him to marry her),—his friendship with M.
de Charlus, which, it was true, had never won him any
very great favour from Odette, but which gave him the
consolatory feeling that she was always hearing com-
plimentary things said about him by this friend in
common for whom she had so great an esteem,—and
even his intelligence, which was exclusively occupied
in devising each day a fresh scheme which would make
his presence, if not agreeable, at any rate necessary to
Odette—remembering all this, he thought of what
might have become of him if these advantages had been
lacking; it struck him that if, like so many other men,
he had been poor, humble, deprived, forced to accept
any work that might be offered to him, or tied dow
by parents or by a wife, he might have been oblig
to part from Odette, that that dream, the terro
which was still so recent, might well have been
and he said to himself: "People don't know when
happy. One is never as unhappy as one thinks."
reflected that this existence had already lasted f
years, that all he could now hope for was tha
last for ever, and that he would sacrifice hi
pleasures, his friends, in fact the whole
the daily expectation of a meeting which,
could bring him no happiness; and he

whether he was not mistaken, whether the circumstances that had favoured his liaison and had prevented its
final rupture had not done a disservice to his career,
whether the outcome to be desired might not have been
that as to which he rejoiced that it had happened only
in a dream—his own departure; and he said to himself
that people did not know when they were unhappy,
that one is never as happy as one thinks.

Sometimes he hoped that she would die, painlessly,
in some accident, since she was out of doors, in the
streets, crossing busy thoroughfares, from morning to
night. And as she always returned safe and sound, he
marvelled at the strength and the suppleness of the
human body, which was able continually to hold at
bay, to outwit all the perils that beset it (which to
Swann seemed innumerable since his own secret desire
had strewn them in her path), and so allowed mankind
to abandon itself, day after day, and almost with impunity, to its career of mendacity, to the pursuit of
leasure. And Swann felt a very cordial sympathy with
sultan Mahomet II whose portrait by Bellini he
d, who, on finding that he had fallen madly in
one of his wives, stabbed her to death in
Venetian biographer artlessly relates, to
of mind. Then he would be ashamed
ly of himself, and his own sufferings
no pity now that he himself held

from her irrevocably, if at
sly and without sepa-
tely have been as-
died. And since
er, he hoped that
knew that her one
was in August and Sep-

tember, at least he had abundant opportunity, several months in advance, to dissolve the bitter thought of it in all the Time to come which he stored up inside himself in anticipation, and which, composed of days identical with those of the present, flowed through his mind, transparent and cold, nourishing his sadness but without causing him any intolerable pain. But that inner future, that colourless, free-flowing stream, was suddenly convulsed by a single remark from Odette which, penetrating Swann's defences, immobilised it like a block of ice, congealed its fluidity, froze it altogether; and Swann felt himself suddenly filled with an enormous and infrangible mass which pressed on the inner walls of his being until it almost burst asunder; for Odette had said to him casually, observing him with a malicious smile: "Forcheville's going on a fine trip at Whitsun. He's going to Egypt!" and Swann had at once understood this to mean: "I'm going to Egypt at Whitsun with Forcheville." And in fact, if, a few days later, Swann said to her: "About that trip you told me you were going to take with Forcheville," she would answer carelessly: "Yes, my dear boy, we're starting on the 19th; we'll send you a view of the Pyramids." Then he was determined to know whether she was Forcheville's mistress, to ask her point-blank, to insist upon her telling him. He knew that, superstitious as she was, there were some perjuries which she would not commit, and besides, the fear, which had hitherto restrained his curiosity, of making Odette angry if he questioned her, of making her hate him, had ceased to exist now that he had lost all hope of ever being loved by her.

One day he received an anonymous letter telling him that Odette had been the mistress of countless men (several of whom it named, among them Forcheville, M. de Bréauté and the painter) and women, and that

she frequented houses of ill-fame. He was tormented
by the discovery that there was to be numbered among
his friends a creature capable of sending him such a
letter (for certain details betrayed in the writer a familiarity with his private life). He wondered who it
could be. But he had never had any suspicion with
regard to the unknown actions of other people, those
which had no visible connection with what they said.
And when he pondered whether it was beneath the
ostensible character of M. de Charlus, or of M. des
Laumes, or of M. d'Orsan that he must seek the un-
charted region in which this ignoble action had had its
birth, since none of these men had ever, in conversation
with Swann, given any indication of approving of anonymous letters, and since everything they had ever said
to him implied that they strongly disapproved, he saw
no reason for associating this infamy with the character
of any one of them rather than the others. M. de Charlus
was somewhat inclined to eccentricity, but he was fundamentally good and kind; M. des Laumes was a trifle
hard, but sound and straightforward. As for M. d'Orsan, Swann had never met anyone who, even in the
most depressing circumstances, would approach him
with more heartfelt words, in a more tactful and ju-
dicious manner. So much so that he was unable to
understand the rather indelicate role commonly attributed to M. d'Orsan in his relations with a certain wealthy
woman, and whenever he thought of him he was obliged
to set that evil reputation on one side, as being irrec-
oncilable with so many unmistakable proofs of his fas-
tidiousness. For a moment Swann felt that his mind
was becoming clouded, and he thought of something
else so as to recover a little light, until he had the
strength to return to these reflections. But then, having
been unable to suspect anyone, he was forced to suspect

everyone. After all, though M. de Charlus was fond of him, was extremely good-hearted, he was also a neurotic; to-morrow, perhaps, he would burst into tears on hearing that Swann was ill, and today, from jealousy, or anger, or carried away by a sudden whim, he might have wished to do him harm. Really, that kind of man was the worst of all. The Prince des Laumes was certainly far less devoted to Swann than was M. de Charlus. But for that very reason he did not suffer from the same susceptibilities with regard to him; and besides, his was a nature which, though no doubt cold, was as incapable of base as of magnanimous actions. Swann regretted not having formed attachments only to such people. Then he reflected that what prevents men from doing harm to their neighbours is fellow-feeling, that he could only, in the last resort, answer for men whose natures were analogous to his own, as was, so far as the heart went, that of M. de Charlus. The mere thought of causing Swann so much distress would have revolted him. But with an insensitive man, of another order of humanity, as was the Prince des Laumes, how was one to foresee the actions to which he might be led by the promptings of a different nature? To have a kind heart was everything, and M. de Charlus had one. M. d'Orsan was not lacking in heart either, and his relations with Swann—cordial if not intimate, arising from the pleasure which, holding the same views about everything, they found in talking together—were more restful than the overwrought affection of M. de Charlus, capable of being led into acts of passion, good or evil. If there was anyone by whom Swann had always felt himself understood and discriminatingly liked, it was M. d'Orsan. Yes, but what of the disreputable life he led? Swann regretted that he had never taken any notice of those rumours, had often admitted jestingly that he had never felt so keen a sense of sympathy and respect as in the company of a scoundrel. "It's not for nothing," he now assured himself, "that whenever people pass judgment on their fellows, it's always on their actions. It's only what we do that counts, and not at all what we say or what we think. Charlus and des Laumes may have this or that fault, but they are men of honour. Orsan may not have these faults, but he's not a man of honour. He may have acted dishonourably once again." Then Swann suspected Rémi, who, it was true, could only have inspired the letter, but he now felt himself for a moment to be on the right track. To begin with, Loredan had reasons for bearing a grudge against Odette. And then, how could one not suppose that servants, living in a situation inferior to our own, adding to our wealth and our weaknesses imaginary riches and vices for which they envy and despise us, must inevitably be led to act in a manner abhorrent to people of our own class? He also suspected my grandfather. Every time Swann had asked a favour of him, had he not invariably refused? Besides, with his ideas of middle-class respectability, he might have thought that he was acting for Swann's good. He went on to suspect Bergotte, the painter, the Verdurins, pausing for a moment to admire once again the wisdom of society people in refusing to mix with those artistic circles in which such things were possible, perhaps even openly avowed as good jokes; but then he recalled the traits of honesty that were to be observed in those Bohemians and contrasted them with the life of expedients, often bordering on fraudulence, to which the want of money, the craving for luxury, the corrupting influence of their pleasures often drove members of the aristocracy.

In a word, this anonymous letter proved that he knew a human being capable of the most infamous conduct, but he could see no more reason why that infamy should lurk in the unfathomed depths of the character of the man with the warm heart rather than the cold, the artist rather than the bourgeois, the noble rather than the flunkey. What criterion ought one to adopt to judge one's fellows? After all, there was not a single person he knew who might not, in certain circumstances, prove capable of a shameful action. Must he then cease to see them all? His mind grew clouded; he drew his hands two or three times across his brow, wiped his glasses with his handkerchief, and remembering that, after all, men as good as himself frequented the society of M. de Charlus, the Prince des Laumes and the rest, he persuaded himself that this meant, if not that they were incapable of infamy, at least it was a necessity in human life, to which everyone must submit, to frequent the society of people who were perhaps not incapable of such actions. And he continued to shake hands with all the friends whom he had suspected, with the purely formal reservation that each one of them had possibly sought to drive him to despair.

As for the actual contents of the letter, they did not disturb him since not one of the charges formulated against Odette had the slightest verisimilitude. Like many other men, Swann had a naturally lazy mind and lacked imagination. He knew perfectly well as a general truth that human life is full of contrasts, but in the case of each individual human being he imagined all that part of his or her life with which he was not familiar as being identical with the part with which he was. He imagined what was kept secret from him in the light of what was revealed. At such times as he spent with Odette, if their conversation turned upon an indelicate act committed or an indelicate sentiment expressed by some third person, she would condemn them by virtue of the same moral principles which Swann had always heard expressed by his own parents and to which he himself had remained faithful; and then she would arrange her flowers, would sip her tea, would inquire about Swann's work. So Swann extended those attitudes to fill the rest of her life, and reconstructed those actions when he wished to form a picture of the moments in which he and she were apart. If anyone had portrayed her to him as she was, or rather as she had been for so long, with himself, but had substituted some other man, he would have been distressed, for such a portrait would have struck him as lifelike. But to suppose that she went to procuresses, that she indulged in orgies with other women, that she led the crapulous existence of the most abject, the most contemptible of mortals— what an insane aberration, for the realisation of which, thank heaven, the remembered chrysanthemums, the daily cups of tea, the virtuous indignation left neither time nor place! However, from time to time he gave Odette to understand that people maliciously kept him informed of everything that she did; and making opportune use of some detail—insignificant but true— which he had accidentally learned, as though it were the sole fragment which he had involuntarily let slip of a complete reconstruction of her daily life which he carried secretly in his mind, he led her to suppose that he was perfectly informed upon matters which in reality he neither knew nor even suspected, for if he often adjured Odette never to swerve from the truth, that was only, whether he realised it or not, in order that Odette should tell him everything that she did. No doubt, as he used to assure Odette, he loved sincerity, but only as he might love a pimp who could keep him in touch with the daily life of his mistress. Thus his love of sincerity, not being disinterested, had not improved his character. The truth which he cherished was the truth which Odette would tell him; but he himself, in order to extract that truth from her, was not afraid to have recourse to falsehood, that very falsehood which he never ceased to depict to Odette as leading every human creature down to utter degradation. In a word, he lied as much as did Odette because, more unhappy than she, he was no less egotistical. And she, when she heard him repeating thus to her the things that she had done, would stare at him with a look of distrust and, at all hazards, of indignation, so as not to appear to be humiliated and to be blushing for her actions.

One day, during the longest period of calm through which he had yet been able to exist without being overtaken by an access of jealousy, he had accepted an invitation to spend the evening at the theatre with the Princesse des Laumes. Having opened his newspaper to find out what was being played, the sight of the title— *Les Filles de Marbre*, by Théodore Barrière—struck him so cruel a blow that he recoiled instinctively and turned his head away. Lit up as though by a row of footlights, in the new surroundings in which it now appeared, the word "marble," which he had lost the power to distinguish, so accustomed was he to see it passing in print beneath his eyes, had suddenly become visible again, and had at once brought back to his mind the story which Odette had told him long ago of a visit which she had paid to the Salon at the Palais de l'Industrie with Mme Verdurin, who had said to her, "Take care, now! I know how to melt you, all right. You're not made of marble." Odette had assured him that it was only a joke, and he had attached no importance to it at the time. But he had had more confidence in her then than he had now. And the anonymous letter referred explicitly to relations of that sort. Without daring to lift his eyes towards the newspaper, he opened it, turned the page so as not to see again the words *Filles de Marbre*, and began to read mechanically the news from the provinces. There had been a storm in the Channel, and damage was reported from Dieppe, Cabourg, Beuzeval. . . . Suddenly he recoiled again in horror.

The name Beuzeval had reminded him of another place in the same area, Beuzeville, which carried also, bound to it by a hyphen, a second name, to wit Bréauté, which he had often seen on maps, but without ever previously remarking that it was the same as that of his friend M. de Bréauté, whom the anonymous letter accused of having been Odette's lover. After all, in the case of M. de Bréauté, there was nothing improbable in the charge; but so far as Mme Verdurin was concerned, it was a sheer impossibility. From the fact that Odette occassionally told a lie there was no reason to conclude that she never told the truth, and in those remarks she had exchanged with Mme Verdurin and which she herself had repeated to Swann, he had recognised the meaningless and dangerous jokes which, from inexperience of life and ignorance of vice, are often made by women whose very innocence is revealed thereby and who—as for instance Odette—are least likely to cherish impassioned feelings for another of their sex. Whereas the indignation with which she had rejected the suspicions which for a moment she had unintentionally aroused in his mind by her story fitted in with everything that he knew of the tastes and the temperament of his mistress. But now, by one of those inspirations of jealousy analogous to the inspiration which reveals to a poet or a philosopher, who has nothing, so far, to go on but an odd pair of rhymes or a detached observation, the idea or the natural law which will give him the power he needs, Swann recalled for the first time an observation which Odette had made to him at least two years before: "Oh, Mme Verdurin, she won't hear of anyone just now but me. I'm a 'love,' if you please, and she kisses me, and wants me to go with her everywhere, and call her by her Christian name." So far from seeing at the time in this observation any connection with the absurd remarks intended to simulate vice which Odette had reported to him, he had welcomed them as a proof of Mme Verdurin's warm-hearted and generous friendship. But now this memory of her affection for Odette had coalesced suddenly with the memory of her unseemly conversation. He could no longer separate them in his mind, and he saw them assimilated in reality, the affection imparting a certain seriousness and importance to the pleasantries which, in return, robbed the affection of its innocence. He went to see Odette. He sat down at a distance from her. He did not dare to embrace her, not knowing whether it would be affection or anger that a kiss would provoke, either in her or in himself. He sat there silent, watching their love expire. Suddenly he made up his mind.

"Odette, my darling," he began, "I know I'm being simply odious, but I must ask you a few questions. You remember the idea I once had about you and Mme Verdurin? Tell me, was it true? Have you, with her or anyone else, ever?"

She shook her head, pursing her lips, a sign which people commonly employ to signify that they are not going, because it would bore them to go, when someone has asked, "Are you coming to watch the procession go by?", or "Will you be at the review?". But this shake of the head thus normally applied to an event that has yet to come, imparts for that reason an element of uncertainty to the denial of an event that is past. Furthermore, it suggests reasons of personal propriety only, rather than of disapprobation or moral impossibility. When he saw Odette thus signal to him that the insinuation was false, Swann realised that it was quite possibly true.

"I've told you, no. You know quite well," she added, seeming angry and uncomfortable.

"Yes, I know, but are you quite sure? Don't say to me, 'You know quite well'; say, 'I have never done anything of that sort with any woman.'"

She repeated his words like a lesson learned by rote, in a sarcastic tone, and as though she hoped thereby to be rid of him: "I have never done anything of that sort with any woman.'"

"Can you swear to me on the medal of Our Lady of Laghet?"

Swann knew that Odette would never perjure herself on that.

"Oh, you do make me so miserable," she cried, with a jerk of her body as though to shake herself free of the constraint of his question. "Haven't you had enough? What's the matter with you to-day? You seem determined to make me hate you. I wanted to be friends with you again, for us to have a nice time together, like the old days; and this is all the thanks I get!"

However, he would not let her go but sat there like a surgeon waiting for a spasm to subside that has interrupted his operation but will not make him abandon it.

"You're quite wrong to suppose that I'd bear you the least ill-will in the world, Odette," he said to her with a persuasive and deceitful gentleness. "I never speak to you except of what I already know, and I always know a great deal more than I say. But you alone can mitigate by your confession what makes me hate you so long as it has been reported to me only by other people. My anger with you has nothing to do with your actions——I can and do forgive you everything because I love you——but with your untruthfulness, the ridiculous untruthfulness which makes you persist in denying things which I know to be true. How can you expect me to go on loving you when I see you maintain, when I hear you swear to me a thing which I know to be false? Odette, don't prolong this moment which is agony for us both. If you want to, you can end it in a second, you'll be free of it for ever. Tell me, on your medal, yes or no, whether you have ever done these things."

"How on earth do I know?" she exclaimed angrily. "Perhaps I have, ever so long ago, when I didn't know what I was doing, perhaps two or three times."

Swann had prepared himself for every possibility. Reality must therefore be something that bears no relation to possibilities, any more than the stab of a knife in one's body bears to the gradual movement of the clouds overhead, since those words, "two or three times," carved as it were a cross upon the living tissues of his heart. Strange indeed that those words, "two or three times," nothing more than words, words uttered in the air, at a distance, could so lacerate a man's heart, as if they had actually pierced it, could make a man ill, like a poison he has drunk. Instinctively Swann thought of the remark he had heard at Mme de Saint-Euverte's: "I've never seen anything to beat it since the table-turning." The agony that he now suffered in no way resembled what he had supposed. Not only because, even in his moments of most complete distrust, he had rarely imagined such an extremity of evil, but because, even when he did try to imagine this thing, it remained

vague, uncertain, was not clothed in the particular horror which had sprung from the words "perhaps two or
three times," was not armed with that specific cruelty,
as different from anything that he had known as a
disease by which one is struck down for the first time.
And yet this Odette from whom all this evil sprang
was no less dear to him, was, on the contrary, more
precious, as if, in proportion as his sufferings increased,
the price of the sedative, of the antidote which this
woman alone possessed, increased at the same time. He
wanted to devote more care to her, as one tends a disease
which one has suddenly discovered to be more serious.
He wanted the horrible things which, she had told him,
she had done "two or three times," not to happen again.
To ensure that, he must watch over Odette. People
often say that, by pointing out to a man the faults of
his mistress, you succeed only in strengthening his
attachment to her, because he does not believe you; yet
how much more if he does! But, Swann asked himself,
how could he manage to protect her? He might perhaps
be able to preserve her from the contamination of a
particular woman, but there were hundreds of others;
and he realised what madness had come over him when,
on the evening when he had failed to find Odette at
the Verdurins', he had begun to desire the possession—
as if that were ever possible—of another person. Hap-
pily for Swann, beneath the mass of new sufferings
which had entered his soul like an invading horde, there
lay a natural foundation, older, more placid, and silently industrious, like the cells of an injured organ
which at once set to work to repair the damaged tissues,
or the muscles of a paralysed limb which tend to recover
their former movements. These older, more autoch-
thonous inhabitants of his soul absorbed all Swann's
strength, for a while, in that obscure task of reparation

which gives one an illusory sense of repose during con-
valescence, or after an operation. This time it was not
so much—as it ordinarily was—in Swann's brain that
this slackening of tension due to exhaustion took effect,
it was rather in his heart. But all the things in life that
have once existed tend to recur, and like a dying animal
stirred once more by the throes of a convulsion which
seemed to have ended, upon Swann's heart, spared for
a moment only, the same agony returned of its own
accord to trace the same cross. He remembered those
moonlit evenings, when, leaning back in the victoria
that was taking him to the Rue La Pérouse, he would
wallow voluptuously in the emotions of a man in love,
oblivious of the poisoned fruit that such emotions must
inevitably bear. But all those thoughts lasted for no
more than a second, the time that it took him to press
his hand to his heart, to draw breath again and to
contrive to smile, in order to hide his torment. Already
he had begun to put further questions. For his jealousy,
which had taken more pains than any enemy would
have done to strike him this savage blow, to make him
forcibly acquainted with the most cruel suffering he
had ever known, his jealousy was not satisfied that he
had yet suffered enough, and sought to expose him to
an even deeper wound. Thus, like an evil deity, his
jealousy inspired Swann, driving him on towards his
ruin. It was not his fault, but Odette's alone, if at first
his torment was not exacerbated.

"My darling," he began again, "it's all over now.
Was it with anyone I know?"

"No, I swear it wasn't. Besides, I think I exaggerated, I never really went as far as that."

He smiled, and went on: "Just as you like. It doesn't
really matter, but it's a pity that you can't give me the
name. If I were able to form an idea of the person it

would prevent my ever thinking of her again. I say it for your sake, because then I shouldn't bother you any more about it. It's so calming to be able to form a clear picture of things in one's mind. What is really terrible is what one can't imagine. But you've been so sweet to me; I don't want to tire you. I do thank you with all my heart for all the good that you've done me. I've quite finished now. Only one word more: how long ago?"

"Oh, Charles, can't you see you're killing me? It's all so long ago. I've never given it a thought. Anyone would think you were positively trying to put those ideas into my head again. A lot of good that would do you!" she concluded, with unconscious stupidity but intentional malice.

"Oh, I only wanted to know whether it had been since I've known you. It's only natural. Did it happen here? You can't give me any particular evening, so that I can remind myself what I was doing at the time? You must realise that it's not possible that you don't remember with whom, Odette, my love."

"But I don't know; really, I don't. I think it was in the Bois, one evening when you came to meet us on the Island. You'd been dining with the Princesse des Laumes," she added, happy to be able to furnish him with a precise detail which testified to her veracity. "There was a woman at the next table whom I hadn't seen for ages. She said to me, 'Come round behind the rock, there, and look at the moonlight on the water!' At first I just yawned, and said, 'No, I'm too tired, and I'm quite happy where I am, thank you.' She assured me there'd never been any moonlight to touch it. 'I've heard that tale before,' I said to her. I knew quite well what she was after."

Odette narrated this episode almost with a smile,

either because it appeared to her to be quite natural, or because she thought she was thereby minimising its importance, or else so as not to appear humiliated. But, catching sight of Swann's face, she changed her tone:

"You're a fiend! You enjoy torturing me, making me tell you lies, just so that you'll leave me in peace."

This second blow was even more terrible for Swann than the first. Never had he supposed it to have been so recent an event, hidden from his eyes that had been too innocent to discern it, not in a past which he had never known, but in the course of evenings which he so well remembered, which he had lived through with Odette, of which he had supposed himself to have such an intimate, such an exhaustive knowledge, and which now assumed, retrospectively, an aspect of ugliness and deceit. In the midst of them, suddenly, a gaping chasm had opened: that moment on the Island in the Bois de Boulogne. Without being intelligent, Odette had the charm of naturalness. She had recounted, she had acted the little scene with such simplicity that Swann, as he gasped for breath, could vividly see it: Odette yawning, the "rock, there," . . . He could hear her answer—alas, how gaily—"I've heard that tale before!" He felt that she would tell him nothing more that evening, that no further revelation was to be expected for the present. He was silent for a time, then said to her:

"My poor darling, you must forgive me; I know I've distressed you, but it's all over now; I won't think of it any more."

But she saw that his eyes remained fixed upon the things that he did not know, and on that past era of their love, monotonous and soothing in his memory because it was vague, and now rent, as with a gaping wound, by that moment on the Island in the Bois, by moonlight, after his dinner with the Princesse des

Laumes. But he was so imbued with the habit of finding life interesting—of marvelling at the strange discoveries that there are to be made in it—that even while he was suffering so acutely that he did not believe he could bear such agony much longer, he was saying to himself: "Life is really astonishing, and holds some fine surprises; it appears that vice is far more common than one has been led to believe. Here is a woman I trusted, who seems so simple, so straightforward, who, in any case, even allowing that her morals are not strict, seemed quite normal and healthy in her tastes and inclinations. On the basis of a most improbable accusation, I question her, and the little that she admits reveals far more than I could ever have suspected." But he could not confine himself to these detached observations. He sought to form an exact estimate of the significance of what she had just told him, in order to decide whether she had done these things often and was likely to do them again. He repeated her words to himself: "I knew quite well what she was after." "Two or three times." "I've heard that tale before." But they did not reappear in his memory unarmed; each of them still held its knife, with which it stabbed him anew. For a long time, like a sick man who cannot restrain himself from attempting every minute to make the movement that he knows will hurt him, he kept on murmuring to himself: "I'm quite happy where I am, thank you," "I've heard that tale before," but the pain was so intense that he was obliged to stop. He was amazed to find that acts which he had always hitherto judged so lightly, had dismissed, indeed, with a laugh, should have become as serious to him as a disease which may prove fatal. He knew any number of women whom he could ask to keep an eye on Odette, but how was he to expect them to adjust themselves to his new point of view, and not to look

at the matter from the one which for so long had been
his own, which had always guided him in sexual matters; not to say to him with a laugh: "You jealous
monster, wanting to rob other people of their pleasure!"
By what trap-door suddenly lowered had he (who had
never had hitherto from his love for Odette any but the
most refined pleasures) been precipitated into this new
circle of hell from which he could not see how he was
ever to escape. Poor Odette! He did not hold it against
her. She was only half to blame. Had he not been told
that it was her own mother who had sold her, when
she was still hardly more than a child, at Nice, to a
wealthy Englishman? But what an agonising truth was
now contained for him in those lines of Alfred de Vig-
ny's *Journal d'un Poète* which he had previously read
without emotion: "When one feels oneself smitten by
love for a woman, one should say to oneself, 'Who are
the people around her? What kind of life has she led?'
All one's future happiness lies in the answer." Swann
was astonished that such simple sentences, spelt over
in his mind, as "I've heard that tale before" or "I knew
quite well what she was after," could cause him so much
pain. But he realised that what he thought of as simple
sentences were in fact the components of the framework
which still enclosed, and could inflict on him again,
the anguish he had felt while Odette was telling her
story. For it was indeed the same anguish that he now
was feeling anew. For all that he now knew—for all
that, as time went on, he might even have partly forgotten and forgiven—whenever he repeated her words
his old anguish refashioned him as he had been before
Odette had spoken: ignorant, trustful; his merciless
jealousy placed him once again, so that he might be
pierced by Odette's admission, in the position of a man
who does not yet know; and after several months this

old story would still shatter him like a sudden revelation. He marvelled at the terrible recreative power of
his memory. It was only by the weakening of that
generative force, whose fecundity diminishes with age,
that he could hope for a relaxation of his torments. But,
as soon as the power of any one of Odette's remarks to
make Swann suffer seemed to be nearly exhausted, lo
and behold another, one of those to which he had hitherto paid little attention, almost a new observation,
came to reinforce the others and to strike at him with
undiminished force. The memory of the evening on
which he had dined with the Princesse des Laumes was
painful to him, but it was no more than the centre,
the core of his pain, which radiated vaguely round about
it, overflowing into all the preceding and following
days. And on whatever point in it his memory sought
to linger, it was the whole of that season, during which
the Verdurins had so often gone to dine on the Island
in the Bois, that racked him. So violently that by slow
degrees the curiosity which his jealousy aroused in him
was neutralised by his fear of the fresh tortures he would
be inflicting upon himself were he to satisfy it. He
recognised that the entire period of Odette's life which
had elapsed before she first met him, a period of which
he had never sought to form a picture in his mind, was
not the featureless abstraction which he could vaguely
see, but had consisted of so many definite, dated years,
each crowded with concrete incidents. But were he to
learn more of them, he feared lest that past of hers,
colourless, fluid and supportable, might assume a tan-
gible and monstrous form, an individual and diabolical
countenance. And he continued to refrain from seeking
to visualise it, no longer from laziness of mind, but
from fear of suffering. He hoped that, some day, he
might be able to hear the Island in the Bois or the

Princesse des Laumes mentioned without feeling any twinge of the old heartache; and meanwhile he thought it imprudent to provoke Odette into furnishing him with new facts, the names of more places and different circumstances which, when his malady was still scarcely healed, would revive it again in another form.

But, often enough, the things that he did know, that he dreaded, now, to learn, were revealed to him by Odette herself, spontaneously and unwittingly; for the gap which her vices made between her actual life and the comparatively innocent life which Swann had believed, and often still believed his mistress to lead, was far wider than she knew. A vicious person, always affecting the same air of virtue before people whom he is anxious to keep from having any suspicion of his vices, has no gauge at hand from which to ascertain how far those vices, whose continuous growth is imperceptible to himself, have gradually segregated him from the normal ways of life. In the course of their cohabitation, in Odette's mind, side by side with the memory of those of her actions which she concealed from Swann, others were gradually coloured, infected by them, without her being able to detect anything strange in them, without their causing any jarring note in the particular surroundings which they occupied in her inner world; but if she related them to Swann, he was shattered by the revelation of the way of life to which they pointed. One day he was trying—without hurting Odette—to discover from her whether she had ever had any dealings with procuresses. He was, as a matter of fact, convinced that she had not; the anonymous letter had put the idea into his mind, but in a mechanical way; it had met with no credence there, but for all that had remained, and Swann, wishing to be rid of the purely material but none the less burdensome presence of the suspicion, hoped that Odette would now extirpate it for ever.

"Oh, no! . . . Not that they don't pester me," she added with a smile of self-satisfied vanity, quite unaware that it could not appear justifiable to Swann. "There was one of them waited more than two hours for me yesterday—offered me any money I asked. It seems there's an ambassador who said to her, 'I'll kill myself if you don't bring her to me'—meaning me! They told her I'd gone out, but she waited and waited, and in the end I had to go and speak to her myself before she'd go away. I wish you could have seen the way I went for her; my maid could hear me from the next room and told me I was shouting at the top of my voice: 'But haven't I told you I don't want to! It's just the way I feel. I should hope I'm still free to do as I please! If I needed the money, I could understand . . .' The porter has orders not to let her in again; he's to tell her I'm out of town. Oh, I wish I could have had you hidden somewhere in the room while I was talking to her. I know you'd have been pleased, my darling. There's some good in your little Odette, you see, after all, though people do say such dreadful things about her."

Besides, her very admissions—when she made any—of faults which she supposed him to have discovered, served Swann as a starting-point for new doubt rather than putting an end to the old. For her admissions never exactly coincided with his doubts. In vain might Odette expurgate her confession of all its essentials, there would remain in the accessories something which Swann had never yet imagined, which crushed him anew, and would enable him to alter the terms of the problem of his jealousy. And these admissions he could never forget. His soul carried them along, cast them aside, then cradled them again in its bosom, like corpses in a river. And they poisoned it.

She spoke to him once of a visit that Forcheville had paid her on the day of the Paris-Murcie Fête. "What! you knew him as long ago as that? Oh, yes, of course you did," he corrected himself, so as not to show that he had been ignorant of the fact. And suddenly he began to tremble at the thought that, on the day of the Paris-Murcie Fête, when he had received from her the letter which he had so carefully preserved, she had perhaps been having lunch with Forcheville at the Maison d'Or. She swore that she had not. "Still, the Maison d'Or reminds me of something or other which I knew at the time wasn't true," he pursued, hoping to frighten her. "Yes, that I hadn't been there at all that evening when I told you I had just come from there, and you'd been looking for me at Prévost's," she replied (judging by his manner that he knew) with a firmness that was based not so much on cynicism as on timidity, a fear of offending Swann which her own self-respect made her anxious to conceal, and a desire to show him that she could be perfectly frank if she chose. And so she struck with all the precision and force of a headsman wielding his axe, and yet could not be charged with cruelty since she was quite unconscious of hurting him; she even laughed, though perhaps, it is true, chiefly in order not to appear chastened or embarrassed. "It's quite true, I hadn't been to the Maison Dorée. I was coming away from Forcheville's. I really had been to Prévost's— I didn't make that up—and he met me there and asked me to come in and look at his prints. But someone else came to see him. I told you I'd come from the Maison d'Or because I was afraid you might be angry with me. It was rather nice of me, really, don't you see? Even if I did wrong, at least I'm telling you all about it now, aren't I? What would I have to gain by not telling you that I lunched with him on the day of the Paris-Murcie Fête, if it was true? Especially as at the time we didn't know one another quite so well as we do now, did we, darling?"

He smiled back at her with the sudden, craven weakness of the shattered creature which these crushing words had made of him. So, even in the months of which he had never dared to think again because they had been too happy, in those months when she had loved him, she was already lying to him! Besides that moment (that first evening on which they had "done a cattleya") when she had told him that she was coming from the Maison Dorée, how many others must there have been, each of them also concealing a falsehood of which Swann had had no suspicion. He recalled how she had said to him once: "I need only tell Mme Verdurin that my dress wasn't ready, or that my cab came late. There's always some excuse." From himself too, probably, many a time when she had glibly uttered such words as to explain a delay or justify an alteration of the hour fixed for a meeting, they must have hidden, without his having the least inkling of it at the time, an appointment she had with some other man, some man to whom she had said: "I need only tell Swann that my dress wasn't ready, or that my cab came late. There's always some excuse." And beneath all his most tender memories, beneath the simplest words that Odette had spoken to him in those early days, words which he had believed as though they were gospel, beneath the daily actions which she had recounted to him, beneath the most ordinary places, her dressmaker's flat, the Avenue du Bois, the race-course, he could feel (dissembled by virtue of that temporal superfluity which, even in days that have been most circumstantially accounted for, still leaves a margin of room that may serve as a hiding place for certain unconfessed actions), he could feel the insinuation of a possible undercurrent of falsehood which rendered ignoble all that had remained most precious to him (his happiest evenings, the Rue La Pérouse itself, which Odette must constantly have been leaving at other hours than those of which she told him) everywhere disseminating something of the shadowy horror that had gripped him when he had heard her admission with regard to the Maison Dorée, and, like the obscene creatures in the "Desolation of Nineveh," shattering stone by stone the whole edifice of his past. . . . If, now, he turned away whenever his memory repeated the cruel name of the Maison Dorée, it was because that name recalled to him no longer, as, but recently, at Mme de Saint-Euverte's party, a happiness which he had long since lost, but a misfortune of which he had just become aware. Then it happened with the Maison Dorée as it had happened with the Island in the Bois, that gradually its name ceased to trouble him. For what we suppose to be our love or our jealousy is never a single, continuous and indivisible passion. It is composed of an infinity of successive loves, of different jealousies, each of which is ephemeral, although by their uninterrupted multiplicity they give us the impression of continuity, the illusion of unity. The life of Swann's love, the fidelity of his jealousy, were formed of the death, the infidelity, of innumerable desires, innumerable doubts, all of which had Odette for their object. If he had remained for any length of time without seeing her, those that died would not have been replaced by others. But the presence of Odette continued to sow in Swann's heart alternate seeds of love and suspicion.

On certain evenings she would suddenly resume towards him an amenity of which she would warn him

sternly that he must take immediate advantage, under
penalty of not seeing it repeated for years to come; he
must instantly accompany her home, to "do a cattleya,"
and the desire which she claimed to have for him was
so sudden, so inexplicable, so imperious, the caresses
which she lavished on him were so demonstrative and
so unwonted, that this brutal and improbable fondness
made Swann just as unhappy as any lie or unkindness.
One evening when he had thus, in obedience to her
command, gone home with her, and she was inter-
spersing her kisses with passionate words, in strange
contrast to her habitual coldness, he suddenly thought
he heard a sound; he rose, searched everywhere and
found nobody, but hadn't the heart to return to his
place by her side; whereupon, in the height of fury,
she broke a vase and said to him: "One can never do
anything right with you!" And he was left uncertain
whether she had not actually had some man concealed
in the room, whose jealousy she had wished to exac-
erbate or his senses to inflame.

Sometimes he repaired to brothels in the hope of
learning something about Odette, although he dared
not mention her name. "I have a little thing you're sure
to like," the "manageress" would greet him, and he
would stay for an hour or so chatting gloomily to some
poor girl who sat there astonished that he went no
further. One of them, who was quite young and very
pretty, said to him once: "Of course, what I'd like would
be to find a real friend—then he might be quite certain
I'd never go with any other men again."

"Really, do you think it possible for a woman to be
touched by a man's loving her, and never to be unfaithful to him?" asked Swann anxiously.

"Why, of course! It all depends on people's characters!"

Swann could not help saying to these girls the sort of things that would have delighted the Princesse des Laumes. To the one who was in search of a friend he said with a smile: "But how nice, you've put on blue eyes to go with your sash."

"And you too, you've got blue cuffs on."

"What a charming conversation we're having for a place of this sort! I'm not boring you, am I; or keeping you?"

"No, I'm not in a hurry. If you'd have bored me I'd have said so. But I like hearing you talk."

"I'm very flattered.... Aren't we having a nice chat?" he asked the "manageress", who had just looked in.

"Why, yes, that's just what I was saying to myself, how good they're being! But there it is! People come to my house now just to talk. The Prince was telling me only the other day that it's far nicer here than at home with his wife. It seems that, nowadays, all the society ladies are so flighty; a real scandal, I call it. But I'll leave you in peace now," she ended discreetly, and left Swann with the girl who had the blue eyes. But presently he rose and said good-bye to her. She had ceased to interest him. She did not know Odette.

The painter having been ill, Dr Cottard recommended a sea-voyage. Several of the "faithful" spoke of accompanying him. The Verdurins could not face the prospect of being left alone in Paris, so first of all hired and finally purchased a yacht; thus Odette went on frequent cruises. Whenever she had been away for any length of time, Swann would feel that he was beginning to detach himself from her, but as though this moral distance were proportionate to the physical distance between them, whenever he heard that Odette had returned to Paris, he could not rest without seeing her. Once, when they had gone away ostensibly for a month only, either they succumbed to a series of temptations, or else M. Verdurin had cunningly arranged everything beforehand to please his wife, and disclosed his plans to the "faithful" only as time went on; at all events, from Algiers they flitted to Tunis; then to Italy, Greece, Constantinople, Asia Minor. They had been absent for nearly a year, and Swann felt perfectly at ease and almost happy. Although Mme Verdurin had endeavoured to persuade the pianist and Dr Cottard that their respective aunt and patients had no need of them, and that in any event it was most rash to allow Mme Cottard to return to Paris which, so M. Verdurin affirmed, was in the throes of revolution, she was obliged to grant them their liberty at Constantinople. And the painter came home with them. One day, shortly after the return of these four travellers, Swann, seeing an omnibus for the Luxembourg approaching and having some business there, had jumped on it and found himself sitting opposite Mme Cottard, who was paying a round of visits to people whose "day" it was, in full fig, with a plume in her hat, a silk dress, a muff, an umbrella-sunshade, a card-case, and a pair of white gloves fresh from the cleaners. Clothed in these regalia, she would, in fine weather, go on foot from one house to another in the same neighbourhood, but when she had to proceed to another district, would make use of a transfer-ticket on the omnibus. For the first minute or two, until the natural amiability of the woman broke through the starched surface of the doctor's-wife, not being certain, moreover, whether she ought to talk to Swann about the Verdurins, she proceeded to hold forth, in her slow, awkward and soft-spoken voice, which every now and then was completely drowned by the rattling of the omnibus, on topics selected from those which she had picked up and would repeat in each of the score of houses up the stairs of which she clambered in the course of an afternoon.

"I needn't ask you, M. Swann, whether a man so much in the swim as yourself has been to the Mirlitons to see the portrait by Machard which the whole of Paris is rushing to see. Well and what do you think of it? Whose camp are you in, those who approve or those who don't? It's the same in every house in Paris now, no one talks about anything else but Machard's portrait. You aren't smart, you aren't really cultured, you aren't up-to-date unless you give an opinion on Machard's portrait."

Swann having replied that he had not seen this portrait, Mme Cottard was afraid that she might have hurt his feelings by obliging him to confess the omission.

"Oh, that's quite all right! At least you admit it frankly. You don't consider yourself disgraced because you haven't seen Machard's portrait. I find that most commendable. Well now, I have seen it. Opinion is divided, you know, there are some people who find it a bit over-finical, like whipped cream, they say; but I think it's just ideal. Of course, she's not a bit like the blue and yellow ladies of our friend Biche. But I must tell you quite frankly (you'll think me dreadfully old-fashioned, but I always say just what I think), that I don't understand his work. I can quite see the good points in his portrait of my husband, oh, dear me, yes, and it's certainly less odd than most of what he does, but even then he had to give the poor man a blue moustache! But Machard! Just listen to this now, the husband of the friend I'm on my way to see at this very moment (which has given me the very great pleasure of your company), has promised her that if he is elected to the Academy (he's one of the Doctor's colleagues) he'll get Machard to paint her portrait. *There*'s something to look forward to! I have another friend who insists that she'd rather have Leloir. I'm only a wretched Philistine, and for all I know Leloir may be technically superior to Machard. But I do think that the most important thing about a portrait, especially when it's going to cost ten thousand francs, is that it should be like, and a pleasant likeness if you know what I mean."

Having exhausted this topic, to which she had been inspired by the loftiness of her plume, the monogram on her card-case, the little number inked inside each of her gloves by the cleaner, and the embarrassment of speaking to Swann about the Verdurins, Mme Cottard, seeing that they had still a long way to go before they would reach the corner of the Rue Bonaparte where the conductor was to set her down, listened to the promptings of her heart, which counselled other words than these.

"Your ears must have been burning," she ventured, "while we were on the yacht with Mme Verdurin. We talked about you all the time."

Swann was genuinely astonished, for he supposed that his name was never uttered in the Verdurins' presence.

"You see," Mme Cottard went on, "Mme de Crécy was there; need I say more? Wherever Odette is, it's never long before she begins talking about you. And you can imagine that it's never unfavourably. What, you don't believe me!" she went on, noticing that Swann looked sceptical.

And, carried away by the sincerity of her conviction, without putting any sly meaning into the word, which she used purely in the sense in which one employs it to speak of the affection that unites a pair of friends: "Why, she *adores* you! No, indeed, I'm sure it would never do to say anything against you when she was about; one would soon be put in one's place! Whatever we might be doing, if we were looking at a picture, for instance, she would say, 'If only we had him here, he's the man who could tell us whether it's genuine or not. There's no one like him for that.' And all day long she would be saying, 'What can he be doing just now? I do hope he's doing a little work! It's too dreadful that a fellow with such gifts as he has should be so lazy.' (Forgive me, won't you.) 'I can see him this very moment; he's thinking of us, he's wondering where we are.' Indeed, she made a remark which I found absolutely charming. M. Verdurin asked her, 'How in the world can you see what he's doing, when he's a thousand miles away?' And Odette answered, 'Nothing is impossible to the eye of a friend.' No, I assure you, I'm not saying it just to flatter you; you have a true friend in her, such as one doesn't often find. I can tell you, besides, that if you don't know it you're the only one who doesn't. Mme Verdurin told me as much herself on our last day with them (one talks freely, don't you know, before a parting), 'I don't say that Odette isn't fond of us, but anything that we may say to her counts for very little beside what Swann might say.' Oh, mercy, there's the conductor stopping for me. Here I've been chatting away to you, and would have gone right past the Rue Bonaparte and never noticed. . . . Will you be so very kind as to tell me if my plume is straight?"

And Mme Cottard withdrew from her muff, to offer it to Swann, a white-gloved hand from which there floated, together with a transfer-ticket, a vision of high life that pervaded the omnibus, blended with the fragrance of newly cleaned kid. And Swann felt himself overflowing with affection towards her, as well as towards Mme Verdurin (and almost towards Odette, for the feeling that he now entertained for her, being no longer tinged with pain, could scarcely be described, now, as love) as from the platform of the omnibus he followed her with fond eyes as she gallantly threaded her way along the Rue Bonaparte, her plume erect, her skirt held up in one hand, while in the other she clasped her umbrella and her card-case with its monogram exposed to view, her muff dancing up and down in front of her as she went.

To counterbalance the morbid feelings that Swann cherished for Odette, Mme Cottard, a wiser physician, in this case, than ever her husband would have been, had grafted on to them others more normal, feelings of gratitude, of friendship, which in Swann's mind would make Odette seem more human (more like other women, since other women could inspire the same feelings in him), would hasten her final transformation back into the Odette, loved with an undisturbed affection, who had taken him home one evening after a revel at the painter's to drink a glass of orangeade with Forcheville, the Odette with whom Swann had glimpsed the possibility of living in happiness.

In the past, having often thought with terror that a day must come when he would cease to be in love with Odette, he had determined to keep a sharp look-out, and as soon as he felt that love was beginning to leave him, to cling to it and hold it back. But now, to the diminution of his love there corresponded a simultaneous diminution in his desire to remain in love. For a man cannot change, that is to say become another person, while continuing to obey the dictates of the self which he has ceased to be. Occasionally the name glimpsed in a newspaper, of one of the men whom he supposed to have been Odette's lovers, reawakened his jealousy. But it was very mild, and, inasmuch as it proved to him that he had not completely emerged

from that period in which he had so greatly suffered—
but in which he had also known so voluptuous a way
of feeling—and that the hazards of the road ahead
might still enable him to catch an occasional furtive,
distant glimpse of its beauties, this jealousy gave him,
if anything, an agreeable thrill, as, to the sad Parisian
who is leaving Venice behind him to return to France,
a last mosquito proves that Italy and summer are still
not too remote. But, as a rule, with this particular
period of his life from which he was emerging, when
he made an effort, if not to remain in it, at least to
obtain a clear view of it while he still could, he discovered that already it was too late; he would have liked
to glimpse, as though it were a landscape that was about
to disappear, that love from which he had departed;
but it is so difficult to enter into a state of duality and
to present to oneself the lifelike spectacle of a feeling
one has ceased to possess, that very soon, the clouds
gathering in his brain, he could see nothing at all,
abandoned the attempt, took the glasses from his nose
and wiped them; and he told himself that he would do
better to rest for a little, that there would be time
enough later on, and settled back into his corner with
the incuriosity, the torpor of the drowsy traveller who
pulls his hat down over his eyes to get some sleep in
the railway-carriage that is drawing him, he feels, faster
and faster out of the country in which he has lived for
so long and which he had vowed not to allow to slip
away from him without looking out to bid it a last
farewell. Indeed, like the same traveller if he does not
awake until he has crossed the frontier and is back in
France, when Swann chanced to alight, close at hand,
on proof that Forcheville had been Odette's lover, he
realised that it caused him no pain, that love was now
far behind, and he regretted that he had had no warning

of the moment when he had emerged from it for ever. And just as, before kissing Odette for the first time, he had sought to imprint upon his memory the face that for so long had been familiar before it was altered by the additional memory of their kiss, so he could have wished—in thought at least—to have been able to bid farewell, while she still existed, to the Odette who had aroused his love and jealousy, to the Odette who had caused him to suffer, and whom now he would never see again.

He was mistaken. He was destined to see her once again, a few weeks later. It was while he was asleep, in the twilight of a dream. He was walking with Mme Verdurin, Dr Cottard, a young man in a fez whom he failed to identify, the painter, Odette, Napoleon III and my grandfather, along a path which followed the line of the coast, and overhung the sea, now at a great height, now by a few feet only, so that they were continually going up and down. Those of the party who had reached the downward slope were no longer visible to those who were still climbing; what little daylight yet remained was failing, and it seemed as though they were about to be shrouded in darkness. From time to time the waves dashed against the edge, and Swann could feel on his cheek a shower of freezing spray. Odette told him to wipe it off, but he could not, and felt confused and helpless in her company, as well as because he was in his nightshirt. He hoped that, in the darkness, this might pass unnoticed; Mme Verdurin, however, fixed her astonished gaze upon him for an endless moment, during which he saw her face change shape, her nose grow longer, while beneath it there sprouted a heavy moustache. He turned round to look at Odette; her cheeks were pale, with little red spots, her features drawn and ringed with shadows; but she looked back at him with eyes welling with affection, ready to detach themselves like tears and to fall upon his face, and he felt that he loved her so much that he would have liked to carry her off with him at once. Suddenly Odette turned her wrist, glanced at a tiny watch, and said: "I must go." She took leave of everyone in the same formal manner, without taking Swann aside, without telling him where they were to meet that evening, or next day. He dared not ask; he would have liked to follow her, but he was obliged, without turning back in her direction, to answer with a smile some question from Mme Verdurin; but his heart was frantically beating, he felt that he now hated Odette, he would gladly have gouged out those eyes which a moment ago he had loved so much, have crushed those flaccid cheeks. He continued to climb with Mme Verdurin, that is to say to draw further away with each step from Odette, who was going downhill in the other direction. A second passed and it was many hours since she had left them. The painter remarked to Swann that Napoleon III had slipped away immediately after Odette. "They had obviously arranged it between them," he added. "They must have met at the foot of the cliff, but they didn't want to say good-bye together because of appearances. She is his mistress." The strange young man burst into tears. Swann tried to console him. "After all, she's quite right," he said to the young man, drying his eyes for him and taking off the fez to make him feel more at ease. "I've advised her to do it dozens of times. Why be so distressed? He was obviously the man to understand her." So Swann reasoned with himself, for the young man whom he had failed at first to identify was himself too; like certain novelists, he had distributed his own personality between two characters, the one who was dreaming the dream, and another whom he saw in front of him sporting a fez.

As for Napoleon III, it was to Forcheville that some vague association of ideas, then a certain modification of the baron's usual physiognomy, and lastly the broad ribbon of the Legion of Honour across his breast, had made Swann give that name; in reality, and in everything that the person who appeared in his dream represented and recalled to him, it was indeed Forcheville. For, from an incomplete and changing set of images, Swann in his sleep drew false deductions, enjoying at the same time, momentarily, such a creative power that he was able to reproduce himself by a simple act of division, like certain lower organisms; with the warmth that he felt in his own palm he modelled the hollow of a strange hand which he thought he was clasping, and out of feelings and impressions of which he was not yet conscious he brought about sudden vicissitudes which, by a chain of logical sequences, would produce, at specific points in his dream, the person required to receive his love or to startle him awake. In an instant night grew black about him; a tocsin sounded, people ran past him, escaping from their blazing houses; he could hear the thunder of the surging waves, and also of his own heart, which with equal violence was anxiously beating in his breast. Suddenly the speed of these palpitations redoubled, he felt an inexplicable pain and nausea. A peasant, dreadfully burned, flung at him as he passed: "Come and ask Charlus where Odette spent the night with her friend. He used to go about with her in the past, and she tells him everything. It was they who started the fire." It was his valet, come to awaken him, and saying:—

"Sir, it's eight o'clock, and the barber is here. I've told him to call again in an hour."

But these words, as they plunged through the waves of sleep in which Swann was submerged, did not reach his consciousness without undergoing that refraction which turns a ray of light in the depths of water into another sun; just as, a moment earlier, the sound of the door-bell, swelling in the depths of his abyss of sleep into the clangour of a tocsin, had engendered the episode of the fire. Meanwhile, the scenery of his dream-stage scattered into dust, he opened his eyes, and heard for the last time the boom of a wave in the sea, now distant. He touched his cheek. It was dry. And yet he remembered the sting of the cold spray, and the taste of salt on his lips. He rose and dressed himself. He had made the barber come early because he had written the day before to my grandfather to say that he was going to Combray that afternoon, having learned that Mme de Cambremer—Mlle Legrandin that had been—was spending a few days there. The association in his memory of her young and charming face with a countryside he had not visited for so long offered him a combined attraction which had made him decide at last to leave Paris for a while. As the different circumstances that bring us into contact with certain people do not coincide with the period in which we are in love with them, but, overlapping it, may occur before love has begun, and may be repeated after it has ended, the earliest appearances in our lives of a person who is destined to take our fancy later on assume retrospectively in our eyes a certain value as an indication, a warning, a presage. It was in this fashion that Swann had often reverted in his mind to the image of Odette encountered in the theatre on that first evening when he had no thought of ever seeing her again—and that he now recalled the party at Mme de Saint-Euverte's at which he had introduced General de Froberville to Mme de Cambremer. So manifold are our interests in life that it is not uncommon, on the self-same occasion, for the foundations of a happiness which does not yet exist to be laid down simultaneously with the aggravation of a grief from which we are still suffering. And doubtless this could have occurred to Swann elsewhere than at Mme de Saint-Euverte's. Who indeed can say whether, in the event of his having gone elsewhere that evening, other happinesses, other griefs might not have come to him, which later would have appeared to him to have been inevitable? But what did seem to him to have been inevitable was what had indeed taken place, and he was not far short of seeing something providential in the fact that he had decided to go to Mme de Saint-Euverte's that evening, because his mind, anxious to admire the richness of invention that life shows, and incapable of facing a difficult problem for any length of time, such as deciding what was most to be wished for, came to the conclusion that the sufferings through which he had passed that evening, and the pleasures, as yet unsuspected, which were already germinating there—the exact balance between which was too difficult to establish—were linked by a sort of concatenation of necessity.

But while, an hour after his awakening, he was giving instructions to the barber to see that his stiffly brushed hair should not become disarranged on the journey, he thought of his dream again, and saw once again, as he had felt them close beside him, Odette's pallid complexion, her too thin cheeks, her drawn features, her tired eyes, all the things which—in the course of those successive bursts of affection which had made of his enduring love for Odette a long oblivion of the first impression that he had formed of her—he had ceased to notice since the early days of their intimacy, days to which doubtless, while he slept, his memory had returned to seek their exact sensation. And with the old, intermittent caddishness which reappeared in him when he was no longer unhappy and his moral standards dropped accordingly, he exclaimed to himself: "To think that I've wasted years of my life, that I've longed to die, that I've experienced my greatest love, for a woman who didn't appeal to me, who wasn't even my type!"

Notes

1   In English in the original. Odette's speech is peppered with English expressions.

2   "Home" is in English in the original, as is "smart".

3   *Reine Topaze*: a light opera by Victor Massé presented at the Théâtre Lyrique in 1856.

4   *Serge Panine*: play by Georges Ohnet (1848-1918), adapted from a novel of the same name, which had a great success in 1881 in spite of its mediocre literary qualities.
Olivier Métra: composer of such popular works as *La Valse des Roses* and a famous lancers quadrille, and conductor at the Opéra-Comique.

5   *Serpent à sonnettes* means rattlesnake.

6   *Pays du Tendre* (or, more correctly, *Pays de Tendre*): the country of the sentiments, the tender emotions, mapped (the *carte de Tendre*) by Mlle de Scudéry in her novel *Clélie* (1654-1670).

7   The rather forced joke on the name Cambremer conceives of it as being made up of abbreviations of *Cambronne* and *merde* (shit). *Le mot de Cambronne* (said to have been flung defiantly at the enemy by a general at Waterloo) is the traditional euphemism for *merde*.

MARCEL PROUST (1871–1922) was born and died in Paris. Educated at the Lycée Condorcet, he did one year's military service and briefly studied law and political science. Proust's charm and ambition gained him entrance to the *salons* of Parisian society—the setting that provides the background for *A la recherche du temps perdu*. After his mother's death in 1905 Proust, suffering from asthma, retreated from active social life and secluded himself in a cork-lined room in his Paris apartment. From 1910 on he was at work on *A la recherche du temps perdu*, publishing the first volume at his own expense in 1913. In 1920 the second volume won him the Prix Goncourt. Until his death in 1922 he continued writing and rewriting his monumental work.